a girl a band a diary

Krys Graf

Krys Graf

This book is dedicated to all those in the Armed Forces who lay down their lives for the sake of keeping freedom, peace and safety for the United States of America, and especially to those who have lost their lives for the sake of your country, my deepest thanks and sympathy to your families.

To our Road Crew: Brian Darabosh (Drax), Tom Uthmeier (Hound), Derrick, Dave B., Tim O Waldron, John Borger, (Slick), Fred Showalter (Showey), Mike, Fred Spence. – our first soundman / roadie/ truck mechanic.

It was not until 1980 when the American Psychiatric Association added Post Traumatic Stress Disorder / PTSD to the third edition of its Diagnostic and Statistical Manual.

To the memories of: Dad: Nick L., Erna Dilcher (Oma), Antonio L.(grandfather), Linda Frank, Kenneth E. Schroeder, Fred Showalter (Showey), Brian Darabosh (Drax) and Ed Huenecke.

Thank you to: to all those who shared their many photos: Marvin Waters, Chapter 12 photo signed by "JR". Prologue and Chapter 19 photo signed by "John Dins". Photos were an afterthought to give a small glimpse of life on the road. Cover art done by author. Thank you to: Pete L. for advice, Laurie W. for your wonderful eyes, and most of all, my family. Thank you to Anna Riabov- I tried to find you when I found your Aretha Franklin album.

This novel may be based on true stories, but this book is a work of fiction. Any references to real people, organizations or locales are intended to give the fiction authenticity. All names and dialogue portrayed in this book are the product of the author's imagination. Any similarity to real persons living or dead is coincidental.

Krys Graf

PROLOGUE

On a warm June morning, Lexa sat at the edge of her bed and brushed a film of grogginess out of her dark brown eyes. A violent thunderstorm ripped through her bedroom and deprived her of sleep. She staggered down the stairway to the kitchen where the clock on the electric coffeemaker flashing 00:00 made no sense as she reset it. A ticking wall clock's dials moved to 9:15 as she sipped warm coffee and ruminated over her plans for the day. At the top of a stairway to the basement, she was confronted by an assortment of papers soaking in the reflection of a brown bookshelf. It took a second for the flood to register and another to understand the impact.

Frantic, she jumped into foot high rainwater, grabbed books and boxes containing personal archives, and gathered them to higher

Krys Graf

ground. Draining a pond from her home stirred feelings of distress as her bare feet splotched through soggy carpet, whirling a cauldron of notes, newspapers and photos. She scooped up armfuls of books and boxes, piled them in heaps up a flight of stairs into her kitchen and was covered in sweat as she dried the deluge of water.

In a waterlogged box that afternoon, she discovered her old diaries, causing memories to rush in wave after wave. The time stamped memoirs written in murkier days of the maniacal years in a band, still haunted her. In being forgotten, cobwebs and dust interlaced the papers and photos. *I can't believe this is in one piece,* she thought, flinging wavy, dark blonde hair off of her forearms to clip it up. *But I don't want it. We are the result of our life experiences and memories, and much of my past is best forgotten.* She picked up a photo, tossed it back, and closed the box. *It feels like time has shoved me forward quickly. Making the best choices possible is not always easy. I've weathered many storms and mistakenly created a few. Desperation causes people to do the unthinkable. Mine was caused by loneliness and feeling isolated though I was surrounded by people, and regrets have given me nightmares.*

She pulled the heavy box to the backyard fire pit, and in a crater of firewood, a private passageway to her past teetered. Clouds gathered overhead as she found a can of lighter fluid, pointed the tip and pressed. A gust of wind caused the liquid to overshoot the container. She sat on the ground and reached for the box where forgotten secrets took another gasp of air. Thick clouds darkened the sky. She looked up and around, noticing rain on the horizon to the south.

Beginning in her childhood, she refused to take advice, viewed the world differently, and connected the dots inversely to others. *I have dreams which come to pass, and premonitions, momentary visions of future events, but I am not always saved from harm.*

She thumbed through old photos and remembered the times her mother told her she was nothing special to look at. "Your sister Candy is the pretty one in your family," her aunt had said often. *Maybe it's why I grew up thinking I wasn't worth looking at,* she sighed.

Heavy raindrops stung her skin and struck the ground. The temptation to dig into past diary entries grew as she dragged the portal she attempted to demolish out of the fire pit and into the house. Pellets of rain pinged on the windows, and she began reading.

Her handwriting appeared foreign and many names and events had washed out of her consciousness. Reading into her past was like viewing a familiar, yet unknown person who wondered if her destination would lead to a hospital, prison, grave, an asylum, or as she hoped, living the life of a rock star, whatever that would be. She picked up a letter she had written to her best friend and never sent. "I think of you often, and there are so many things I want to tell you..." A nearby crack of rolling thunder boomed, and she stopped reading to watch the downpour streaking on the glass panes.

Those days disappeared like lost toys. At the time, we were entwined by our music, each of us haunted by things we were unable to resolve. She thumbed through portraits like a detached, casual observer of her history. *We were catnip to the kitties, caffeine to the somnolent, nicotine to the smoker. We drew them out by dangling the musical cheese before the mice.*

She held up a photo. *You, the killer of happiness, destroyer of whatever joy I could muster.* She ripped it into small pieces. *There are some who give us comfort, and there are those who create scars. I never want to hear your name again. I started a diary to document my rise to fame in the music industry, and ended up documenting my survival guide. One more time I slid out of death's grip. I wonder how many chances I get. In the beginning, it was the hands of another around my neck and at some point, they were replaced by my own.*

His grasp intended to silence me by ending my life. No breath able to enter or leave my lungs, in a blink of clarity, I knew what I had to do.

CHAPTER 1

HEADSTONES

The vision would not stop; a girl lying in the alley, skin cold, heavy and white as the glare of the overhead street lamp illuminating the darkness. Fear waxed and waned down Lexa's spine. When she brushed her long, light brown hair, when she closed her eyes to sleep, and held her head when she awakened during the night, the image remained. It was the first time a mental imprint grabbed her by the throat and would not relent.

Her brother Nathan tapped on her shoulder. She jumped.

"What is going on? You've hardly eaten or spoken much these past two weeks," he said.

"The usual school issues…mean classmates, crabby teachers, and too much homework."

"It never bothered you before."

"It does now," she said as she climbed the stairs to her bedroom, and closed the door. The girl looks like me, she thought. I need to prepare. And as always, she took it to the extreme.

She kept her Swiss army knife in hand on all walks, scanned all directions, ran one to two miles daily, wore running shoes at all times, and bought a loud whistle. She practiced karate moves in the mirror, and did push-ups to strengthen her arms.

Wednesday, August 26, 1970
My screams dispersed into darkness when he squeezed my neck. I thought I would never see daylight again. What made me think begging for help would open one door in that - don't bother us we-won't-get-involved neighborhood? Makeup does not hide my battered face. I did not feel them getting ripped out, and my silver earrings are gone. My earlobes are bleeding. I lost my knife and whistle. Numbness has settled over me and dulls my pain. It's strange to feel so disconnected, like I'm not fully here. Because I was not in an alley, I thought I would be safe.

A tall, gray-haired detective in his forties who sat behind his desk, slid five heavy mugshot books in front of her. "We need any kind of information you can give us. Are there any features you can remember?"

"I tried to look at him, but it was dark, and he grabbed my head and screamed at me to turn away. I saw his hair and I'm not certain, but I believe it was brown," she said to the man dressed in navy slacks and short-sleeved blue shirt. "And I remember his red car."

"Maybe someone in these photos will jog your memory."

Lexa flipped the cover open and turned pages, overwhelmed by a plethora of black and white two inch by three inch faces. Within minutes, their features blurred into one another. A vent above her head sent an air conditioned chill down the back of her neck forcing her to wrap her arms around the shoulders of her cap-sleeved blue peasant blouse. Wishing she had not been out the night before, the white walls in the claustrophobic room closed in on her.

"I don't recognize anyone," she said.

Another detective in a gray shirt and slacks walked into the room and sat in a chair to face her and his partner.

"Any leads? Miss, are you five three? Was he a lot taller than you?"

"I am, and I'm guessing he was about 6 feet tall. I wish I could identify the man and the make and model of his red car, but I'm sorry I can't. Can I leave?"

"Not yet. This guy tried to kill you by strangulation. You said you played dead. You do want us to capture him, don't you?"

"Yes. If you had voice recordings attached to the headshots, I'd remember the tonality, the sound," she said.

"We need to get a few photos." They led her into another room.

"Turn your head farther to the left, Miss. Okay…look straight ahead…now all the way to the right. Good…"

Bright flashes winced her bruised eyelids.

"If anything comes to mind, here's our number. Call right away."

"Yes sir," she said as she arose, took his card, and straightened her denim bell bottoms. "His tone and speech patterns are distinctive. He had a German accent."

"We will keep it in mind. You are the only survivor we have."

Hovering over her, the muscular detective was accompanied by his partner who slid his arms into a gray suit jacket and escorted her to the back of a silver unmarked patrol car. "It's too bad you didn't get a decent look. He's probably looking for you."

"What happened to me won't be in the newspaper, will it?"

"Not unless you inform them," he said.

She was returned to her parents' doorstep where she looked up to her seventeen year old brother's marbled blue eyes staring at the entourage as she walked into the beige stucco house.

"What really happened to you and who are those men?" he said turning around to follow her. "You said you fell down the stairs. Who are they, the stair cops?"

"The FBI questioned me about your illegal activities Nathan," she said pacing through the living room, up a stairway to her right, through a hallway past two bedrooms and turned the key on the lock inside her bedroom. "I hope you have an escape plan."

"Oh, X, you and your cute little stories," he said into the door jamb. "You like someone shoved you down the stairs."

"I told them you did it." She threw her sandals into the closet, buckled onto the floor, and the swelling in her face created a spinning sensation. She fixated on the underwater mural she had painted on her double hung sliding closet doors in hues of blues and greens of seaweed shimmering upward in the foreground of a castle, coral and caverns. Encircled by hair, her palms wove through dark blue shag carpet in the room where she spent endless hours studying song books to learn how to play her guitar, and music of her own was documented in notebooks. She was startled by her brother's scream.

"X, get the phone! It's Sam Lynnch."

The telephone dangled on a spiraling cord in the kitchen, where she reached down to bring the white receiver up to her ear. "Hello?"

"How did it go? I thought you said you were going to call me when you got back from the police station. I shouldn't have let you get on a city bus so late last night. I feel terrible. I need to be with you."

"Don't blame yourself. You don't need to come over." She sat on the floor and braced her back against the wall. "It isn't your fault."

"I need to see you. I'll be there as soon as I can. I love you, Lexa."

"I shouldn't have left your apartment at 10:30," she said.

"We should be able to walk down a street and not worry about being injured or murdered no matter what time it is. See you in a bit."

She sat in motionless for a few minutes.

Sam Lynnch, who attended the Milwaukee School of Engineering was three and a half years older than Lexa, and had met her six months ago at Amadeus Amped, the music store where he worked. Because of his charm and attention to her, she visited his workplace often for guitar picks and strings. He asked for her phone number, invited her to his friend Drake's party and his plans included her from the time of their first kiss.

In her bedroom, the shifting patterns of the lava lamp on her dresser cast a subtle glow in the mirror. She placed the Cheap Thrills album on her turntable, and permeating the walls was the passion in the voice of Janis Joplin. Despite her charisma, she was as self-critical and insecure as Lexa was.

She picked up her guitar, strummed it, and a soft knock interrupted 'Piece of My Heart'. "Come in." She looked up to a 5'10" man and met Sam's sad blue eyes. Despite not being the best looking man she had known, he had qualities she was attracted to, and being the polar opposite of her father was one of them.

His slender body sat beside her; his breath swirled over her skin. He kissed her indigo forehead, the bloodied scratch marks on her neck, savored her soft innocence, and glided his hands down her back.

She inhaled his Polo cologne, and brushed her fingers through his short, wavy blonde hair as she unbuttoned his shirt and pressed her lips onto his creamy tan chest. The taste of apple was still on his lips. On the floor, she rested her head sideways on his legs and stroked his legs. "I'll only be sixteen in November. It seems like it'll be forever before we'll be on our own."

"I want to spend the rest of my life with you and live in a peaceful quiet countryside someday. No crowds or creeps," he said brushing his hand over her long, light brown hair and back. "You know how I feel about you."

"The silver earrings you made for me are gone. I looked for them early this morning, but they have disappeared," she said.

"I promise I'll make another pair."

"Last night keeps replaying in my head. He knows what I look like, but I won't recognize him. I may never get over my anger for him."

"Don't worry, you will. I'll always be there for you. Always." Jolting off the floor by her father's voice echoing up the stairwell, he kissed her and buttoned his shirt. "Meet me tomorrow. I'll call you."

He hurtled down the hallway, bumped into the stairwell railing, said goodbye to Mr. and Mrs. Laudon and slammed the back door.

Adjacent from her bedroom, in the bathroom she glimpsed into the mirror to cause a double take before she lowered her head to splash cold water onto her face. She wondered if she would ever look the same again. *I need to get out of here, take a quick run outside, or sit on a swing at the school down the street.* The shower curtain pushed aside, she climbed into the bathtub to open the window and invite the humid summer air to surround her in the second story of the house. She grabbed onto roof shingles above her and balanced her hips on the ledge. Alarmed by three hard raps on the wooden door, her upper body slipped downward. Almost falling to the ground, she clutched the windowsill with her fingertips while her feet scissor kicked to regain her balance.

"Your mom wants help setting the table, and it's time for supper." Dad's commands rumbled like an avalanche, and the twisting brass door knob groaned. "Young lady, do you hear me?"

Dangling upside down, the throbbing in her head intensified, and a dizzy sensation overcame her. Across the street, sun's rays flickered off of headstones. It was the first time she realized how close she lived to the deceased in regaining control of her grip.

"Lexa Jean Laudon, answer me now," he said.

She pulled herself back into the tub. He did not use her full name unless he was angrier than usual. She stood behind the locked door. "I'll be there soon. I don't feel well." *Nathan told him.*

She hesitated down the steps and walked into the kitchen, where she sat at Nathan's side and avoided everyone including her little sisters Candy and Abbie on her right. Across the table, her mom, dad, and grandmother ate in stunned silence. Her dad's dark brown eyes stared at her intensely. He glanced at her Mom's frightened blue eyes.

"What in the hell happened to you? I can't believe your face and neck, and whatever else is black and purple because you fell. I forbid you from seeing him again. Do you understand? Where else do you have bruises that you won't let us see?"

She glared at the black-haired man who sat across the table and stood up. "I fought off an attacker when I walked home last night. Sam would not hurt me," she said taking her plate and fork to wash at the sink. She jogged to her room, consumed as to where else she could live, and in her room, she picked up her notebook.

"What are you writing?" asked Oma, in her half German and English accent who stood in the hallway.

"I'm sketching an ocean scene."

"Like the one on your closet?"

"No, I'm drawing waves, of how they move and catch the light," she said peering up at her frail grandmother who had been slipping away over the past year. "Come in. I'll show you. Thanks for supper. I wasn't hungry, but your beef Rouladen always tastes so good. How do you feel? You look a little pale."

"Es geht voruber. Auch dies geht vorbei."

"Yes, this too shall pass," said Lexa.

"Are you going to tell me what caused your injuries?" asked Oma who sat down on Lexa's bed.

"I was followed by a red car after I got off the bus on 27th Street. I ran as fast as I could, but he knew there would be no place for me to hide. I'm worried his next target may not be as lucky as I was."

"Lucky? You got a beating and you're lucky?"

"I'm lucky he believed I was dead."

"You don't read the papers like I do, but three women have been murdered in the past two months. He'll wonder why there isn't an obituary, why your death wasn't reported in the paper or the news. He will realize you're still alive."

"I'm in trouble," said Lexa.

"He will be looking for you, but may get a different car, wear glasses, change how his hair is styled, or even change his hair color to continue harming others. There is no fairness in this world, only vigilance," said Oma. "You must always watch out for yourself. Always be prepared for the worst."

"No, fairness, so be aware of who is around me," said Lexa.

"Even though his hands are no longer around your neck or harming you, never let the hands of another be replaced by your own.

"My own?"

"When something terrible happens, it gnaws at us, and we do or say things that hurt ourselves in some way, but the worst thing is we are not aware of it. Do not punish yourself. This was not your fault."

"You lived through the war in Germany," said Lexa. "It must have been horrible."

"Your grandfather was killed in the war, and all I had was your mom. Sometimes I can still hear the bombs falling, and your mom being shot at by French pilots as she ran through the field. She was ten. Always live in peace, but be ready for destruction. Watch your back, heighten your awareness. And if something unforeseen happens, move forward. Do not let it get under your skin and destroy you. He may still be watching for you, but it doesn't mean you should live in fear. Live boldly and remember to do whatever the right thing is and what will make your heart happy."

"I will."

Thursday, September 3, 1970
The wickedness of the world may always disturb me, but I am not alone. Though I may feel voiceless and insignificant at times, I never lose hope that each step I take leaves an indelible footprint on this earth.

The unhappiness Sam tells me he feels because my parents refuse to let me see him equals how I wince every time I look in the mirror. I wish I could avoid everyone's judging eyes until my face is no longer a purple balloon. The man who thinks he killed me struck again in this city. The newspaper article is alarming. My classmates are dying their hair blonde, and I'm keeping mine pinned up.

Lexa was the object of whispers and stares for weeks, while Oma, who battled fatigue, chemotherapy, loneliness and pain, had done her best to pass on her wisdom, cooking and sewing skills to her granddaughter.

In October, Nathan and Lexa found Oma unconscious in her bed and ran to tell their mother who hurried into the room and spoke to her as though her mama would open her eyes and respond. There were still breaths being taken, there were still fractions of seconds remaining in her mother's life. She ran to the phone and called an ambulance.

At school Lexa told a few classmates of her grandmother's death, but their condolences were empty words as the day went on the same way as the day before, as though faces Lexa passed in hallways should care that a longtime part of her life would now be gone forever.

Thursday, October 15, 1970

When death approaches, sometimes earthly rules bend. As I watched Oma's irregular breaths, we tiptoed along the tops of a white picket fence. She was a young woman again, and for a moment she faltered. I followed behind her, wondering if she would fall into the ethereal blue-green grass, and instead, she turned around, blew a kiss to me, and vanished into the dust particles falling downward from the light streaming through her bedroom window. My mother called out to her, not once saying her name, or referring to her as her mother, instead she repeated, "Oma", as if she would awaken, "Oma, Oma..."

Friday, October 16, 1970

Some don't live past the womb, some take several gasps, and others endure struggles from their first breath. Today I grieve for someone interwoven around my heart who left a loss so great it will take years for my heart to mend. I will honor her request to move forward and do what it takes to feel happiness.

Lexa stood at an unmarked grave remembering her mother's sole surviving lineage, a skilled professional seamstress who endured World War II. After her husband's death and the annihilation of her home, she clung to her blonde daughter and meager clothing. Food was scarce where they lived in the underground bomb shelter, and missiles shook the earth around them. To survive the horrors of war, "Es geht voruber. Auch dies geht vorbei", this too shall pass, had become her anthem.

Though Lexa clasped the lapels of her coat, she was unable to stop shivering. Faint sobs encompassed her ears as she tossed a red rose into the six foot opening.

"Auf wiedersehen, Oma." *Farewell. So many things I already miss about you.* Frigid droplets filled her eyes as she read the names etched into granite, and the tombstone of Julette Zadrik, age 32, wife, daughter, and mother was beside Oma. *If I didn't play dead, I would lie alongside them.* She turned her body full circle, taken by the sadness of those who had once stood in this field of engraved markers when she saw her name carved into a small concrete headstone next to where she stood. The latter date was the night of her attack. As she moved her hand toward it, it vaporized.

"What are you doing?" Nathan turned to her.

A blank look on her face, she spun around, "I...My name was on..."

"What did you see this time?"

CHAPTER 2

FOREWARNINGS

"**O**ne of the headstones disappeared," she said into widened eyes, a mix of white and light blue sky on a summer day.

"What was on it?" asked Nathan.

"My name, and the dates of my birth and death."

"I'm glad it's gone," he said.

He shared Lexa's grief as they sat at her bedside that evening during a discussion of life and death before she nodded off to sleep.

Oma's presence dissipated in the walls she once occupied, where Lexa opened the drawers of her sewing desk. Silver spikes in a pincushion lit up through the curtains. She pulled out a long hatpin and held it up to examine its sharpness. Her grandmother had often spoken of women who tucked the long pins into the sides of their purses when they walked alone at night. "It made us feel safer," Oma used to tell Lexa. She wove one into the fabric of her handbag.

"X, get the phone. The police want to speak to you," said Nathan.

"Hello?" Lexa paused. "Yes, but I have no transportation to the station. Yes, sir."

"What do they want?" asked Nathan.

"They're going to pick me up to see if I can identify someone in a lineup. Don't tell Mom and Dad where I am."

Thirty minutes later, she stood in the presence of the previous detectives staring at six men identified by numbers. As much as she struggled, she was unable to pick out any distinct features. "He has a foreign accent. I can only remember his voice," she said.

On September 18, 1970, James Marshall Hendrix passed away at the age of 27, and on October 4, 1970, Janis Joplin, also at age 27, was found unresponsive by her road manager.

Lexa's favorite performers dying at the peak of their careers crushed her dream of attending their concerts. With how often she strummed her guitar, she did not fret over scrapes that dulled the luster of its shine. It had become her tranquilizer and surrogate friend.

Thick clouds covered the month of November and Sam's clandestine visits were the highlight of her days. She had become skilled at sneaking out of and into her family's home and met him at a designated time in the alley behind the house, where he waited for her in his red Corvair.

Sam kissed Lexa's cheek. "Let's stop for ice cream. How are you?"

"I'm okay. Dad hasn't said one word to me for six days. Not even 'Hello'. He's been ornery for so long, he may be unable to feel happy again. I don't think my mom can stand it."

"I'm glad I don't have to live with him. Let's go to the lakefront later." He opened the car door to wait in line.

"Sure." She glanced to her right, and a red vehicle was beside theirs. She flattened her body downward, and her muscles trembled. She rolled her window down to listen for voices. *Is it him?*

Sam returned holding the cones. "What are you doing?"

"Something's on my boot." Her head between her legs, she reached for her cone.

He closed the door and licked his ice cream as hers dripped onto her hand, with the heat being directed toward it.

"Why is the window open? I'm freezing," he said.

"Let's get out of here." A crushing feeling overcame her like the night her world was altered last month. Fixated on the car she had seen, the ride through the city was silent. At the waterfront her gaze met his, and their caresses steamed up the inside of the dark car.

"I will never love anyone as much as you," said Sam. At midnight, he gave her a soft kiss before she exited in the alley.

She closed the door quietly, and looked up at her parent's house. To her left, near the garage, a darkened lump of clothing fluttered in the wind. As she approached it, the form of a body came into view.

Lexa bent down and the light in the alleyway illuminated a woman who appeared to be sleeping, but her body was rigid, her skin icy cold. Her long brown hair covered a beautiful, smooth face, and nylon stockings were tied around her young neck so tightly, Lexa was unable to loosen the knot. Lexa's muscles twitched, and then shook uncontrollably. A slain girl was dumped at her home, and Sam may have driven past the car of the killer as he pulled into the alley. She was supposed to be in her bed, and could not call the police.

Sucking in a deep gasp of air, Lexa grabbed the woman's arms, dragged the body two houses down, crossed the stiff arms over the chest, and she knelt down. "Do you have brothers and sisters, a kitty, a dog? Where is your Mom and Dad? I'm sorry your sweet life ended this way. You are now free to fly off to majestic and indescribable places. I wish you peace in the heavens."

"Find him."

Startled at the voice, Lexa fell backwards and looked around. She touched the stone-cold body and there was no pulse.

"Find him," she heard again. *Earthly rules bent for a split second.* "I…," said Lexa. "I will try for the sake of all who have been harmed." She ran behind a garage as headlamps streamed into the backstreet. She climbed up the uneven bricks and long gutter which she had always grabbed onto to steady her ascent, and in her room, she pulled her duvet over her throbbing head.

Unable to sleep, at 4 am she walked to the to the alleyway which was flooded by police and six light-flashing squad cars. *He could have put the body anywhere. He knows where I live. I need to tell Nathan we must safeguard our little sisters.*

In the news the following day, on the second page was an article about an eighteen year old waitress who worked at Captain's restaurant five miles from where her body was found. Her name was Milyana Milevic, and she would have graduated from high school in June. She was survived by her Mom, Dad, a brother, a sister, and grandparents.

Lexa took a long, hard stare at the black and white photo of the smiling young woman who could have been her twin, her hair long, wavy and what appeared to be brown. She clipped out the story, folded it, and put it in her wallet.

Upon hearing the news, her parents tightened their reign on Lexa, who feared being caught whenever she scaled the house to escape. She told no one of encountering the girl in the alleyway, or the disembodied voice. The words had to be her imagination, or maybe it was her desire to bring justice to someone so wicked.

"I'm going ask a friend to make a fake ID for you, so Drake and I can get you into bars to see our band," said Sam. "Pin your hair up, wear lots of makeup, and do not smile."

Lexa examined the card which stated her age was twenty-one, and wondered if club owners would accept its validity. *It would give me, a sixteen-year-old access to nightclubs to watch bands and drink whatever I please.* She looked up and out of her parent's large living room window. A red two door car drove past the front of the house, and her knees buckled. Dammit. Her heart echoed into her eardrums. She sat on the floor clutching the card for a few moments wondering if it was him and if he saw her.

She arose and hid behind the drapes, peering at the man who sat behind the wheel and the red vehicle idling in front of her house. Maybe he followed her home from school to stalk the girl he failed to kill. His thick fingers grasped the steering wheel, his indistinct face, brown hair, and broad shoulders leaned toward her home. *He is looking for someone, possibly me.* For ten minutes the car sat beside the curb, and she was motionless, peeking through curtains until he drove away.

She wished she had asked her grandmother what she meant by living boldly. *Maybe I should have walked outside near the car, gotten the license plate numbers and called the detective who gave me his business card. I failed at it today. But how can I prove to police this is the perpetrator? If they find nothing, he will be free to kill again.*

In fear of the five mile walk to and from high school, she pleaded with a schoolmate who had a car and said he would pick her up and drop her off in her neighborhood. She offered to pay for gasoline. Preoccupied by what was around and behind her, especially red cars, she ran through the alley into the kitchen, and slammed the door. When Nathan saw her, he asked why she was always out of breath.

"I was jogging," she said.

"I bet you're afraid of the guy who is murdering women," he said.

"Maybe. You're lucky someone isn't killing young men."

"Oh yea? Nam is, and I could get drafted any day."

The room was somber when her Dad explained why he was packing to leave for Vietnam. *It's why he has been so quiet, and Nathan may need to go to Nam next,* thought Lexa.

"I need you to be responsible now Nathan, keep an eye on your sisters," Dad said. "I have to leave for one year".

"Why will you be gone so long?" Ten year old Candy asked. Her long, dark brown ringlets bounced as she ran to grab her mom's hand.

"Sometimes our job makes us do things we don't want to," said Mom.

"How far away is that place?" asked six year old Abbie who twirled wisps of her blonde hair as she held Lexa's hand on the way to the airport.

"Farther than you can imagine," said Lexa who stood near her mom and grandparents at Mitchell Field Airport.

They waved to him as his ticket was collected and he waved back as he headed into the first of many planes to land him halfway around the globe. All had exposure to war correspondents who detailed the daily death toll on TV news reports which instilled a sense of dread of never seeing the 5'10", 180 pound man in the olive green dress uniform and polished black shoes in one piece again.

Long Binh, Vietnam was postmarked at the top of a letter dated November 10, 1970. As she read the letter at her light tan desk in the corner of her room, she imagined Dad's voyage beginning in Milwaukee to Honolulu, Hawaii, to Kadena Air Base in Okinawa, Japan, landing in Bien Hoa Vietnam, onward to Long Binh. He elaborated on his living quarters, the intense heat and conditions of the barracks. Later notes described the attire of Vietnamese women, a long dress split at the waist, under which they wore loose fitting slacks. He explained how he had to make a mandatory inspection trip to Pleiku, An Khe and Qui Nhon and would follow up on how it went. He felt as though he was imprisoned and detailed incidences of 'Charlies' sneaking onto bases, killing fellow soldiers.

Her mom, who worked full time, had kept in close contact with her husband during his time in Vietnam and kept his homecoming secret when he returned for a brief visit in June. "Look who's here," Mom said wiping her tears as all entered the dining room.

Shocked at how his appearance had changed, Lexa pretended she was unaffected. A mummy who had shed a sarcophagus stood before her, and she wondered if it was why he was sent to the U.S. for a two week furlough. She stared at a man who had become a shadow of his former self, evincing sunken cheeks and dark circles under his charcoal eyes, testifying the hell he would be forced to return to.

She did not receive another letter. Being submerged in a battle zone for six more months, by the end of his tour, visions of war were imprinted to his core.

Wednesday, November 17, 1971
Dad's writings showed a side of him I never knew existed. His experiences in a distant country and job in the army has shaped a man who is angry and separated from those around him. He had a bad temper before, but my fear of him has intensified. Army sergeant + Vietnam + constant back pain + life / job stressors + depression + heightened temper, rage and outbursts = stay far away.

Because her mother insisted that Lexa start first grade upon her family's arrival at the Army base in Heidelberg, Germany at the age of five, she graduated from the tenth school she had attended in June of 1972 when she was 17. The last glance of her school was liberating, and having spent her life on army bases, she and her classmates had little in common. College classes now occupied her time.

On the first Friday of March, Lexa looked up to admire a glistening, opalescent moon as she walked outside to her parent's car in the alley. A woman's spectral voice whispered into her ear, "Find him."

"Milyana, is that you?" she asked, but heard nothing. "It's not as easy as you think it is. Please help me." She remembered the night she hovered over the pale, lifeless girl as she drove to the Catacombs Coffeehouse, her guitar packed in its case.

Since practice was a daily ritual, she felt prepared as she tuned the strings of her guitar. She perspired under the heat of a large floodlight above the stage, and sang songs she had written as well as her favorites by Tina Turner, Janis Joplin and Joan Baez.

Into her fifth song, the B string snapped and having forgotten a spare, she remained steadfast, refusing to glance at the dangling sting.

By her last tune, sweat poured down her temples, and the twenty some patrons in the club applauded as she struck the last chord of 'Sounds of Silence'. Because she had forgotten to pack spare strings, her confidence was shattered. She disliked being out alone late at night, and the pay would not be enough for food and rent.

Her image of a sultry singer was replaced by a white-uniformed woman caring for patients in a hospital. Lexa wrote out detailed notes during lectures and most of her time was spent studying in a quiet library, where she could avoid the conflict at her parents' home.

Her parents had dismissed Sam, hoping she would meet someone else, but weekend evenings belonged to him without their consent.

She and Sam joined Drake Dority at a bar where their conversation was drowned out by live amplified sound. Sam's long time best friend and former childhood neighbor who stood at 6'2", was easy going and loved to party. He pounded the bass guitar in 'The Raving Redwoods', who rehearsed and took whatever gigs they could grab.

"I'm getting off on the babes, but it's too damn loud. I gotta get outa' here," Drake roared. "Are you coming to our jam on Friday?"

"I'll be there," Lexa shouted back.

"Let's hang out at my pad. I can't hear myself think," said Drake.

"So it's okay when your band is this loud?" She laughed.

"You better believe it!"

"They aren't as good as we are," said Sam. His comprehension of algebraic equations, physics, trigonometry and calculus earned him high grades at the Milwaukee School of Engineering.

What distressed Lexa was his taste for hallucinogenic drugs in his quest for the ultimate high. He had insisted his drug using days were over long before a flask of homemade LSD dropped out of his partially unzipped back pack and splattered onto his bedroom floor. He panicked and rushed for towels.

"Why didn't you tell me you made a bottle of Acid?" she asked.

"I was going to surprise you," he said.

"Were you going to sneak a splash into my drink and not tell me?"

"No. My friends and I were going to take a swig to make our music more interesting."

"I don't want to impair my ability to think clearly," she said. "What if someone drank a little too much and flipped out?" she asked during their ride on the icy roads to Drake's east side lower flat.

"Come on, my friends aren't stupid."

"I hope none of your smart friends end up dead or in a mental ward," she said as he parked the Corvair.

In the spacious room, she was in awe of the musicians who possessed mastery of their instruments. All of her practicing aside, she knew her skills did not match theirs. An inch taller than Sam, his slender older brother Tedrick, similar in stature, who inherited his father's brown hair and eyes began warming up.

Lexa sat beside Ted's girlfriend Debra, whose graceful, sculpted 5'3" body, shoulder-length curly brown hair, big brown eyes, and full lips drew everyone's attention as she spoke. She was as beautiful as she was kind. Because she knew almost everyone in Drake's living room where The Raving Redwoods rehearsed, everyone laughed at the private jokes they shared.

The peace sign and symbols covered the walls, bottles were popped open and sipped, Mad Dog wine was poured into plastic cups, and a joint was lit up and handed around the room. Fascinated by the loud, pulsating music on Murray Avenue, the door was open to all who crammed inside. Amplifiers warmed up, guitars were plugged in, pickups adjusted, the turning of pegs tuned vibrating strings, and the drum time signature began in 4/4 time. A mild tap progressed to a frenzied rhythm, while Drake's bass guitar pounded a riff in tempo to the slam of the bass drum and Sam's white Stratocaster wailed a soulful melody, all reaching for the ultimate crescendo in unison.

"You all blew my mind," said a friend who took a sip of beer.

"I did a compound triple meter and the rest was 4/4. I had to play that whole last part with half a stick," said the drummer.

"Man, that was heavy," he said to Sam. "You infused a lot of Hendrix. Where'd you learn to play guitar?"

"I grew up watching my mom play our baby grand piano. She hired a tutor to come to the house every week to give me and my brother lessons, but my uncle showed me how to play some sweet sounding chords on his guitar, and I begged for one until they gave in."

"You like a Strat?"

"It has a compound radius fretboard for easy string bending and three hand wound pickups," said Sam.

"Far out, man."

Sam's mother adored the younger of her two sons, and doted on her "angel" whose wavy golden hair and blue eyes matched hers. Though she was kind to Lexa, she questioned her son's choices, especially his girlfriend.

Sam called Lexa daily to remind her why he rented the apartment. The sole reason was so they could be together.

The charismatic persona of Jimi Hendrix epitomized what Sam craved to become. Both were left handed Stratocaster guitarists. Both loved the wall of noise, distortion and synthesizing of guitar feedback through a screaming crowd. Lexa had written out what Jimi had said, 'When the power of love overcomes the love of power, the world will know peace,' and taped it on the mirror of her dresser as the war in Vietnam dredged on.

Following her evening of Sam's jam session, as she went to the kitchen for breakfast in the morning, she thought nothing of a red vehicle driving eastbound past her house. She left to walk her little sisters to school 20 minutes later, and the same car headed westbound. *A red two door Plymouth. There are probably hundreds of them in the city. I wish I got the plate number.*

That night she told Sam about what she had seen.

"Did you tell your parents?" he asked.

"No, I don't want to worry them, but I am fearful for my little sisters."

"I don't think he's interested in children. Most likely the struggle gives him sense of power over his victims. I doubt if any of them went down easy. It seems young women are his preference."

"I hope you're right," she said.

In the half-lit dimness of dawn she awoke upon hearing her voice moan, "Candy, Abbie." She jolted upward, pushed her curtain aside to scan all she could, in being awakened by a vivid dream of a dark-haired man in a red car who stood beside her little sisters. He smiled and said, "They belong to me now."

She brushed the sweat off of her forehead, got up and went to her little sister's bedroom, sat on the floor, and watched them sleep.

Nathan awoke, walked past their room and whispered, "What are you doing, X?"

"I couldn't sleep."

"What did you see this time?"

"I had a disturbing dream. Someone kidnapped them."

Days later she stood in the foreground of smoke laden skies, ashen trees and blackened landscape. Shelves in charred grocery stores were empty. Distraught, panic-stricken crowds ran in pandemonium. Adults were blood stained and maimed. Children were crying. Sam's hands, full of weed and pills, gestured to open her mouth, and a woman's voice repeated, "Find him." *What a realistic dream.* She wiped the sweat off her brow. *I was surrounded by chaos and madness. I hope it's not another premonition.*

As the days ticked closer to her eighteenth birthday, Sam jingled the keys to Lexa's freedom, tempting her to grab them to be at his side in his apartment. He called her from a pay phone at MSOE daily to tell her how much he hated living alone, and she would be far away from the man who almost ended her life.

For all the times Lexa walked in the alley, she never heard the ghostly voice say 'Find him' again, despite wishing she would. Maybe the spirit of the deceased woman had moved on, but Lexa did know this much; her task was to find the perpetrator.

CHAPTER 3

BAILED

Nathan refused to leave Lexa's side on the warm June afternoon of 1973. As the twenty-year old pleaded, aware of the consequence of her departure, his 5'9" frame remained behind her in the kitchen through the dining room, up a flight of stairs and down a hallway to her bedroom.

"Please X, don't leave," said Nathan who stroked his fingers through thick brown hair and held them on the top of his head, agonized by Lexa strewing his memories into a bag and ransacking her dresser and closet. "Mom and Dad will freak," he said brushing the shirttails of his white shirt aside to stick his hands into the pockets of his jeans.

"Where's my guitar?" she asked Nathan. Lexa peeked into the bedroom of Candy and Abbie, who were absorbed in the game they played. She blew a kiss toward her little sisters. Bye-bye my sweeties.

"Mom locked it up in her bedroom last night. Why didn't you come home? Will we ever see you again?"

"I'm moving in with Sam. I'm done listening to Dad's put-downs and threats. I'm sick of being punished for everything they think I do that's wrong. I'm tired of feeling scared all the time. Sam loves me. Mom and Dad don't." Her love for Nathan was not enough to stay.

"Mom and Dad dislike Sam, and now they will never forgive him. They'll blame him forever for how you left," said Nathan.

"Maybe if I go, Dad will stop his endless reprimanding. Maybe he'll stop his constant foul moods." She had called the previous evening to explain her intent to return in the morning, and her dad's bitter voice pinged through the earphone like bullets she needed to dodge. What worried her was how Dad sounded in repeating that he would kill her the next time he saw her. "The guy who almost murdered me lives around here. Please watch over Candy and Abbie."

She turned back to take a last look at Nathan's anguish as she headed to the alley for one last chance of hearing the soft, eerie voice. She stood at the garage where she had knelt over Milyana's body, and walked to the house where she first heard the ethereal whisper, but all was silent. "Goodbye sweet girl, I'm sorry I could not help either of us." Lexa headed down the street, and waited at the bus stop.

She sat in the closest seat, and rested her head on the window as her belongings vibrated in a bag on her ripped jeans. She watched vehicles below, in envy of passengers cruising to their destinations before she exited on Twenty Seventh and State Street.

In a small fifth floor dwelling, Steppenwolf's "Born to Be Wild" leaked into the hallway where she turned the key in the lock and was greeted by Sam who smiled and reached out to wrap his arms around her. She brushed his shoulder-length, wavy blonde hair back and kissed him, in a small dining area inside the door. To her right was a built-in mirrored china hutch beside a refrigerator and white cabinets in a kitchenette were to the left of the entrance. Soon, Sam, Drake, and Tedrick fought to restrain a heavy, used green sofa up the long, twisting staircase to be part of the living room.

In leaving food and transportation behind, Lexa's college pursuits crumbled. The engine of Sam's Corvair blew up and was towed to a junkyard. She applied for and got a job as a waitress at Captain's restaurant, and when all she had to eat for the day was an apple, she felt no regret for leaving her parent's home.

Screaking crickets no longer filling her ears, wails of sirens besieged her apartment. To save money, she hitchhiked to her job where she scavenged a meal in between waiting on tables.

At the end of her shift near the time clock, Lexa overheard two waitresses discuss a former coworker named Milyana. "Her boyfriend's obituary was in yesterday's paper. He was killed in Vietnam." They sighed deeply. "What a shame," said one of the women. "She and I worked together. I miss our laughter."

"What do you remember about her?" asked Lexa.

"She was kind, smart, and planned on going to nursing school."

"No one deserves to die like she did," said Lexa. "No one."

Her shift ending at 11:30 pm, she grabbed her jacket, and walked to the northbound corner of 27th and Morgan Avenue, stuck out her thumb, and a car stopped. A plume of gray exhaust billowed from the tailpipe of the revving eight cylinder engine, and the radio blared Led Zeppelin's 'Whole Lotta Love'. The window opened, smoke swirled out in plumes, and she asked four guys in their late teens where they were headed. "Wherever you want." She climbed into the back seat.

"Thanks for stopping. I've had a long night of waiting on tables to snobs who get off on harassing me, then leave a crappy tip."

"You're not scared to get into a car with four delinquents?"

"Why should I be afraid of you?" she asked. "Drop me off on State Street," she said to the driver.

"What would you do if we don't let you out? I might not let you go if you were in my car," said the back seat passenger leaning toward her. "Maybe we should abduct you."

"Knock it off. One way or other, we pay a price for our choices," she said as she got out. "Dude, at your age, all girls are tempting."

"At my age? How old are YOU? Fifteen?" he shouted, hanging his head out of the window.

"No, I'm eighteen. Too old for you."

"Wrooong!" He screamed as the tires shrieked down the road.

Tuesday, June 26, 1973

The squealing tires sent the risk of not leaving a stranger's car in one piece. When the door latches, tingles of fright crawl up my spine. I'm at the mercy of men who sit a breath away. The red car is still out there. I'll take the bus, be vigilant about who is around me, and keep my pin in hand until I get to my door.

The following day, she stepped off of the bus, and on the short walk to her apartment, Lexa was seized from behind and dangled off the ground. Massive arms were wrapped around her and a hand was clenched over her mouth.

"Do not scream," he gurgled.

The smell of decaying teeth and stale beer gagged her while thick arms clutched her torso and reached under her blouse. Fighting to free herself, her anger intensified as she felt the grit on his dirty hands rubbing over her breasts and the other down her jeans. She knew better than to beg for help. She knew playing dead could be her demise this time and swung her right foot between his legs.

His chin-length, dark, greasy hair, and beard shook as he coughed, bent forward, and dropped her on the ground, giving her time to squeeze behind a dumpster.

"You don't stand a chance," he raged in heavy wheeze-like snorts.

Unable to budge, she sucked in the dark, musty night. Her heart pounded into her ears.

He fought to reach her face through the space between the brick wall and metallic enclosure, kicking hard on the steel and slurring profanities in realizing his body was too corpulent to grab her. "If I ever see you again, I'm gonna kill you," he shrieked.

"Then get in line you pathetic idiot." Her voice echoed around the concrete.

"What did you say? Damn you!" he repeated as his fists banged onto the garbage container that echoed into her head like gunshots. He kicked at her steel shelter and swore she will be dead if he laid eyes on her again.

I should have hitchhiked and kept my mouth shut. Great idea I had to carry a pin. A lot of good it did me with my arms in a bear lock, she thought, worming her way out an hour later and walking up the back metal stairway.

"What happened to you? I was worried," said Sam.

"I had to work late. I'm going to brush my teeth, shower, and go to sleep. I'm tired."

During the time it took for her bruises and scratches to fade, men loitered in the dark of all day dreams where she turned to look over her shoulders at any movement in her vision, both real and imagined. Always there, they were ready to grab and injure her no matter how fast she ran. A liquor store was within a block of her apartment. *The advantages of the drinking age being lowered to 18. I don't need a fake ID anymore.* Cabernet, Pinot Noir, Merlot, Zinfandel, she was going to try them all. Maybe one would calm her fears which infused almost all destinations, despite a long pin woven into the outer fabric of her purse.

For weeks She and Sam scoured classified ads to buy an affordable car, and she felt content to park a used gray Volkswagen Beetle in the back alley alongside an empty storage building.

A few days later, Sam confronted her upon his discovery in the garbage. He held up an empty bottle. "A wine flask has been in the garbage every few days. Why are you drinking so much? You're becoming an alcoholic."

"I don't drink any more than you do."

"I care too much about you. It upsets me to see this," he said.

"Okay, don't worry. I will cut back." Someday. "What happened to your right hand?"

"What are you talking about? It's fine." He held his hand up.

"Your hand was bandaged up a few seconds ago. Be careful."

Sam arrived home that evening, his right hand bleeding by a puncture wound. "I tried to be cautious, but a string snapped and went straight through my palm." He bandaged it the way she had seen it.

Drake's announcement of his new job as an insurance underwriter created the gloomy summer of 'The Raving Redwoods' disbanding and Sam frequenting Amadeus Amped every few days to study the bulletin board. A month later, he ripped off a notice, auditioned for and became the lead guitarist in a band named 'FX of Violinz', to take his familiar steps onto a stage at night. Their set list was full of upbeat rock and roll music, and filled clubs wherever they performed.

Sam had one trimester to go at the Milwaukee School of Engineering, and having heard how much money he could make, was hired part time as a driver at Courteous Cab Company. His new boss, an ex-drill sergeant, who had a habit of rubbing the stubble of his crew cut, hurled an ultimatum. "If you don't cut your hair, you cannot work here. No one's gonna take a ride with a crazy looking hippie behind the wheel."

Sam explained his dilemma to Lexa during dinner as sunset seeped into their apartment through the beige curtains. His long hair was part of his stage identity, and he refused to chop it off. "No one has short hair in the band. They might replace me. What should I do?"

"I have an idea." She purchased a short-haired blonde wig matching his hair color, but what solved one problem created another. He put the black hat on his head and it teetered on top of the wig. He pulled on the visor until the fabric began ripping away. At the start of his shift, the manager told him it was about time his hair looked decent. He asked what idiot gave him the wrong hat size.

Sam said he was starving at the end of his workday. He grabbed a plate and dug into a rice and vegetable casserole which sat on the kitchen table. "I hate my job. I'm worried the wig will fall off."

"I'm not surprised. By the way, I got a call from Doctors hospital on Wells Street. They want me to start next week."

"Are you quitting the restaurant?"

"No, nursing assistant during the day and I'll waitress at night."

"Why are you working two jobs? Our rent is only $65.00 a month."

"I'm going to get my degree," she said.

"As far as I'm concerned, you're smart enough. There is no reason for you to finish college," he said.

"Dropping out was one of the worst days of my life. Why the double standard? You're attending an engineering college. Do I need your permission to become a nurse?"

He gave no reply.

On her days off, Lexa accompanied Sam to watch FX of Violinz pack night clubs, and overheard many secrets of his fellow musicians in dressing rooms during breaks and at the end of shows. Band members and their girlfriends accepted invitations to numerous events, including a party given by the manager of the band, Sha-Na-Na in the Prospect Towers overlooking Lake Michigan. Lexa slathered on extra eye make-up, and chose her best jeans and black shirt.

Thursday, July 5, 1973

The elevator opened at the top floor into the penthouse. I was awed by the high ceilings, expansive rooms, artwork bordered by ornate frames and extravagant furnishings. I felt intimidated by the musicians who I recognized and have heard on the radio. Because I had too much wine and champagne, my vision blurred, and I stumbled once or twice.

Wednesday, August 8, 1973

At the restaurant this evening, a patron asked me if my name was Milyana who waited on him the last time. He did not read about her murder. I explained she no longer worked here. He insisted we look the same and he stared at me until he left. I asked for a shot of Jim Beam as the bartender was closing up. I may be on track to join the people who sleep in my back alleyway, cradling their bottles.

Sam's day job as a cab driver followed by his rock and roll persona on a stage three to four nights weekly to pay his way through MSOE, left Lexa alone most evenings.

Her steps echoed off the bricks on the outside metal lattice stairway to the edge of the rooftop, where the breeze sailed her long mane. She often sat overlooking the city, sipping on several glasses of Merlot.

She watched traffic weave through the street, listened to frightful cries of children in nearby apartments, and felt surrounded by brutality. The greasy-haired bearded beast who held her captive in her alley walked below, and her heart raced into her ears. It took every ounce of restraint not to drop her wine bottle on the top of his head.

Every aspect of her surroundings overtook her thoughts, to where she began a vigorous exercise regimen to improve her strength and agility. She ran up and down the steps to her fifth floor apartment on the inside, and on the outside metal lattice stairwell.

Thursday, September 6, 1973

The parties Sam and I attend acquaint me with different wines, the flavors, dry, sweet, white, and red. Lines of coke get snorted, weed is shared in a circle, and people pop uppers and downers like candy. I think the dealers don't ask for cash for all the drugs they dole out because they want to become the best friend of every musician. Sam and his bandmates get lots of attention.

In September, Lexa applied for tuition aid, was relieved to be accepted, gave her resignation at the restaurant, and cut her hours at Doctor's hospital to accommodate her class schedule.

Sam sat adjacent from Lexa at the kitchen table where they ate the spaghetti and salad she had prepared on Sunday evening. Pushed out of the way as they ate, her thick books were pulled back to where she studied under the light of a hanging lamp.

"Lexa, you hardly pay attention to me. Your head is always buried in your books and I see your back more than your face. When are you going to drop out of school and stay home to take care of me?"

"Your mother told you I should drop out of school, didn't she? Is it what you want? Should your girlfriend be like your mother?"

"Do you have something against my mother?" he asked.

"No, not at all."

Monday, December 3, 1973
Before I left the restaurant this evening, I asked the bartender to give me a shot of Jack Daniels. I'm getting 5 hours of sleep a night because of working long hours and studying. My empty wine bottles go in the back alley dumpster, and I hide new ones under an old blanket in the basement locker room. Sam thinks I don't drink anymore. His mom says I'm not the perfect girl for her angel. I worry about my grades and where I'm going to get enough cash to get through school, and I haven't made time to hunt down Milyana's killer.

Her boots clunked down the metal stairwell to the alley where Lexa brushed off eight inches of snow which had accumulated on her VW. Her first class ending, she went to the cafeteria for a cup of coffee. The Milwaukee Sentinel newspaper dated Monday December 17, 1973 headlined a plane crash into a neighborhood and the murder of a police officer. She picked up the paper, thumbed through it, and stopped on page five in grasping the article: **'South Siders Tense after 2 Slayings'**. Lexa read the story twice upon realizing a former high school classmate and another young woman was strangled in a two day time span, within a five mile radius. The photos of both young, smiling women broke Lexa's hesitation. *They were beautiful. My attack was near there. It has to be the same person doing this for the past three years. He continues to elude capture. Maybe Oma is right about him* *changing his hair color and style. I need to tap into the nature of a murderer.*

Stunned by the death of her gentle classmate, Lexa felt apprehensive, knowing her attacker remained at large. At her apartment, her first stop was to unlock the door to the basement. On the rooftop, she sat cross-legged on the snow, sipped on her wine and ruminated how she could lure the city's serial killer. She returned her cup to the basement before the five story climb.

"Vietnam War, Watergate scandal, and women are strangled, not very far from here. There's so much violence lately," she said, slamming her books on the kitchen table. "And now gas is going up to 90 cents a gallon because of an oil embargo," she said to Sam, who sat on the sofa strumming his guitar.

"Don't get worked up about it. It's not your problem. There will always be people who do bad things."

I'm going to hunt down this criminal. I will never forget his voice. I may be the only survivor. I'll check the areas where bodies were reported. She visited a sporting goods store, browsed aisles looking for any useful item to help her quest, and purchased Mace and a Rapala knife for filleting fish. She admired the razor sharpness of the blade which would serve a more important purpose. She opened a map of Milwaukee, and penciled X's where the murders occurred, including her attack at Mt. Olivet cemetery, and discovered a common thread: a close knit group of graveyards.

The attacks near cemeteries may be deliberate. Arlington to St. Adalberts, about a mile. Arlington Cemetery to Mt. Olivet, roughly a mile. Arlington to Good Hope Cemetery, about two miles, and from Arlington to Forest Home Cemetery, less than two miles.

On Thursday, December 20, Sam was at his show. She parked the VW and walked through the neighborhood on Howard Ave. between 35th St. to 27th St. She began at 10:30 and ended at midnight. Cars whirred by, ignoring her. She took a similar path on Friday night and walked through snow-topped headstones. On Saturday the 22nd, she began street walking at 10:30. At midnight, a dark-haired man in his early thirties, driving a blue car, swerved towards her, and rolled down the window, eyeing her.

Touch me and I will slash your wrists. She clutched the knife behind her back.

"Miss, you shouldn't be walkin' alone. Der's a lot a' kooks out 'ere. You need a cab or sumpin'?" he asked, leaning out of the window. "I can give ya a ride."

"No thanks. I'm parked up the block," she sighed.

"Okay, but ya gotta be careful dese days," he said, as he drove off.

That was a waste of time, she thought, and started the ignition.

In her dark apartment, she swigged down several glasses of wine and wondered if her paranoia would evolve into confidence.

Sam returned home fifteen minutes later and set his guitar case down. "How was your evening?" he asked peering into the garbage.

She had already tossed the empty bottle outside in the dumpster. "I've been reading. How was your show?"

"Great as usual. We're probably the best band in the city," he said reeking of booze and cigarettes. He approached her to kiss her.

She held her breath as they embraced. Her teeth were brushed, and she had sprayed Wild Lily cologne on her neck. *Soon...I will be able to suck in a deep breath and feel a sense of calm...soon.*

Saturday, December 22, 1973

I'm not sure what's more disconcerting, being attacked without a weapon or having a weapon and not being attacked. I will be prepared for predators and continue my search for the man who took those young women, my classmate, and Milyana out of this world too soon. May your souls rest in peace.

CHAPTER 4

ETHEREAL TRAVELS

They planned a sleigh ride on Sunday, February 17 to meander through snow topped trees, evergreens and hilly powder coated country sides.

"Did you hear what our neighbor said?" Sam asked.

"I can't hear her in here," she said in the bathroom where she towel dried her hair.

"I made breakfast for us. They're my special recipe pot pancakes."

"Shhh…If we can hear what's going on in the next apartment, they can hear us." She frowned at the plate of green doughy slabs. "No, thanks. They look disgusting."

"Oh, come on, try one. I did. It'll make the sleigh ride more fun."

"No, I don't want one."

"Try one. They taste fine. I'll pour some maple syrup on yours." He took his fork, stabbed a piece and put it near her mouth, looking into her deer-in-the-headlights eyes.

"It doesn't look appetizing. I don't want to get sick."

"Come on, try a little. Just one bite."

She opened her mouth and chewed his concoction.

"Do you like it?"

"No. It's horrid," she said. "I don't want any."

"I'll put more syrup on it." He forced it into her mouth.

"It doesn't taste good. It's like musty seaweed." She grimaced.

"Oh come on, have some more." He held the full fork to her lips.

She ate everything he offered. The THC of the cannabis kicked in, and all laughter silenced. The room spinning, she grabbed the back of the chair and steadied her limbs to the ground where she melted into a cold wood floor. Chills shot through her. She remembered a vast empty space before floating toward the glow of a hypnotic bright light, until she was awakened by Sam who repeated her name, alarmed at how pale and unresponsive she had become. Her tether to earth hung in the balance as she drifted in and out of consciousness, and light melted into darkness. Her mind struggled for clarity.

"Why…why?" She repeated, rolling side to side, unable to lift her head off the chilled floor. Sam, who ingested as much as she had, was as weak, lying beside her, but managed to drag them both into the waterbed, where they collapsed.

By Monday, the undecipherable scribble in her head was erased, but the memory of an ingestion bringing back images of Joplin and Hendrix and an ethereal light remained. She remembered the bottle of Lysergic acid, the hallucinogen Sam had made and realized he would have insisted on her drinking it also, had it not smashed open on his bedroom floor. She believed Oma was watching out for her that day. It was time to go her own way, having grown tired of his drug use. Their eight months of living together was enough, and she informed Sam she was leaving. She feared that either he would unintentionally place her in harm's way, or accidentally kill her.

"Lexa, will you marry me?" he asked.

"Are you asking because I said I'm leaving you?" She sat on the edge of the waterbed.

"Please don't leave. I love you and only you through eternity. There will never be anyone else. Will you marry me?" He sat beside her.

"No, I can't marry you. We're not right for each other. We should go our separate ways."

"What are you talking about? We've been together for forever. My life won't be the same without you. I will change. I want to take care of you. You have to believe me. No one is like you," he said.

"Let's see how things go for the next few months," she said.

A month passed and Sam asked, "Will you marry me? I love you."

Lexa let out a deep sigh. "Our three years together have been good. I know you love me and I love you. After you graduate, things will be better, and we will have a great life together. Yes." She kissed him.

"You have nothing to worry about." He wove his fingers through her hair and down her back, igniting the friction between them. The smoothness of his skin embodied pleasure and familiarity to her.

Drake Dority was the best man, and Lexa asked a coworker to serve as her witness. In a short conventional ceremony, "I do's" were exchanged and the officiating judge snapped a photo of the group.

The Milwaukee County courthouse behind them, they returned to their apartment. Sam picked up the ringing black telephone and spoke to his brother Ted and girlfriend Debra, who had been living in the mountains of Colorado for the past eight months. They discussed how much they would like a visit and gave directions to their location.

Sam asked Lexa about traveling to see his brother and girlfriend, and she agreed, saying the trip would be a honeymoon.

Debra drew a detailed map they received in the mail a week later. "Milwaukee to Denver, to Colorado Springs to Pueblo. Continue west on Hwy 50 to San Isabel National Forest. Drive to a small white sign posted on the right of a dirt road stating: Old Monarch Pass. Take it 2 - 4 miles to the top of the pass and keep going. About eight miles at the top on the left, I will leave a white piece of cloth as a marker. On the next dirt road, drive 100 feet, turn left, you see our camp."

In early June, they packed the back seat of their Volkswagen bug, and maps guided them to their destination near a mountain summit.

"The views are amazing," said Lexa. Debra's shoulder-length, wavy brown hair and five foot three inch frame appeared trimmer, toned and darker skinned than the last time Lexa had seen her.

"Set your tent up anywhere around the van. We'll start a campfire and make some chili," said Ted. "We'll show you our favorite spots." He lit up a joint and passed it around.

They traversed up mountain sides, beginning in the morning and arriving at the top in darkness, and slid down steep terrain to get back to the campsite. On their last hiking expedition up a steep incline, the group spent a few hours pioneering the wilderness, when Sam frowned, patted his clothes down and ransacked through his pockets.

"Lexa, do you have the VW keys?"

"You drove us here. You had them. We will freeze to death up here if we can't start the car," she said shivering.

Sam's face became haggard as he zigzagged across the mountain in the darkening sky. Tall grasses and flowers that appeared pastoral in one moment became obstacles to spying the glimmer of keys, the value of which increased by the minute. As light diminished, the more desperate they felt as the night and frozen mist swirled around them in the bitter cold.

"I found them!" The wind whistled through Debra's scream. "My Mom always says to pretend I found something I lost. She says to picture it like it already happened. It always works for me."

Her overwhelming relief made Lexa wonder if she imagined capturing a killer strongly enough would pay off. It had to be harder than locating keys, but she devised a plan on their drive home.

Back in Milwaukee, Sam was glued to his Stratocaster, the guitar that validated his skills at popular clubs. Lexa gave little thought to him relishing local rock star fame and the attention of devout groupies, both men and women who showered trinkets upon him. He showed Lexa a Hendrix T-shirt, a Led Zeppelin, and a Pink Floyd album, and lyrics were given to him to transform into a song. The gifts distracted him long enough for Lexa's covert study time.

In her VW she heard a gruesome news broadcast on the radio, and Lexa became engrossed in tracking the man who wreaked terror on the dark streets of the city. The razor sharp knife and Mace would either harm or subdue him long enough for her to run and call police.

Sam rarely returned before 2:30 am during shows, which gave her from 11:00 pm until 2:00 am to become bait. The sites were in close proximity. Her walk began at Arlington Cemetery, where she spent 30 minutes as vehicles streamed by. Two cars stopped. One driver asked if she needed a ride, but his gray hair and voice was not a match. She said she was "almost home". The second stop was a driver who opened his door and asked if she was looking for money. She said she was going to help her mother who lived nearby.

"Sweetie, the only people around here are dead."

"Not my Mom." She sprinted to her car.

At St. Adalberts, she walked for 45 minutes, and a woman stopped to ask if she was okay. Lexa said she was "almost home".

Twenty minutes into her walk at Mt. Olivet Cemetery, within a block of her attack, she glimpsed a blonde male a driver who stopped to watch her. She heard a door slam, and footsteps walked toward her. She picked up her pace; his stride was long and heavy. She grasped her knife and Mace, and the long pin was woven into her jacket. She ran into the graveyard, and dodged between monuments. In the dark, she hid behind a tombstone and listened for breaking twigs. Folded like a fetus, fear crept into her as she took in long quiet breaths.

"You're playing games, aren't you?" screamed a man's voice.

She did not respond. It was not the man who tried to strangle her.

"Oh, I have all night. How about you?" his voice echoed off of the marble and granite.

She wished she was in her apartment, as she flipped the red switch on the Mace to the open setting.

"I'm going to get you, and when I do, you're going to either be real sorry or real happy," he said. His voice was near.

She held the Mace in her right hand, and worried it may be defective or not work. In her left hand was the fishing knife. Whether it was minutes or an eternity, she felt pale and clammy as she recalled her grandmother's words to live boldly and in prepared vigilance. Twigs broke; his footsteps became louder. She peeked out.

"Babe, you are easy to find," he said.

She remained steadfast and ready. "So why will I be sorry?"

"Honey, I'm bigger and stronger than you are."

She knew he was close. The ground scrunched under his steps, and she closed her eyes to calm her racing heart.

He tapped on her shoulder, and she sprung to her feet, sprayed Mace into his face, and ran. Her body was shaking as she started up the VW and drove home. She had no idea what time it was. For all she knew Sam was waiting and wondering where she was. She ran up the steps to an empty apartment and sighed in relief.

Sam returned home five minutes later, and showed her the new guitar strap someone had made for him. She admired the design, and he leaned in to caress her.

Friday, May 31, 1974

My quest to find a needle in a haystack became a cat and mouse game. This was a new cat. My plan failed, and there won't be a next time. I'm guilty of creating the cat, and this mouse escaped. I haven't had wine recently, but tomorrow I will select some I haven't tried yet. Milyana has probably given up on me.

Lexa opened the fraying article about Milyana and reread it. She stared at the photo and returned it to her wallet, sadly disappointed.

That night Sam was given a plastic bag full of Quaaludes. Lexa batted twinges of insecurity away, especially at the sight of sweaty women, who smiled and danced at his feet during shows. They stared up at the musician, magician of sorts, who entertained them by navigating his long fingers on amplified nickel plated steel core wire.

"There are women who stare at you all evening. I understand why they look at you, but what bugs me is how they look at you," she said.

His whiskey breath hit her nostrils. "You have nothing to fear. How many times do I have to tell you you're the only girl I'll ever want to be with? I could spend the rest of my life looking at your pretty face."

They laughed about how drunk and scantily clad some women were, and how they would slither and grind in front of the stage.

"Promise me you'll tell me if something I do bothers you. And if there is someone else you have stronger feelings for, be up front about it, okay? I want honesty," she said.

"Of course I will." In their waterbed, he smiled, reached over and kissed her.

Sam graduated magna cum laude, submitted a resignation to his boss at the cab company, and shelved the blonde wig. He was hired by an electronics firm, and because his workday was 9 am to 5 pm, 'FX of Violinz' performed on weekends. Their bass player needed more income, and set his sights on California, and Sam convinced Drake Dority to take his place.

Sam heeded all of Lexa's premonitions especially after she predicted his hand injury. Though her family's relationship was distanced since she had left, Lexa continued her college studies, worked at Doctor's Hospital in the evenings, and Nathan married his high school sweetheart, Polly. Lexa's dad refused to look at her, and her guitar was returned per a meeting arranged by her mom. The records, record player and clothes she left behind were gone and in wanting reconciliation, she did not question it. Her underwater mural vanished under wallpaper and most traces of her past were gone.

Lexa asked Sam if he had thought about moving out of the apartment. She feared the day may arrive when the bearded beast who held her captive behind the dumpster would finish what he attempted.

"Our finances are good. Let's start looking for a place," he said.

They bought a house which had separate living quarters on the upper floor. In the lower living room, they set their glass topped coffee table before a brick fireplace and settled a tan and brown sofa to face two matching chairs as well as a seven foot high by eight foot wide bookshelf Sam had built it in their apartment and had to disassemble it to move it into the house. He had carried each piece of cut pine up the winding apartment stairway, needing Lexa's help for heavier pieces. It occupied almost an entire wall of the living room and faced the front entrance, where copper-colored drapes hung over a large window. A rust-toned shag carpet wove throughout the connected living and dining rooms, separated by an archway.

For as old as the structure was, all they thought it needed was to apply a sealant to the wood on the outside back stairwell, fresh paint in the rooms, and an electrician to repair the light fixture in one of the bedroom closets. Alongside the entrance, inside of the house, the stairwell that lead to the upper flat would be locked.

The upper unit had a kitchen, living room, bathroom and one bedroom who they rented to Janie, a friendly, young working woman who met the criteria as an ideal tenant.

They cleaned and painted their turn of the century duplex, noticing random noise and static spewing on their radio, and an electrical voltage problem of a closet light that spewed sparks.

"I've had nightmares of a dark-haired woman staring at me, and I don't know who it is," Sam said.

"I'm having similar dreams," said Lexa. "Maybe it's why the last owners were in a hurry to leave. Tonight, while you're out, I'll get our clothes hung up and finish unpacking."

Because of the faulty light socket, she used a flashlight and stood on a kitchen chair to wash off dusty, spider webbed shelves. Her hand touched a slick metallic dagger. Confused, she brought the heavy sword down, and inspected a long silver, triangularly-shaped blade. A vision of blood dripping from it caused her to drop it.

Sam returned hours later repeating her name. "Lexa, where are you?" He walked into the bedroom. "I worried about you all night. I envisioned you clenching a huge knife. I rushed to get home to see if you were alright. We need to get a phone hooked up here."

She walked him into the living room. "This long bayonet was on the upper shelf of your closet. Maybe the property has more history than we are aware of."

He mused over the dagger. "I don't like it. We need to get rid of it."

While Sam was at work, she tucked it into the opening between the wall and her waterbed. Her hands were small enough to reach into the gap and grab it.

Her classes done the following day, Lexa parked her VW, and to her left, a white-haired, plump woman who stood near her back entrance, signaled, waved and introduced herself. Lexa did the same.

"My husband and I lived here for the last 30 years, and your house was here before then."

"How well did you know your previous neighbors?" Lexa asked.

"Before you arrived, the couple lived there for a year and other families stayed for around three years at most. One remodeled your home into a duplex, and about twenty years ago, a lady died in the back bedroom."

"Her son Shane was a good friend of my son, and he had the most beautiful dark eyes and jet-black hair I have ever seen. A month after his mom's death, someone new moved in. Are you newlyweds? It will be nice to see babies and kids in the neighborhood again."

"Do you remember how old the lady who died was?" Lexa asked, wondering if it was the face she had seen in her recent dreams.

"Julette was in her early thirties. She was lovely, and had stunning, long, dark hair."

Lexa relayed the conversation to Sam. She didn't mind her occasional dream of the dark-haired woman, but did not understand why and how long the dreams would continue. She recalled a small part of the dream, "You must help me find..." but a loud noise outside startled her, and she woke up.

Sam asked where the sword was, and she said it was on the floor, tucked beside the wall and waterbed.

"Why did you put it there?" he asked.

"It's for our protection in case we need to use it on an intruder."

"I don't think we should keep it," he said as he flexed and moved his fingers on vibrating steel and silver wire on the neck of his guitar. After securing his Strat in its case, he changed into blue jeans and a fitted black Henley shirt, and left to join 'FX of Violinz' for a show.

That evening while she read school books and sipped on wine, Lexa's mother called.

"We bought a house in Florida, and will be moving as soon as we can sell this place."

"You never told me you were looking for another home."

"Every time I look into Oma's bedroom, I feel sad. I see her sitting at her sewing desk like she always used to. And Dad always has so much pain in his back. Shoveling snow has become too difficult for him. He's always worried about icy weather and body aches. Nathan has his own driveway to clear out and a toddler to think about, so he can't help us, and I hate it, especially after a long day at work."

"Mom, do you think Dad will ever speak to me again?"

"He won't let us mention your name. I'm sure he'll get over your leaving someday."

As Lexa hung up, she felt a haze settle over her at not being able to watch her sisters grow up. Candy, six years her junior, Abbie was ten years younger. Though she had stopped in to see them monthly, this distance made her fearful of becoming insignificant, a remote sister who meant nothing to them. She reached into her closet for one of the bottles of wine she had hidden under a blanket, and poured a few more glasses.

The following evening she approached Sam. "My family is moving to Florida. It's going to be tough not to see them. I'd like to visit."

"Sounds fine. Let's ask for time off from our jobs."

Lexa informed her mom of her arrival time. Her intent was to visit before her dad got home at 6:00. Her sisters and mother were happy to see her, and gave a tour of the house, property, pool, and dock that overlooked a waterway, aware of their short time together. Lexa assured them she would visit at the same time for the remainder of the week.

In the morning's heat, Sam shoved bricks under the back tires of the VW, parked on a slanted driveway to replace old brakes and use the tools and equipment he had packed. Tired of working on the car, Lexa's eyes followed his stride through the motel toward her.

"You're staring at me. I heard you gasp," he said. "What's wrong?"

"I saw blood gushing down your arm, starting at the top of your left shoulder. I was ready to grab a towel and rush you to the ER."

"I came in for water, but was about to go back outside, reach under the front passenger tire and if the car slipped, the rim would have ripped my shoulder open." He repacked his tools, refused to touch the vehicle, and decided they should relax at the beach.

The sand and ocean were reminders of living at the water's edge when her family had lived in Fort Monroe Virginia, where as a teen she had received a lifeguard certificate and was trained on techniques for holding her breath.

She swam out to the horizon, the shore becoming distant faster than she remembered, and turned back. Her surges of tenacity were no match for a vicious undertow crushing her in each wave. She held her breath and jumped up to gasp for air. Getting pulled out into deeper waters, she choked as milky froth was sucked into her lungs.

Her consciousness fading, the sight of Milyana in the alley and the memory of hands wrapped around her neck returned. The attempts she made to catch a killer had been futile. Turbulence forced her eyes shut, and she felt at peace in letting go. She drifted downward. Sam swam out and yanked her arms to give her another lungful of air and they muddled their way to shore.

"I got to you as fast as I could. How are you?"

She bent forward, knelt on the sand, coughed and wheezed. "Thanks for coming to my rescue. I thought it was over for me. Why do I keep knocking on death's door?" she gasped.

"This time you were pounding."

Tuesday, July 30, 1974

Waves topple like gargantuan dominos by the breath of a cosmic force, making all entities equal in nature's dimension. A fragile thread kept me connected to this life as the solution of mineral salts filled my lungs and whispered to surrender to it. I remember the day Sam was the reason for my glimpse of the other side, and today he pulled me back.

My year of lifeguard training paid off in being able to hold my breath for so long before going under. Three minutes made the difference between life and death today and on that night in August four years ago. I'm reminded of Debra's words on the cold hillside and at times I can still hear the soft voice whisper, "Find him." I will devise another plan.

Sam insisted they saved each other. She was curious as to whether her visions would continue, and was jabbed with worry as to why she had no insight regarding herself to avoid drowning. Maybe it was a lesson she needed to learn, to be aware of a sign reading: Dangerous Undertow.

The premonitions had been sporadic, like envisioning her headstone beside her grandmother's after her attack, the sirens and red lights as she watched kids building their snow fort, seeing Sam's arm bleeding heavily when he worked under the VW, and stopping a child who was about to drink antifreeze. There had to be a way to hone in on the brief visions.

In returning to Milwaukee, Sam's days were spent at an electronics firm. Most evenings 'FX of Violinz' took up his time and Lexa sat in classrooms, libraries and beside the bookshelf on the floor, immersed in studying, to pass state board exams. She cut back to one glass of wine daily, despite craving more due to the stressors of her job, housekeeping, cooking tasks, and lack of sleep.

Friday, August 9, 1974

I had a visualization of the faceless man who almost killed me. He looked upward and blew a kiss. I was on the top of a stairway or a platform which could mean our paths may cross again.

Today President Nixon resigned to avoid impeachment for illegal wiretapping. Stepping in will be Gerald Ford who served on the Warren Commission and accused the CIA of destroying information connected to JFK's murder.

Wednesday, November 6, 1974

On the second page of the newspaper was a small article and photo of a woman who was strangled. Her hair was long, just like the rest. I am certain detectives are working to solve these murders, but no details were given, which makes this more alarming, since I am aware of the killer's tactics. Maybe the clues are gruesome, or homicides are becoming too common. Today I tried new wines, and have no plans to stop.

Wednesday, April 30, 1975

The capture of Saigon by the North Vietnamese was broadcast on all airwaves. Watching the finality of the war and the breaking of the peace treaty, American and civilian military personnel and tens of thousands of South Vietnamese are being evacuated in one of the largest CH 46 and CH 53 helicopter missions in history.

a girl a band a diary

Tuesday, May 6, 1975

Those who burnt their draft cards are condemned and those who fought have not fared well on US soil. Their scars serve as war's lifelong reminders.

A ticker tape parade was held in New York in 1946 after World War II, but Vietnam vets returned to a nation of apathy. No newspaper headlined a welcome home. Soldiers appear to voices ranging from hatred to indifference as the days go on the same way as the day before, as though the faces they pass on the streets should care they sacrificed their lives for their country.

Lexa and Debra were at a show where Lexa and the manager struck up a conversation. She happily accepted a date to entertain on a coffeehouse stage.

Wearing patched bell bottomed jeans, a beaded fringed vest, peace sign earrings and long colorful beads under spot lights, she strummed her guitar. She sang her original songs for two hours and her yearning to be in a band was rekindled as she stayed to watch musicians who shared their gifts of song and talent. It was her best performance.

"Sam, it's the seventies. Nothing surprises anyone anymore. I could get on stage wearing only masking tape all over me. No one will care. Doing a great show on stage is hard to explain. I feel more alive and my senses are heightened. I'm going to look for thigh high black boots and check AA's musician's board to join a band looking for a singer."

"Amadeus Amped is always crowded. You'll find something."

She stuffed a few phone numbers into her purse. In dreams, air raid sirens often rang in her ears, she smiled at Oma's visits, and though many mornings large hands around her neck awoke her, the dark-haired man who stalked her day dreams now pointed a sword in her direction. The names of bands auditioning singers sounded intriguing.

CHAPTER 5

INVITATION

Lexa purchased the required white uniforms and cap, and as her graduation date neared, her application as a graduate nurse at Deaconess Hospital was accepted, where she would work second shift. Her white shoes walked antiseptic hallways, as she checked vital signs, gave medicine, performed CPR, held hands and spoke last words to those who could no longer hang on to the fragility of life.

At 2:30 am, Sam approached her as she studied for the state board exam. He paced the bedroom floor. "This evening our singer said he's quitting, so the guys and I discussed…having you take his place."

"Your band? Me…the lead singer of 'FX of Violinz'? Yes!" She felt joy tingle through her veins.

"We have a rehearsal scheduled on Saturday. Think about what songs you want to sing. Also, we don't want anyone to know you and I are married, so consider using another last name."

Thursday, May 9, 1975

Though singing in a band is within my grasp, I feel as much uncertainty as confidence, and as much anxiety as excitement. I'm at 4 glasses of wine a day.

The seventies has brought major changes in dynamics of relationships. America's divorce rate started climbing in the late 60's, but has now skyrocketed. Women are demanding equality in all facets of life, and if an intimate disease is contracted, an injection, pills, or antibiotics are the magic cure-all.

Wednesday, May 14, 1975

The body of a 22 year old woman was discovered yesterday near a garage on 20th and Cleveland Ave, near the Forest Home Cemetery. Police found white pantyhose wrapped around her neck. She was strangled the same way Milyana was, and never made it home after working second shift as a nursing assistant. Her husband must now raise their one year old son. All of the deceased women have long hair, and either pantyhose or rope is used. He strikes intermittently and targets specific women in the dead of night.

Lexa's passion for music began as a child, watching her uncle pick up an accordion, adjust straps around his shoulders, and using his hands to bring an entire room to its feet. Songs had always triggered a memory and 'Stand By Me' by Ben E. King stirred her desire for Sam during their first slow dance at a nightclub.

Sam, on lead guitar and keyboards, his brother Ted on rhythm guitar and keyboards, drummer Grant Slanik and Drake Dority on bass, all believed their band's marketability could be increased by adding a female musician.

Krys Graf

Tuesday, May 22, 1975

We had the taste of youth on our tongues as six friends piled into Ted's Chevy Impala. On a mission to get to the music store before it closed, we felt entranced by the trembling of the old engine, or maybe we were consumed by exhaust seeping through holes in the floor. Lightheaded and dizzy, we inhaled a lungful of the brazen colors streaking above us, the last remnants of daylight, before we flashed the headlamps to illuminate the dark streets. Our rehearsals are sublime. I'm anxious to begin and will use the name: Lexa Loxx.

Monday, May 25, 1975

Our upstairs tenant, whom I quietly call double D Janie, said she enjoys our music rehearsals which is fortunate because of how loud we are, and we invited her to watch our sessions in the basement. She said she will bring her friends to our shows.

I passed state boards and received my nursing license in the mail. As happy as I felt is as annoyed as Sam looked. He said nothing, but I had a private celebration, a few glasses of wine in my closet, and maybe Milyana is smiling. I'm changing nursing jobs to a clinic where I don't have to work evenings or weekends, because of shows and rehearsals.

Patrolmen visited the Lynnch residence during amplified rehearsals usually into the fourth song. The repeating doorbell rang off key, ignoring the time signature. Sam and Lexa got to meet all of the second shift officers.

"Good evening, Officer Arrestem, how can I help you? We're not too loud are we? Any requests? Another ticket? Noise Disturbance? No, we haven't practiced any of those tunes," said Lexa.

Starting up her VW parked at the curb, she saw that her wiper blades were bent and twisted away from the windshield. She got out to examine the damage. *Only massive, nasty hands could have ruined them.* "You haven't heard full blast yet!" She shouted toward the neighbor's home to the north as she drove into the open wooden double doors of the garage, closed them and secured the padlock.

She was certain the devious act was done by the white-haired 6' 2", elderly ill-mannered male neighbor who was built like an English Mastiff. He had always scowled at her and Sam, and refused to acknowledge them in any way.

"Sam, what do you think it'll cost to get the metal arm of my wipers fixed?"

"I'm not sure. At our next jam session, let's notch up the volume for fifteen minutes and open all the windows facing his house."

"I wonder how his wife can stand him. What's he like to the other neighbors? Let's dedicate the first song of our next rehearsal to him."

The band opened the north windows of the basement, timed their watches, maxed out the volume on all amplifiers and microphones and started Chuck Berry's Jonny B. Goode. "Way down in Louisiana, close to New Orleans…"

By the time the officers rang the buzzer, the street was silent.

"Can I file a claim for harassment?" Lexa asked.

"Not in this case, ma'am."

She stepped outside to get the mail in the morning and the heavy concrete garden flower pot was splattered on the walkway below her doorstep. In the hour it took to clean debris of dirt, chunks of cement and flowers, she realized a power struggle had begun and assured the band to keep rehearsals as loud as amplifiers would allow, but to stop in fifteen minutes, before police arrived.

The elderly lady was oblivious to her husband's bad behavior, and continued flagging Lexa down to converse as though she needed a sympathetic ear to listen to random details of her children and grandchildren's lives, neighborhood gossip, and the stories about a little boy named Shane.

An agency managed club bookings of 'FX of Violinz' prior to her replacing the lead singer, and on a warm day in June, the group snapped an assortment of poses on a grassy hillside behind Grant's house. Their favorite was sent to a printing company, and the glossies would be given to the agents who promoted the band at their shows.

She notified her bandmates of the smashed van window and the missing box of 8 x 10 photos. Annoyed at having forgotten to hide them, she resolved to be more careful. There was no proof of who did this, but she had a strong suspicion.

The glass was replaced, and Lexa hid the reprinted 8 x 10 photos in a box at the back of the van under the bed Sam and Grant had built.

Drummer Grant Slanik's rock solid beat and 6'1, 180 pound body was chiseled by years of performing in numerous bands. He demonstrated great showmanship skills in slamming the snare, toms and cymbals, holding a look of serious intensity as though the drum set was a tormentor in need of reckoning and deserved the beatings. In his left hand, he twirled his drum sticks high in the air and rhythmically struck double-ply drum heads using the other. He and several former bandmates had studio recordings on albums. From 9 to 5 he worked at an office equipment company in the repair department of large format copiers.

A foot taller than her, Drake Dority continued his day job as an insurance underwriter. He had a young son and beautiful wife, who made her unhappiness evident because she was not asked to join the band, since she could sing also.

Friday, May 30th was Lexa's first time on stage. The road crew set up their gear and she sighed, paced and wondered, *will my voice hold up? Will I forget lyrics?*

Song lists were taped to the four front stage monitors, positioned to face each singer in order to hear every voice, separated through drums and guitars. Grant taped his set list to a music stand. Her mouth caressed the metal mesh wires of the microphone and the taste lingered like the feel of rough skin.

"Testing, testing, 1, 2, 3... Check... check... 'Break another little piece of my heart now baby! O Lord, won't ya buy me a Mercedes Benz,'" she sang as mics and monitors were set up.

The microphone sent sound to loudspeakers, a Public Address system, also known as the PA, and gave her voice a dynamic intensity. The device she held in her hands changed the persona of her as a singer in coffeehouses to one whose voice could fill an auditorium. To add to her stage presence, she dressed in tight silver slacks, a black tank top, and high heels for her first show.

Lexa had become her idyllic singer for a moment, and marched across a stage, mic in hand, singing 'Piece of My Heart' and 'Move Over'. *Maybe this is what Joplin felt like at her first concert.*

Determined to do whatever was needed to improve her voice and stage presence, she cut back to one glass of wine a day, did vocal exercises and ran two miles daily.

A glass of whiskey jiggled on top of Ted's amplifier while he tuned and tested the sound of his guitar before a show. "Drinking helps me act and feel normal," he said, setting up his gear. "I get relaxed enough to laugh and speak my mind. When Sam and I were in our first band, girls chanted our names, asked for autographs and made me feel invincible. I couldn't stand any other job afterwards, and always quit within a few months."

"What about the book binding business? Doesn't your dad want you to manage his company?" she asked, plugging in her mic and adjusting the height of the stand.

"No, being in a band is the only job I'll ever like. I don't even own a suit. By the way, did Debra tell you about our Terrier? We have two puppies now. The neighbor's Border Collie jumped the back fence for her. You should stop by and see them."

"I want the white one," Sam said.

"We're gone too much. It wouldn't be good for a dog," said Lexa.

"A dog has always been part of my life. I've been wanting another one for a long time," said Sam.

"And you haven't mentioned it before?"

"Let's see them tomorrow."

"Please, let's not get a dog," said Lexa.

"You'll change your mind by the end of the week. I'm bringing her home. What should we name her?" Sam asked, admiring a white, fluffy, bouncing puppy, petting her soft fur.

"She's cute, and I understand why you would want to keep her, but our calendar keeps us so busy. It would be one more thing we would have to worry about."

Ebbie grew to be 17 inches tall and 20 inches long, and Lexa read library books on dog care and training. Ebbie did not seem to mind her small patch of grass around the house, nor the long trips in the van. Surrounded by people almost constantly, her barks took on human-like words, so teaching her to 'speak' was easy. She slammed her paw on her heavy plastic bowls when she was hungry or thirsty, and learned to roll over, jump through hooped arms, and do back flips on command.

The schedule of performances was full for June and they rehearsed for their show at Summerfest, a festival near Lake Michigan. Security personnel checked their passes and signaled them to enter into the grounds. Boats opened sails and some revved engines in the nearby harbor while numerous stages showcased entertainment, starting at noon and ending at midnight. They stood backstage waiting to begin at 8 pm in 74 degrees, speckled clouds, and a breeze off the waves. An announcer introduced 'FX of Violinz' as they waited at their mics. Spotlights were aimed at the musicians giving them an ethereal glow.

The crowd stood shoulder to shoulder, and Lexa felt an electrical charge flow into her as she sang. The surge of the high Sam had so many times tried to explain, awakened in every particle of her being.

"Who wants to party?" she shouted as the show began.

Whistles and screams were heard in response.

She held up her arms and waved to a panorama of hands being waved in return. Lexa threw out kisses. Kisses were thrown back. The sun's rays diminished and lights illuminated halos around each performer. In the darkness, lighters glistened throughout the crowd, igniting the band to play several encores to whistles and screams of "FX, FX, FX", awakening an almost dizzy feeling of elation. She had never experienced anything remotely similar to the love and adrenaline shared by the mass of admirers.

At the end of the concert, Sam played the Jimi Hendrix' version of the 'Star Spangled Banner' lick for lick and people roared, cheered and chanted, "Hendrix, Hendrix, Hendrix," as band members waved, threw more kisses and exited the stage.

While gear was hauled to the van, party invitations were offered. Howls of, "I love you," and requests for autographs made for what Lexa thought was a perfect evening.

"Sam, you sounded great tonight. You're keeping the memory of Hendrix alive," she said as distant cheers and whistles echoed. A cloud of reefer hung over the crowd and permeated the stage, while security police closed in to scatter people in all directions.

Friday, June 27, 1975

Those who were captivated by the amplified sound shared an energy which has seeped into my being. The altered state of this new enlightenment is like a mystical potion and makes me feel alive in new way, like I'm able to hold onto a rainbow or walk on clouds. For a moment, I matter to someone. The transient gratification my fellow musicians create seems to generate an outpouring of devotion and is as seductive as drinking the elixir of love itself.

After a club performance, Lexa was approached by several fans. "Hi, can I get your autograph? I like your band," said a burly 6', brown-haired man whose brown eyes were vacant like a discarded doll. "I took a photo of you at Summerfest. Sign it to Aldar. Where do I send fan mail?"

"I'll give you the address of our agency," said Lexa.

As her head bent forward, she felt his breath on the back of her neck and a tightness in the pit of her stomach that she was unable to explain as he repeated her signature, "Lexa Loxx."

Aldar's voice is like a punch in the gut, she thought. She looked up at him and stared. *I know him from somewhere.* As she was about to speak, she was tapped on the shoulder to sign another autograph, and she watched the man wander through the crowd.

"Sam, what address should we use for fan mail?"

"Let's discuss it on our breaks at our show tomorrow."

She realized her days of being invisible were over. She took a few vocal lessons, began a rigid strengthening exercise routine and started to feel good about herself for the first time she could remember.

Lexa acquired a P.O. Box, and the band placed a notebook on the sound board for fans to sign up on a mailing list, which was announced in between songs while on stage. Fans received a monthly itinerary on a 4" by 6" postcard including the address where correspondence could be sent, to begin in August.

Being in a band in 1975 without being immersed by some kind of drug was like trying to take a bath without water. Attending parties after shows became familiar rituals of entertaining strangers who shared their dubious intoxicants. 'FX of Violinz' members were invited to parties of fellow musicians, radio disk jockeys, new friends and fans, where Sam was in his element. The offerings during and following performances included cocaine, weed and now Quaaludes, a prescriptive relaxant. It was the reward for having been entertained and given a transitory sense that any dilemma they faced could be eradicated in the time they engaged themselves in the band's music. It was the carrot before the horse. "Come to our party, keep entertaining us. Here's a Lude." In the vast array of pills, pipes, bongs, uppers, downers, and alcohol knocking out inhibitions, the need for a "bottle in front of me, rather than a frontal lobotomy" was satisfied.

In their living room, Sam pulled out one of his gifts, deciding his friends would have more fun if everyone popped a white pill and play a game he called change partners. Lexa said "No," and backed away which served as a cue to the partiers; she needed more persuasion.

"We have a prude. Take a Lude. Relax. Maybe you'll remember how to laugh," Sam replied stepping closer to her. "We took one. Look how happy we are, except for you."

Backed into a corner, the more she turned down the offer, the louder they got. She wondered if Sam had already done this. Maybe it was a test to determine how she would react, so he could stop her if she moved her hand toward her mouth to say it was a joke.

"Are you going to avoid us all night, or are you going to join us?"

Sweat dripped down the sides of her temples under her hair as she looked at Sam, but no sympathy was in his eyes. The group was persistent until she swallowed the tablet and gulped down the remainder of red wine in her glass.

In the morning she awoke in her waterbed, confused as to how she got there. It was her first lapse of memory and the previous evening was missing, starting thirty minutes after the chemical landed in her stomach. In her struggle to get up, spinning filled her brain and weakness ravaged the muscles she needed to pry her body upward to the bathroom mirror, in wonder as to how rough she would look.

She clung to her desk near the doorway and hallway walls to balance her unsteadiness, turned the faucet wide open and stuck her face under cold running water. To stop the swaying, she grasped the sink and could not remember feeling a stronger desire to sleep as she stumbled to the refrigerator where she rifled for a piece of bread. She ate it on the way back to bed.

At 4:30, her bandmates arrived on schedule for their show in Rockford Illinois, suitcases and guitars in hand. Lexa was able to get dressed, but was unable to walk to the van unassisted. Her back hit the seat, and she became incoherent. Drake woke her up, pulled her arm around his shoulder, and step by slow step, got her into the club. The room was spinning as she grasped her mic stand and buckled onto the stage. Her vision blurred, and the band's indiscernible voices echoed. Unable to sing, she remembered someone carrying her into the van where she slept, and was assisted into the house. At home she fell into a void for the next twenty four hours.

In a half wake, half dream state, her brain positioned the needle on a broken record. Over and over it repeated, *'I will change. You're the only girl I'll ever want.'* The words wouldn't silence as she crawled out of bed to eat, forced herself to dress two days later, slugged down a pot of coffee, and walked the length of the Capitol Court shopping mall, back and forth until the grogginess faded. She sat in the VW feeling lost, and wondered whether the pills Sam's acquaintances offered him had caused him to become self-absorbed, or if it was she who had stagnated.

Wednesday, July 9, 1975

Apparently I need to rethink the values I've been taught to fit into the music scene. These parties have been going on while I pursued anatomical facts. The Lude made me sleep solid for almost three days and I can't shake the grogginess. I have no memory of my life since Saturday. I'm starving. My coordination is off. I drank a pot of coffee, took deep breaths and walked the halls of the Capitol Court mall until I felt alive again.

Sam said, "You think you're so special, Miss Nurse." It felt like a barb striking my chest. I remember all of his critical comments about my schooling, and asking him not to force me to take a drug I didn't want. He does not keep his word. I regret marrying him. We have a house, a band business, and a dog. At the clinic today, I closed the bathroom stall and cried my eyes out.

The fan named Aldar who asked for my autograph had his breath on my shoulder and his hands on my hair. I backed away and pretended it didn't bother me, but I hated it.

photography by
Marvin Waters

CHAPTER 6

SHOVED

Airwaves took on the voices of Ian Anderson's Jethro Tull, Eric Clapton, Bob Seger, Queen, Pink Floyd, and Steve Winwood, and roars of V-8 engines filled streets with muscle cars like Camaros, Challengers, Chevelles, Gran Torino's, Chargers and Firebirds. Sam and Lexa lived on 40th St. near Congress Street, in the North West side of Milwaukee where members of 'FX of Violinz' met, parked their cars on a large area of concrete alongside the garage near the alley and loaded all of the equipment into Sam and Lexa's new maroon van.

A few days later, the van's front tires were slashed, and Sam went into the a fit of rage. "We can't park on the street ever again," he said. "And I'm going to talk to Grant about rehearsing in his barn.".

Grant was in agreement, and the gear was hauled to the barn on his property in Waukesha.

At 3:30 am, Sam and Lexa were awakened by a young man screaming and pounding on the back door.

"Fire! Your garage is on fire! People get up! Fire! Fire!"

Afraid to respond, they feared that some crazed madman had wandered to their house. Sam moved the bedroom curtain aside, gasped and moaned, "Oh, no, no." Billows of black smoke streamed and expanded upward around the garage. He stumbled out of bed to call the fire department. Waiting for his call to be connected, his hands were shaking as he tried to get the kitchen window open. Smoke seeped around garage windows as bursts of hissing flames shot above the roof. He hung up, they grabbed robes, and ran outside to pops, crackles, and an increase in the volume of sirens until it pierced their ears. Throbbing red lights oscillated over neighboring faces, until each onlooker was bathed in the glow of flashing flares.

Thick yellow jackets protected the men who shouted over the drone of sirens. Glass sprinkled onto concrete, and garage doors were smashed by long handled axes. Fear widened the distance of watchers who awaited a gas tank to explode splinters at them while streams of water soaked the plywood structure, dampening a raging blaze to smoldering gasses.

The smoke clearing at daybreak, Sam and Lexa gathered enough courage to walk into the charred garage to touch the skeleton of the melted van. Clumped black glass solidified into drips and looking upward, they viewed clouds moving through gaping holes in the roof. The four chairs Sam and Grant had installed, the bed built into the back, carpeting, pillows, sleeping bags, music tapes, flashlights and road equipment had become powdery ash.

"I'm relieved our gear was in Grant's barn. Do you think someone would deliberately torch the van thinking our valuables would be in it? What could have caused the fire?" asked Lexa.

"I'm not sure," Sam replied.

The neighbor? Lexa thought.

The new aluminum overhead garage door opened by the push of a button on a remote and replaced the old wooden double doors.

An empty shell of a yellow van served as a replacement. Small ottomans were thrown into it for seating and slid around during drives like a theme park ride in magic teacups. It was fun until the evening a Lincoln Towncar ran a red light and broad-sided their vehicle, sending Lexa flying into the front window. The top of her skull took a hard hit. Her memory of the trip to the emergency room in the ambulance was sketchy.

"You were so wet, I thought you were covered in blood," said Sam.

"Your cup of water splattered all over me." Her hair and clothes dripped in the darkness, and the ambulance attendants covered her on the cot. "I guess we're going to miss the party."

The doctor in the emergency room asked her to squeeze his hands, and he pointed a light into her pupils, telling her to track it. He asked her to respond to a few questions, and gave her strict orders to take it easy for the rest of the evening and next few days. She had a trip planned to see her grandfather, and would take it easy once she landed in Florida, but learned about the effects of a concussion on the plane ride.

"Flying makes you sick? asked the stewardess.

"Head concussions do," Lexa replied.

Returning to the clouds of Milwaukee, Sam picked her up at Mitchell Field Airport, and she gave him the bleak news about her grandfather, who had moved to warmer weather to help him feel better, but it was futile. His new doctor told him he had leukemia.

"He looked so gray while he slept. I stood near his bed to check if he was still alive. I knew he was seriously ill, but didn't have the courage to tell him what he has meant to me and how much I love him. I felt so scared I was immobilized."

"Don't worry about it. He's going to be okay."

"It's why they asked me to visit. The doctors don't think he has much time. What did I miss over the past week?"

"You didn't miss anything. We're going to rehearse 'I'm Down, by the Beatles, and Janie asked if we would learn Mustang Sally."

"Janie, our tenant?"

"She thinks you'd do a great job singing the background vocals."

"It's so nice of her to take good care of our upper flat, and it's cool she's become a fan of the band," said Lexa as he drove.

At 10:30 pm, she pulled a blanket over her shoulders, closed her eyes, tossing and turning as the image of her grandfather flashed in her mind. She glanced upward as smashing, pounding and mayhem began.

The outside door of the upper flat slammed shut and an inside cabinet crashing sound was followed by pots clanging, more doors banging and feet stomping. The crackling of breaking glass alarmed Sam to where he bounded out of bed and ran up the inside stairs to a flat which was usually locked.

Lexa lifted her head and rested it on her knees, bewildered. Muffled wordy sobs wafted down the stairwell, where she tiptoed to, baffled by the sequence of events. She trembled to hear a woman's voice in such distress, but her body began to shake, as she became engulfed in the knowledge of Sam having an intimate relationship up a short flight of steps. Her mind scrambled and her heart ached as her reality disintegrated. The delicate globe of the imperfect life she dwelled in was shattered. Nothing could console or comfort her.

Infinite hours were spent at evening music rehearsals. Her band had a constant string of shows, and on weekdays her nursing job ended at 5:00. Most names in her address book were smudged and erased. She had nowhere to go. Her parents lived over a thousand miles away. She stepped into the night's humid thickness, turned the key in the Volkswagen and steered down the alley, having no clue as to where she would head at midnight other than Nathan's house, a 30 minute trek through Milwaukee. On the radio, the melody of Armageddon's "Silver Tightrope" resonated.

She parked in her brother's driveway. In retracing Sam's dialogue and previous events, the punch in her gut caused shock to crawl down her spine and she sat motionless, unable to ring the bell and awaken Nathan, his wife Polly, and their young son.

She closed her burning eyelids which were weighed by exhaustion. As the glow of sunrise washed the horizon, salty droplets on her gray t-shirt and jeans were illuminated. Above, cobalt clouds dotted the heavens, some as dark as the turmoil weaving through her. Tall streetlights came alive, hung their pale heads low, and a shrugged shoulder held a lamp to direct her journey homeward.

Memories orbited of the talks she and Sam had about having children, where they planned to live in the future, and the boat they intended to navigate waterways together. He had once lavished his love in affection, promises, personal secrets, and words of adoration. She remembered the times he had walked or given her a ride to work to ensure she got there safely, and was always on time waiting for her at the end of her shift. They had conversed effortlessly, and laughed about all aspects of their world, but now it had no meaning. Parking the VW, she sat frozen in the seat for ten minutes and opened the entrance leading to the kitchen.

Sam stood in the doorway looking ragged. "Where did you go?"

"So you're pretending to care? Get away from me," she said, glaring at him. He stepped closer and her tone notched up. "Do not touch me."

His footsteps faded as she fell backwards onto the water bed, unable to relax, as though her skin had been torn off. She thrashed, paced, turned on the TV, threw herself back onto the bed, flung her limbs and punched her pillow on and off throughout the day in an effort to embrace the dreamland she had taken for granted. There was now a fissure which became the vessel in which adrenaline poured, filling her pores and cells, destroying all the peace she had known.

Thursday, July 24, 1975

Today marks 72 hours since I last slept, and I'm losing track of time. I've done 24 hour sleepless stretches to study for exams in college, and always thought we sleep if the brain gets tired enough. My body has never been this drained before, and my mind has not been so flipped out it won't shut down. I've called in sick to work and can't lose my nursing job. I read that three or four sleepless nights can cause hallucinations, and I may be not aware of it. 100 proof vodka did nothing to calm me down. The crazier I act on stage, the larger the crowds get. They gawk at the maniac, drunk singer.

Her heart rate increased into the hundreds, and Lexa called her doctor for a prescription to help her sleep. She said would try anything.

Standing at the pharmacy counter, she opened a bottle labeled Valium 5 mg. *Ten pills? It doubt if it will be enough.*

In the bedroom where the dagger was discovered and a woman named Julette had taken her last breath, Lexa swallowed a yellow tablet and drifted to a dream where she was tied in a dark room. Thick fingers became snakes slithering around her neck and her screams were silent. She awoke, her mouth open, panting out a weak, dry yell. She got up to splash cold water onto her skin, and as she looked in the bathroom mirror, the light of the window illuminated a young anguish filled face.

Friday, July 25, 1975

My mirror reflects a lost face trying to understand betrayal. I dangled on a fraying rope which was cut free, and down I plunged. I brushed off every sign, bought into every lie, every faked kiss. My radar failed me because I wanted to see the good in him. I did not feel the knife he stuck into my back until now. A brazen bitch giggled and boozed it up at all of our parties while she screwed my husband and laughed at me. My hatred for them is difficult to contain. The twists and turns of my life has now hit a brick wall.

Sleep is gone. I'm unable to swallow because my throat constricts. Again I am sinking under water and struggle to stay afloat. I have sacrificed who I am for acceptance from the only person who said the words, 'I love you' to me. No one is ever prepared to have their heart crushed by the person they trusted. Like Oma said, be ready for destruction, don't let wicked things destroy me, and move forward no matter what.

Sunday, July 27, 1975
*I returned from our break at our show tonight, and a note was taped to my mic stand: **'I know where you live. I have been watching you.'** Someone wrote this so I would feel threatened. I ripped it up.*

She sat on the floor in the corner beside the bookshelf and heating vent wall examining the Valium, and decided to break them in half. She let the bitter pill dissolve under her tongue, and swigged down a half a bottle of wine.

Lexa's mother called a few days later to give the details of her grandfather's passing. Though Lexa was aware of his timeline, the finality left her despondent. His death was as quiet as his life had been. He was a man of few words but his smile possessed the gift of making insecure children feel loved. He had been the one person in her childhood who pushed her on swings, hugged her, and gave her an affinity to an adult male figure. Leukemia had no mercy on him and took him quickly. Lexa was unable to travel to his memorial service where he had spent his final days.

As she stared at the dark ceiling and walls, slumber avoided her despite desperate efforts to restore it, and she gravitated to the corner between the bookshelf and heating vent, resting her head on her knees, where warm air swirled around her, brushing hair over her ankles and feet.

Debra phoned Lexa to vent her frustration and worries. Her wedding was two weeks ago, and Ted has been more confrontational than usual. She is debating if she wants to get divorced. They have been living together for the past year in her parents' upper flat.

Lexa wondered why Debra didn't ask Ted to leave, especially in how miserable she had become, spilling unending tears during most conversations, but Lexa knew endings are not easy. *I think we fell down the same rabbit hole, and I haven't told her what is going on in my life. For all she knows, Sam is the perfect husband. I don't think he plans to tell his family what he has done any time soon.*

She had difficulty sleeping, swallowing, and her weight dropped, which triggered a coughing, wheezing, muscle-aching virus which lasted a week before she went to visit her physician's office.

The sullen doctor stood over her in a starched white lab coat which matched his hair. "Miss, you're 97 pounds and for five feet three, you should weigh at least 120 pounds. You need to eat more. I'm giving you a shot of penicillin."

"Can I have a prescription for something to help me sleep? I'll try whatever you suggest."

"You don't need it," he replied before walking out. "Some people complain about everything. You'll feel better in a few days."

His nurse entered the room clenching a silver syringe on a matching tray. Buck up and grit your teeth, Lexa thought. The scent of rubbing alcohol filled her nostrils.

Friday, August 8, 1975

Physicians are considered figures of authority, and no one would dare question an injection intended to spare a body from death, but that guy doesn't listen or give good medical care. I will never see him again.

*Another note was taped to my mic stand while the band was in the dressing room. **'Your VW doesn't stand a chance against*** *my 8 cylinder. Your small body is no match for mine.' I showed this to my bandmates. They laughed. I didn't.*

Sam soon had the same condition and went to the same clinic.

"How does your butt feel?" Lexa asked as he walked into the dressing room.

"It feels fine."

"The shot didn't hurt?"

"I didn't get one."

She swirled around to face him. "Why are you so special?"

"I told the doctor my symptoms and I knew he'd make me get a shot. The nurse came into my room holding the silver tray, and I said those shots are prohibited by my religious beliefs. I'm not allowed to get them," he said.

"And what religion did you say you were?"

"I told her I was a Hindu."

"Hindu's can't get shots?" she asked.

"I don't know, but neither did they. The nurse rushed out to tell the doctor, and he gave me a prescription for penicillin pills."

Sam got well in the same amount of time as she did. He may as well have said he was a Baptathlic or a Sexbeterian. Lexa had a clearer picture of his manipulative abilities. He had numerous unsuspecting victims, his mother being the first, whom he could persuade into doing almost whatever he wished by portraying his helpless, 'pity me' act. And just maybe Lexa didn't buy into it the way he had expected her to.

Plotting an escape from Sam and his conquest who resided steps above them, preoccupied her thoughts.

As she walked to the garage, she was startled by the matronly woman to her left.

"Isn't this a picture perfect day? My grandchildren are coming over soon," said the elderly white-haired neighbor, who hung her laundry. "Are you pregnant? My kids were the cutest babies. I thought you might be expecting by now, hauling in a crib."

"I'm not ready for babies."

The neighbor continued divulging snippets of her life and stories about a raven-haired child named Shane.

Lexa checked her watch and listened for as long as she could stand to, and said she had an errand to run.

Fatigue held a firm grip on her during shows. She walked to the bar and waited behind gossiping barmaids. In overhearing them refer to her as a "skinny bitch", she cleared her throat and said, "Excuse me." They turned around. "I'd like a glass of altruism, but apparently you have none."

She returned to the stage to wrap speaker, guitar, mic and amp cords, and while packing them into a heavy, wheeled trunk, she tripped on a cord, landed on her wrists, and scraped her palms and knees.

"You and your band aren't worth the insomnia, throat tightness, and being called foul names," she said to Sam. "Start looking for someone to replace me." The ride home was soundless.

The coworker who sat beside her at the clinic mentioned she was looking for a roommate to help cover expenses in her two bedroom apartment, and Lexa asked if she could see it. The rooms were spacious, ceilings tall, and light spilled into every corner. She signed the lease and began packing.

Lexa pet Ebbie, knowing Sam would take good care of her, no matter how he treated anyone else. Her sorrow was replaced by surges of anger that struck a match to a plan as simple as a trip to a grocery store. In ten minutes, she placed the raw foods in various locations, and turned the key to lock up. She looked back at the white siding, and a smile crossed her lips for the first time in a month as she thought about the aroma of decay which would overcome the house.

Lexa arranged her sparse belongings in an ivory colored bedroom, where she slept on blankets placed on the wood floor. Her new roommate and boyfriend preferred his apartment, restaurants and clubs which gave Lexa ample quiet time.

Eight cylinder cars bore down around her, especially after shows when she drove home alone. The words 'Your VW doesn't stand a chance' alarmed her. She purchased camouflage which was easy to slip on, smoothed her long hair into a ponytail, tucked it under a hat, wrapped a scarf around her neck, and kept the items in her glove compartment.

Polly mentioned how ill Nathan was in a phone conversation, so Lexa stopped in to visit. Confused by the peculiar person, Polly closed the door on Lexa.

"Wait, it's me," she said removing the mustache, thick eyebrows, rubbery nose, dark-rimmed glasses, bolero hat and neck scarf.

Lexa explained why she bought the disguise and Polly giggled, invited her in, walked into the bedroom where Nathan slept, and shook his legs. "Nathan, wake up. The doctor is here."

His face, imprinted by folds of his pillow, peered over his blankets.

"Sir, how do you feel today?" asked a deep voiced Lexa.

He glared at the foreign visitor and pulled the covers over his nose. That strange nubbin of a man was not touching him even if he was a doctor. She took her camouflage off and her hair fell to her waist.

"I should have guessed," he said throwing off the sheets.

"I stopped by to see my new nephew. May I hold the baby?"

Despite admiring the newborn and her attachment to her brother Nathan and his family, she felt misplaced like a lost child. She had not taken many belongings to the bedroom where she strummed her guitar.

At shows, she avoided Sam and made little eye contact, which stretched the tension among her bandmates to a thin thread.

"You okay?" asked Grant who packed up his drums.

"I'm alright. I hate seeing Sam's bimbo in the crowd. Does she show up to antagonize me, because he's going to head for her? She definitely has her hooks in him, and is probably thinking 'Ha, ha, he's mine now. I won.' There's a knot in my gut and I hate them."

"Do you want some company?" asked Grant. "You look like you had too much to drink."

"I'm not looking for sympathy. All the fun has been sucked out of me by the Dracula I despise. I've gotta get the hell out of here." In the VW, she slipped her disguise on.

Lexa awoke and opened the window of her living room to watch children playing on the sidewalk below, inviting recollections of her childhood. Appearing was the sweet face of a dark-haired boy who sat near her in her first grade class, and was the only friend who joined her at a playground on the monkey bars and swings. *So much sadness was in your face the day you said you were moving to another Army base. Everyone we grew attached to, we had to let go of and leave.*

Although she studied psychology and knew the dynamics of betrayal, in her daydreams, she pulled the trigger of a silver handgun pointed at men who had aggrieved her. Her right palm clutched the gun, as her left held onto and kissed her classmate's hand. Five gunshots echoed into flesh. Blood splattered through the air. Smoke rose off the weapon. The man who tried to kill her when she was 15 got an extra bullet to the forehead. Her young friend smiled and kissed her cheek.

"Good shot, Lexa."

"I killed the men who harmed me. Even though we were so small, it was you who understood and cared about me, didn't you?"

"Completely."

Wednesday, August 13, 1975

In some relationships, wings grow in loving arms. Let's fly somewhere together. In some, wings get clipped but can heal and fly off to a better place. But in others, not only do wings get ripped off, a steel anchor is locked onto a leg as a reminder that for the time you remain, you will be watched, controlled, manipulated and injured physically or emotionally.

My untethered bonds sent me to the underground cave of Hades where Charon, the ferryman calls me to him. He waits for me on the other side of the Acheron and Styx rivers that divide the world between the living and the dead. He senses my insomnia, sees emptiness in my eyes. I can almost reach him.

I haven't yet learned the rules for confronting deceit, but my first one is: always be prepared for something horrible, and when it happens, scream and drown myself in distractions. My crying spells are not because I lost someone good, but for believing a charade, kissing the lips of a liar, and being made a fool of. My To-do list: Repair the breaks, fill the empty, become whole, expose the truth, and track down dreamland.

Alone at her apartment after her day at the clinic, she initially ignored the ringing doorbell, but it persisted. She peered through the glass spyhole, and was startled by the visitor who stood in the doorway.

CHAPTER 7

DILEMMAS

Confused by the slender, brown-haired man who rang the buzzer in the heat of an August evening, she opened the door halfway. "Who told you where I live?"

"Drake did. I wanted to run some new songs past you and I wanted to ask how you're doing." Grant smiled down at her.

"Isn't it a long way for you to commute to discuss? Wouldn't it have been easier to call me?"

"Do you always ask your friends fifty questions? I happened to be in the area. Are you going to invite me in?" Grant's thick, low voice stammered.

"Okay, come in," Lexa stared upward into his deep brown eyes. "Can I get you something to drink?" She walked him to the sofa in the living room. "I can offer you some water. My fridge is empty."

"I brought some wine," he smiled. "Where are your glasses?" He poured some for each and blurted his speech of songs he had in mind, and exaggerating a smirk, began impressions of foreign accents.

The glass of wine in her hand began to shake as she noticed herself doing something she had not done in a long time. *I'm laughing. If he came to cheer up the lead singer of his band, he's succeeding.*

"So…you're here because you want to talk about songs?" She handed the glass to him. "Pour a little more, please."

"Ted, Drake and I were told you want out. All my bands busted up over dumb things, but since you joined, we've had an increase in our audience and cash flow. So are you quitting?" he asked.

"I'm thinking about it."

"Can you at least hold on for a few more months? We're finally getting really good. Can you put your Sam situation aside and stay in the band?"

"I have no idea."

"You can't be serious. I won't be able to stand this band if you're not in it. I'll probably start looking elsewhere."

"What are you talking about? Sam is a first rate guitarist and Drake is a rock solid bassist," she said.

"Yea, but you add that lick of sugar. Guys show up just to see you, and the girls come to pick up those guys who don't stand a chance in hell."

"Have you told your wife you're here?"

"No, I didn't. I'm not sure how much longer we'll be together. I don't get what Sam sees in Janie. Her overly painted face and mousy shoulder-length brown hair are nothing special to look at."

"Beauty is in the eye of the beholder, and Sam loves her big, bouncing boobs," said Lexa.

In his foreign accents, Grant brought out more laughter that evening and reassured her he would be there for her.

He returned in a few days bringing lighthearted conversation and a bottle of Pinot Noir. They sat and talked for hours while her roommate was out. In the course a few visits, she had a synopsis of his childhood, the Catholic schools he had attended, which they had in common, and his close family relationships. She heard about his previous bands, details of what broke them up, his recording sessions and famous musicians he worked alongside. He said he would bring a gift at his next visit to guarantee a good night's sleep in seeing the lethargy in her eyes.

The following week, Grant stood before her, holding his lighter as smoke encircled them. "Take a hit. It doesn't get better than this."

She moved toward him, and he held the joint at her mouth as she inhaled.

"Just wait. In about a minute you'll feel like you're melting."

Her head fell back against the sofa and she closed her eyes. He offered her another hit, then another. She looked at Grant. "Why are there two of you? What is in that stuff?" She closed her eyes, and felt as though she was floating on water.

"Can I kiss you? I've wanted us to be alone for so long."

His voice became a distant echo. Though she felt the heat of his body, somehow, he was far away. She frowned as his fingers moved across her chest. Her thoughts repeated "No," over and over, but her mouth would not move. His hand was behind her head and his lips formed a tight seal over hers. The sensation was intense and tingly.

She struggled to turn away. "I think you'd better leave."

"I can't. I'm too stoned." He closed his pleading eyes and moved toward her. She braced herself, shut her eyes, and his mouth softly suckled on her lips.

Though her thoughts were jumbled, she pushed him and raised her head off of the sofa. "Please, Grant, you have to leave. I can't get the image of your pretty blonde wife sitting in a chair petting your cat. My conscience is still intact, and I'm sure yours is too."

Friday, September 12, 1975
Either Grant is trying to take advantage of my vulnerability, or he wants to move in on the newly free Lexa. Would he go so far out of his way just to cheer someone up? Yea, he doesn't

*want me to quit – keep me happy to hang onto the band's cash
flow.*

Grant called Lexa on Monday. There was something he needed to
confide, and he knew he could trust her. Their liaison was confidential,
but she had no one to tell anyway. Presenting cheer, a bottle of Merlot
and a meal, he relayed his story in between bites. His wife was cold
and distant. They were not in love anymore, and he felt lonely. Lexa
was helping him get through it. His foreign accents and humor drew
her to him. She craved to be touched, and before her was a warm body
being freely offered. His kiss became more intense. In using the image
of Sam's rejection, Grant lured her to the bedroom where a sleeping
bag, pillow and blankets served as her bed. He pulled her shirt off and
saw the unhappy and absent look in her face.

"You don't have to do this," he said. "Maybe some other time."

"No, it's okay…it's just that I've been with someone else for so
long, it may take me longer than I thought to warm up to you." What
Sam and I had is gone. I don't owe him anything. I'm fine, just uneasy.
I'm not sure. Tell me what brought a married man to my apartment. I
never flirted or led you on in any way."

"You have no idea how hard it is to watch how you move on stage
in front of me. I want to reach over the drums and rip your clothes off.
All I can think about is sex. My wife is constantly rejecting me. I'll
never speak about this to anyone. You can stake your life on it." He
kissed her cheek and trailed his mouth to her lips.

Lexa wondered if he was trying to convince her or himself. By his
fifth visit, Grant's laughter and body spent the entire evening in her
bedroom, taking short breaks to confess whatever secrets came to
mind. Though he was a diversion, she could not shake her sadness.

Her mirror did not hide the dark creases under her eyes, and
reminded her of father's return from Vietnam. She applied extra
makeup. Shopping in children's and teen's departments for clothes,
she overheard coworkers and fans comment about how emaciated she
looked, and her scale would go no higher than 97 pounds.

Her boss scolded her for coming to work ill, and sent her home, intensifying the stress of her clinic job. She was told to stay in bed, but she was not sick. Her uniforms now hung on her small frame.

"Grant, do I look scrawny? I'm hearing a lot of comments."

"You're sleek. Don't take what other people say personally. Wrap yourself around me, and I'm in heaven. "

Monday, September 22, 1975

My 'crazy-rock-star-singer' persona contradicts my calm-nurse profession. I must always watch my actions to avoid losing the nursing license I worked so hard for.

A note was taped to my mic stand this evening which said: **'Watch your back. I can see into your windows.'** *Our road crew never noticed someone handling our equipment. They go to the bar in between sets and I don't blame them for wanting to party, but I wish they had seen something. I hope none of them sold my personal details to someone who is stalking me now.*

Wednesday, September 24, 1975

I mused over the note on my mic, and wondered if the person has the house or apartment address, or if I had been followed. I'm going to find a bodyguard.

Drake's melodic bass beat, Grant's steadfast drum rhythm and Sam having mastered the songs of Jimi Hendrix, pack the clubs where FX of Violinz headline.

My self-worth is attached to my stage identity. Alcohol is soothing my loneliness and a stepping stone for climbing out of the darkness I'm swimming in.

Into her second month at the apartment, Lexa picked up the phone and was puzzled by Sam's voice.

"I've had a lot of time to think about what I've done. I want your forgiveness, it will never happen again. Please come back."

"What? Is this a joke? I don't think I can," she said. His words caught her so off guard, she sat on the floor, almost speechless.

"I told Janie it's over. I discovered the smiley faces you drew on the wall next to the bookshelf. I miss you. Please give me a second chance. I want you back. I'll be better. I think about us all the time. You mean more to me than anyone ever could. I messed up so bad."

Lexa sat in silence.

"Hello? You still there?" he asked.

"You're joking."

"No, I'm serious," he said. "I'm so sorry for hurting you."

"I don't think so. I may never trust you again."

"I'm a changed man. I really mean it. You'll see. I will be so much better to you than I have ever been. I swear."

"Do not expect me to return until your girlfriend is out of the house, and out of your life. I never want to see her again."

"She's gone. I asked her to leave. I told her only love you and not her. I'd like to give to you a gift tomorrow. Can you stop over here?"

She drove to her house after work and Sam displayed a box containing a heavy turquoise and coral inlay sterling silver bracelet.

"Is this a gift to profess your love or a bribe to come back?" she asked, admiring the design. "Why couldn't you tell me you didn't care about me anymore?"

"I always cared, but I was tempted by the flesh of another woman."

"And you thought it was okay for me to find out the way I did?"

"I had no idea what to do. I made a huge mistake and I'm sorry. It won't ever happen again."

"How long have you been seeing her?"

"It's been awhile. You were at work every night and I was alone. At first it was some innocent visits, and then it got out of hand. It got more disturbing over time, and I had a difficult time trying to end it, and I hoped I didn't have to tell you."

"What does awhile mean? I hated working second shift. I called home at 10:00, and you didn't answer. I felt scared and had no idea where you would be so late. Whether I conveyed it or not, I believed in you. I may not be able to trust you again," she said.

Monday, September 29, 1975

Sam's apology did not calm me, but because I believe the band can succeed, I'll try to work things out. I'm done paying the bills on the house plus rent on the apartment. It probably wasn't difficult for Janie to seduce Sam. She helped me realize who he was. His lies are imbedded in the walls. Had it not been for her, I may not have experienced the kind of sensuous physical pleasure Grant offers. He has taught me to observe how a man moves, how they dance. It will speak volumes.

Before returning home, Lexa bought cleaning supplies, long plastic gloves and garbage bags. She was overcome by the smell wreaking as much as she anticipated, and opened all windows and both doors before removing rancid peeled eggs which had been hard boiled, from behind the refrigerator. The raw chicken at the top of the bookshelf and under Sam's dresser in pie tins a few months ago had become green fuzzy slime. She gagged as each foul smell was tossed into bags and hauled outside. While she sprayed cleaning solution and scrubbed, a fan blew the stench outside. She opened the furnace in the basement to remove the opened can of liquefied sardines, and though she emptied spray bottles and pine fragrance, the putrid smell lingered.

Her roommate gave notice that she was moving into her boyfriend's flat in a month, giving Lexa enough time to move her belongings out.

Grant suggested they continue their rendezvous at The EZ Sleep Motel, where he handled room reservations. He accompanied her to the room they shared for the evening, where he brought quarters to drop into a slot for the bed to vibrate.

New clubs requested the band's performances, and the agents who managed the schedule asked the band to travel longer distances, prompting Sam to suggest hiring another roadie to assist in tackling their demanding work load. He and Grant installed reclining, high-backed chairs in the van, and Lexa bought new pillows and blankets for the bed they constructed behind the chairs.

Working forty-plus hours at the clinic left her drained and worn out. By Friday evening, after unloading, organizing equipment and sound check of vocals and instruments, Lexa wanted a short rest. On a nearby piano bench, she folded her arms across her chest and dozed off.

Awakened by a salivating mouth on her lips, her feet shot upward. Unable to push the strong young man away, she squirmed, turned sideways and fell onto the floor. Bent over her was a thirteen year old boy, surrounded by curious friends who stared down at her in wonder.

"What the hell?" she screamed. "Get out of here!" Using her sleeve to wipe the unwanted drool off her mouth, she watched the boys laugh as they ran away. She pulled herself off the ground.

'Me and Bobby McGee' started the first song of the set where Lexa watched the return of their curiosity bathed in stage lights.

"It's odd for a kid wanting to kiss someone my age. And why does something always have to interrupt what little sleep I get?" she said to Drake in the dressing room.

"His dad owns this club. If I was his age, I would kiss you too."

Preoccupied by the teens on her way downstairs to do laundry, she felt a draft in the basement and saw the glint of glass sparkle on the concrete. In approaching it, sharp fragments glistened around her feet, a carton and the smell of a dozen splattered eggs wafted off the floor. She ran hot water into a bucket, poured it over the debris, soaked down an old towel, and wiped up ground glass.

Friday, October 3, 1975

In my travels, I've seen homeless who cradle alcohol to numb abandonment, and crave food to quiet their aching insides. The eggs were an act of anger. My thoughts of who would break the window point to the neighbor whose back door is a few feet away. No rehearsal has been at the house in months. I opened the phone book and called Same Day Glass Service.

When we got to the Cavalry Club this evening, I realized it is near the Union Cemetery where my grandmother is buried. After our show, the black-haired manager gave me a plaque he said he made. My picture was in the center of a piece of wood, covered by clear lacquer. I pretended to admire his gift and I thanked Mr. Zadrik. He said he prefers to be called Shane. I've heard his name before but I don't know where. He offered champagne which was chilling in his office. I had a few glasses, and laughed at his jokes. He asked if anyone in the band wanted some good weed or cocaine. I told him to ask them, not me.

I admired the life sized photo of Hendrix near his desk and if I wasn't in such a hurry to leave, I would have asked where he got it. A colorful beaded, fringed guitar strap hung near the photo -- he said it once belonged to Jimi Hendrix – yea, I'm sure. I worked on the books in the van after our show as usual.

Aldar approached the dressing room tonight, but the road crew would not let him in. His fixated eyes are murky pools spilling darkness onto everyone around him.

At the desk in her bedroom, she opened utility bills and fan mail. A letter addressed to her written on yellow lined steno paper was so disturbing, she dropped it on the floor before she finished reading it. The glow drained out of her face, the room darkened, and hands were tightening their grip around her neck as fear suffused her thoughts. For a moment she sat in the alley hovering over a beautiful young woman named Milyana.

CHAPTER 8

ULTIMATUM

It was difficult to read the disturbing words her name was attached to. Fan mail had been directed to the P.O. Box for several months, making Lexa wonder how dangerous this person is.

Lexa,   *October 3, 1975*
They all scream. Every one of them. Some blacked out quickly, and some thrashed like banshees. I hear you scream every time I watch your band. There is something satisfying about that luscious sound. It instills a sense of power. I cannot get enough of it. I return to the times when females screamed at me, especially my mother. She hated me because I

killed my gerbils and the parrot. She wouldn't allow me to have any more pets. I don't like having a blefarospasm. It was an evil punishment for having been born. You didn't seem to notice when I asked for your autograph. You look a lot like a little girl I had my hands on many years ago. I often wondered if there was any woman I could care about. I've come the closest with you.

A davoted fan   P. S. I took your nielons as a souvineer.

She opened her hand, and it sailed to the floor. After sitting for a moment, she crumpled the yellow paper, and threw it across the room. She ransacked her suitcase to discover nylons and red lace socks were missing. The envelope was dated and ink stamped in Milwaukee and there were no other clues as to who wrote it. She wanted to rip it into shreds. *This person has spelling issues, and it's what the note on my mic, 'Watch your back I know where you live' meant. They have my home address. Did someone ask for an autograph who had eye problems?*

She straightened the page and showed her band members.

"All libraries have a directory, so it's easy for people to look up your name and address," said Drake. "If someone has your address, they can easily get the information of who owns the house."

"This note would be more entertaining, had it been sent to the P. O. Box. Some psycho knows where I live and he or she had access to our dressing room. They took my nylons, but I had money in the suitcase and my ID was in my purse." At that moment she knew how they got her address. "They went through my wallet. You better watch your bags in the dressing room from now on and how much cash you leave in your wallets. Whoever did this may know where you all live also," she said. My medical dictionary said a blepharospasm makes someone blink often or look like they're winking. Have any of you noticed someone who has eyelid problems?"

"I never take a close look at anyone," said Ted.

"Most club owners don't pay attention to who goes into the dressing room. They probably figure it's a band person or roadie," said Karl.

"Lesson learned," said Lexa. "Either we leave our valuables locked up in the truck, or we put our suitcases backstage."

"Since neither our roadies or we can make time to watch what happens backstage, we'll have to lock our things up in the truck," said Karl. "The van windows are too easy to break."

She stuffed the wrinkled letter into the fan mail box, but caught herself watching the crowd more intensely for anyone who had eye issues. She analyzed both women and men, and realized that in joining a band, standing in the center of the stage, singing and screaming, she had become a target for the sane and the insane.

It wasn't that the letter included animal deaths and blacking out, but 'they all scream' most likely referred to the women he had murdered.

Determined not to let sickening phone calls and letters affect how she dressed or performed, she decided to hire a security guard.

Numerous calls to agencies and discussions of their rates led her to try Dependable Security who would ensure her safety during shows.

In the dressing room, she met a 400 pound, 6'5" male wearing blue jeans, snakeskin boots and a sleeveless jean jacket over a white t-shirt that displayed bulging muscles. He introduced himself as "Tiny". Smelling like a mix of locker room and Aqua Velva, his blonde uncombed hair and scraggly beard jiggled as he spoke. His waistline hung over his belt, and he sounded as though he possessed an extra set of vocal chords.

"Hi, nice to meet you, can I buy you a drink?" she asked.

"Not while I'm on duty."

"Lighten up Tiny. Have a little fun while you watch the band. Drinks are free for us."

"Yes ma'am."

"What would you like? And please call me Lexa, not ma'am."

"I'll have a Milwaukee's Best Premium." He licked his lips.

"I'm sure you are the best at your job, and if anything seems suspicious, I trust you will tell me. It might sound odd, but watch for someone who winks or blinks a lot. Please try to be as inconspicuous as you can," she smiled, thinking it would be difficult for someone who looked like a blonde gorilla to hide in any crowd.

"Okay," he said in his bear-like voice.

He approached her at the end of the show. "Not just men stare at you. I saw women evil-eyeing you. There's a few folks I think could be trouble, especially a guy who scowls and has dirty brown hair."

"Thanks. Here's the cash I owe you and the dates and clubs I'll need you for."

Though they did not notice anything out of the ordinary that evening, she felt like she could relax, having someone watch over her, at least while they were in the club at the same time. It would be difficult for her to fight a strong attacker even though she had attended a self-defense class and carried Mace.

At her show the following day, Lexa told Tiny about a man named Aldar who kissed his hand and blew it towards her while she sang.

"He is not an ordinary fan. He stares as though he is looking into my skull. His eyes are nefarious," she said.

"Huh?"

"Eyes like the devil. Like he is out of his mind deranged."

"Oh. I think it's the same person I'm concerned about."

Friday, October 10, 1975

My Grant time is a brief escape and our weekly workouts bring the sweet sleep I once had, but reality returns and I sit in dark walls of deceit for lack of anywhere else to go.

My home does not feel the same. I will never trust, believe or love Sam again. I am dumping my empty bottles in a dumpster down the street.

After a dream of Julette, the dark-haired lady who died in my bedroom, I am confused. I don't know what she wants. She tried to speak to me, but I woke up. "You must help me…" If I knew, the dreams might stop.

If Lexa hadn't bent down to pick up a piece of trash, she may not have discovered a plywood plank filled in by nails driven through it, the spiked points upward, she would have destroyed her tires. *My neighbor is taking his hatred of us too far. We haven't rehearsed at the house since July.* She wondered if this was connected to the letter, the fire and smashed eggs.

For several weeks Lexa deliberated about how she could acquire something to help her decompress. *I'm not sure if I'm having panic attacks, but chest pain and difficulty catching my breath started after being stalked and the nail spikes incident. No matter how much I drink, it is not enough.* She dialed the phone to speak to Debra, who said her and Ted's arguments edged up a notch, and he dislikes how her parents treat him.

"I'm sorry," said Lexa. "He's a difficult person to be around. I hate to ask, but you said you were taking Nembutal, so if you have extra, can you can sell some to me? Insomnia is beating me up. I need to sleep. I'm tired all the time."

"I'll give you some. I understand how it feels to be flipped out," Debra said sweetly.

"I appreciate this and will pay you back," said Lexa. They arranged a luncheon for the transaction.

"You're a lifesaver," said Lexa as she stuffed the pills into her purse. "I'll pick up the tab. I wonder if you could do one more favor, and I'm asking a lot. If I arrange an appointment for you to visit my doctor, and whatever you say to yours, could you repeat it to mine?"

"Sure, I can."

"I will call his office tomorrow. What time and day works best?"

Debra visited Lexa's doctor as arranged, and left the office holding a prescription for thirty 10 mg Valium tablets, six refills, and another for as many Nembutal capsules. Black eye liner tear stains smudged Debra's cheeks.

"Debra, you're my best friend. You told him the story didn't you?"

"Doctors will do anything to get me out of their office. They check their watches as soon as I begin the hysteria and tears," said Debra.

"You are a great friend," said Lexa. "Please take some of these."

Thursday, November 6, 1975

The neighborhood kids are pathetic. The bodies of a soft brown gerbil and a green and yellow parrot were lifeless on my doorstep this morning. I put on plastic gloves, and as I scooped each one up, I admired their velvety beauty. I buried them beside the rose bushes in my garden. I wanted to knock on every neighbor's door to ask if they had owned these pets, but I would have doubted anyone's honesty. I almost told Sam, but he wouldn't care. Grant is kind, but there are no words he could utter to end human aggression. Debra, I love you. Tiny, you are cutting into my paychecks. Wine, Rum, and Gin, you sooth me. Sam, I need to leave you.

Monday, November 8, 1975

Sam gave us an ultimatum at our rehearsal today. He wants to join a full-time band that travels across the US. If our band won't do this, he will leave. He said we'll never progress if we keep playing the same clubs; that we need to change our songs, our name, work on original material, and upgrade our show. Drake said he will not quit his job. He has a family to support, and has worked his way up the corporate ladder.

The band began doing shows four and five evenings a week, which led Lexa to submit her resignation at the clinic. She agreed to continue doing the books, receipts, and payroll.

Ads were run in local music papers, bassists auditioned to replace Drake, and the group decided Karl Slater had the best skills and voice. In packing away his Rickenbacker after rehearsals, Ted complemented Karl on how quickly he learned new songs.

"I've played guitar for five years in other bands, but knew I needed to play the bass to be in 'FX'," said Karl. "The day I showed up for the audition, I stumbled out of my car, a six-pack under my arm, my bass case in one hand and an open beer in my other. My fingers slapped at the strings like a maniac, I was so nervous. Sam and Grant told me I diddle a lot, but they like my voice. I worked in a machine shop for three years, inhaling fumes every day, and now I'm breathing in second hand smoke in these clubs."

"Are you from around here?" asked Ted.

"I grew up on the north side of Milwaukee," said Karl.

Thursday, December 4, 1975

It's was a rare day when Drake did not smile. I will miss his humor and stage presence. Our new bassist is a, shy 20 year old, has chin-length brown hair and looks to be 5' 9". Karl is the eldest of a brother and two sisters, and is close to his dad, a physician who lives in Oconomowoc on a lake.

Weeks of meetings have been spent deciding on a new band name and of our long lists, 'Word Locket' was chosen. Grant and I designed a logo to hang above his drum riser and arranged a photo shoot at a studio.

The band rehearses almost daily to learn original songs, and at a friend of Grant's studio, the revamped band recorded a two song 45 rpm record.

After the photography session, three hundred copies of the photo were printed to be sent to clubs as well as fans who requested it.

Burt, who was introduced to the band by one of the booking agents, having connections in local radio, signed on to be their manager. He saw the band's potential and the 45 was soon being aired on a regular rotation. Convincing the band they would become big stars if they continued writing marketable songs and touting his experience in the music business, meetings now included him.

Word Locket's name was announced each time their song hit the airwaves, drawing in larger audiences to the shows. Burt sent a promotional flyer to stations resembling a telegram about the release of the single and gave photos to radio stations, extras for DJ's who requested it and arranged live on-the-air interviews for the band.

Lexa felt ecstatic to hear her voice on her radio and she cranked it up every time the song aired.

The stage and lights magically galvanized ordinary people into entertainers who were given license to step outside the box, destroy stereotypes, create their own roles, and crush the norm without consequence. But Lexa's life had become a double-edged sword, and changed directions so many times, she was unsure where to turn next. She thought about leaving the life of a performer.

Grant had become a comfort to her, and his affection relaxed her into a night of slumber. She was not expecting him to call. On the phone, he spoke quickly and sounded alarmed.

"I messed up. My wife knows...about us. She noticed my motel receipt in the garbage while she was cleaning, checked the date, and went ballistic," Grant's deep voice wavered. "I had told her my friends and I were hanging out, but she confronted me, and I confessed."

"You threw the receipt in your garbage?" Lexa's throat constricted. "Why didn't you leave it in the hotel room? Why didn't you say you were seeing someone else?"

"I never thought my wife be looking through trash," he said.

"Your visits made me happy, but I guess it wasn't meant to last. Everyone will hear her version, including all of her friends and any distant acquaintance," said Lexa, pacing on the kitchen linoleum as far as the phone cord would allow. "I have to go."

Debra called several days later. "We go way back, so I thought I could trust you, but I can't. I told you about my rape when I was a teen. I will never tell you anything again, and I won't do any more favors for you."

"I'm not sure what you're talking about," said Lexa.

"Why are you gossiping about me? You gave your word to keep my secret. I thought we were good friends."

"Seriously…I don't remember telling anyone about what happened to you," she said as her mind raced.

"Leave me alone. I will never trust you again," said Debra.

Lexa placed her head into her hands. She had no awareness of telling anyone the details about a brutal rape. Then she remembered an intimate conversation and something she told Grant. She suspected he enhanced the story in relaying it to his wife, who salivated her version to Debra.

At their next gig following sound check, Lexa backed Grant into a corner. "My friendship with Debra is forever damaged. Of all the women who despise me, one was my closest friend. I have no other job, so I can't leave, but our meetings are over. There is nothing you can say. I'm done." She walked to the dressing room.

The intimacy they shared vanished like chalk murals in a rainstorm. His spouse had become a victim of her misjudgment, and was seeking revenge. Lexa pondered how to stretch the pills Debra gave her. She opened a Nembutal capsule, licked the harsh powder, and rejoined it.

Wednesday, December 17, 1975

I did not seek Grant out. He came to me. He may have been lonely, and attempted to ease my bitterness by using his body. But his wife has left no stone unturned in announcing her husband's betrayal to every person she can think of. Debra's hatred of me is a high price to pay for hoping to be consoled.

I've been looking through local papers for jobs and ads auditioning singers, while trying to figure out a way to tell Sam what transpired before someone else does. I will never feel badly about having a liaison while Sam and I were apart. All the while I thought we were finished.

Last night I dreamt his firm grip held my head under the water of our waterbed, the lining of which had become a pool. He pulled me up for air, he said, "I love you." His face grew dark and again he shoved my head under water. A dark-haired woman who had indistinct features stared at me in the same nightmare, kneeling and asking for help. I sat up, aware of why I had violent dreams of Sam, but did not understand the sorrow of Julette.

It seems long ago when I found Milyana's body and read of my classmate's strangulation. Though guilt drifts over me for not keeping my promise to expose who their killer and my attacker is, remorse has been added to my conscience because Grant's mistake has been life altering. I will always miss Debra.

CHAPTER 9

CONFESSIONS

For several days, Lexa agonized how she would break the news to Sam about her hookup, and she mused over numerous scenarios. She had no reason to feel regret. He had spent many months with another lover doing whatever he pleased while she was at work. The truth was disclosed soon after Lexa switched to a day shift job, putting a crimp in his upstairs romps.

Announcing he was going to AA, Lexa said she would join him. She slipped on her long, tan leather coat and jumped into the passenger seat of the van, where she decided to fess up. A book on the van's dashboard caught her curiosity as to what he was reading. Janie's name was written on inside the front cover.

"So…when did you see her? I thought you said it was over."

"What do you mean?" he asked.

Lexa's voice notched up as she read: "Return to Janie." As her anger intensified, she threw the paperback at him. It bounced off the driver's window and slid across the dashboard. He held his arm up to shield his head. "This book wasn't in the van the last time I was in here. What new lies to you want to clear up?"

"I felt sorry for her, 'cuz she kept calling, so I went to see her."

"Oh untruthful one, you are spewing garbage. You don't have your own private phone and I never heard ours ring for you. What does 'I want your forgiveness, it will never happen again' mean to you? I spent days in fear about how you would react to hearing about me. Though I've ended my affair, you can bet there will be gossip."

"What affair?" He stared at Lexa. The van swerved over the center line.

"I was seeing Grant. You were busy shagging tenant lady, so I moved out. He came to cheer me up long before you called to tell me you wanted to get together again. I wasn't going to push him away. Did you think I was sitting alone crying for you? Oh, you felt pity for me, so you called to ask me back. You and Janie are still sleeping together and now I have the evidence. Care to clear the air about anything else?"

"No. I can't believe you would screw Grant. Someone I have to see almost every day. You jeopardized the band. I'll never be able to look at him the same way again."

"Ironic. Your bimbo is at our gigs, our parties, and at places where I run errands. She even accompanied us to the music store. You said you want me back and yet, you're still banging her. Am I part of your harem?" she said. "Ask Grant why he came to my apartment. Why he kept visiting me. Why he wanted my affection. Sam is playing his Lexa-on-a-string game to see how long he can keep me dangling, isn't it?"

She threw her back into the seat. *The chauvinist lives by double standards.*

The remainder of the ride was silent and though they sat an arm's length away, they were light years away. Crowds were being drawn to both of them and each needed the other for their venture to continue.

Where did I put that needy chick's rental lease? It should have enough information for me to do some damage. She hates me anyway.

On Monday, 12/22 Lexa called the workplace of her husband's mistress. "Hello, this is the Cristoph Collection Agency. Yes, the spelling is correct...the CCA. I would like to leave a message for Miss Milonski...her landlord will be taking her to small claims court if she continues to be delinquent on her rent, and the bank will be seizing her vehicle to pay for her shopping debts. What was your name? Well you sound much nicer than what Janie Milonski said about you. Have her call this number, thank you." Lexa left the phone number for the Milwaukee County Courthouse, and wondered what a one year subscription to Smut Girl magazine would cost...delivered to her workplace. She picked up the phone again.

Lexa knew the memo to her enemy's employer made little sense, but would be sufficient in getting the ball rolling on office gossip, especially when porn magazines are delivered under Janie's name, and would be worth every penny. If she discovered any new involvement of Sam and that woman, Lexa planned to call the references listed on the lease.

During sound check on Wednesday evening, Grant adjusted drum heads, appeared anxious, and paced across the stage to the equipment trunks. "My drums sound terrible tonight and I can't find my new sticks."

"Where did you have them last?"

"My thoughts are a mess. I've been given an ultimatum. Either I quit the band, or my wife will leave. She said she'll file for divorce."

"You got off easy. She'll take you back if you quit? Maybe you should go."

"Lexa," he said as his voice cracked. "You won't care if I'm gone?"

"Do what's best for you. I should never have touched you."

"Our time together was great. Even though I wished for more, I was willing to settle for friendship," he said.

"It was fun, but it's an unfixable break," she said walking away.

Thursday, December 25, 1975

Sam asked me to join his family's party this evening. I did not want to stay home alone. He has not told his parents about his indiscretion, so I was expected to pretend all is well like a good little girl. The evergreen tree in their living room in lights and ornaments brought back childhood memories, and I thought about my family who is far away, the gifts they exchanged, their festivities. I doubt if they mention my name.

We all cringed every time Sam's mother said she wished she was young and in love like we are. I took long sips of wine and choked. Often.

Ted's inebriation plastered a smile on his face, but Sam's jovial mood ended during Ted's twelfth beer. He complained the entire way home about his brother's drinking. Debra refused to speak to me, but we did roll our eyes at Sam's mother's oblivious comments.

Tuesday, December 30, 1975

Tension between Sam and Grant has become so thick, they avoid looking at one another. We are forced to communicate on what needs to get done during weekly scheduled conferences in trying to run the band as a business. We sell promotional materials at shows: our record, pictures, and the band's logo on t-shirts. I am handling bookkeeping and expenses, as well as artwork for the ads in music newspapers.

We've added two road crew members to replace the previous ones. Ted's neighbor, whose long, wavy, golden hair, muscular build and structured features reminds me of Thor, the Marvel Comic book hero. I'm tempted to buy him a red cape and winged hat.

We hired a quiet man named Frank to be our road manager. He'll repair the truck, maintain and haul equipment, and adjust levels at the sound board during performances. Our crew has become the hardworking backbone, getting the work of transporting, sustaining, stacking and setting up the heavy PA. Tiny has been protecting me from crazed fans who carry guns.

The pop, punk rock, heavy rock, and heavy metal music of 1975 includes disco. Word Locket refuses to deviate from our roots, keeping Zeppelin's 'Rock and Roll' as one of the encores on our set list. None of this matters unless we can write a song worthy of airplay.

Sam doesn't care how much I drink, and has thrown our old memories in the trash. I finish a wine bottle daily. Climbing out of darkness has not been easy.

My New Year's resolutions: Prepare for the unexpected, watch my back, elevate my awareness, and if something bad happens, keep moving forward. Live boldly and remember to do what the right thing is, like Oma said, but it would be easier to follow her advice if I wasn't standing on a crumbling ledge.

The letters on yellow steno notepaper made her wince. The claws of this letter began scratching the surface of her skin, only to dig deeper as she read on, leaving long, jagged lacerations.

1/2/1976

Happy New Year, Miss Loxx. No one will dezire you like me. I like to watch you on stage and how your hair flails like a whip. I imagine it lashing me and tying me up. Did you notice that there haven't been any murdered women lately? I love to hear you scream. In grade school, the girls used to scream when I pulled their hair out. I didn't use my rope on them until I was sixteen. The grade school girls were lucky. Your shiny hair turns time back for me.   A davoted fan.

I've become a target because of my occupation. This person is inept at spelling, and it's someone who gained access to our dressing room. I recall reading about the murder of one of the women last year where rope was discovered. Maybe it's him.

I open fan mail almost daily, and most are short notes saying they enjoy watching the band, or suggestions for songs they want to hear, and often a request for an autographed photo, but this is a stalker.

The common thread between the letters is no name or signature, no address, yellow lined stenographer paper sent to my house instead of the P.O. Box, misspelled words, a fixation on screaming women, and signed by a 'davoted' fan.

Lexa ransacked the fan mail box and was soon holding the similar one. She held them together to compare handwriting. In her view, it matched. She mused over the words as though there was a secret message, but was unable to decipher it. *This is the eye-twitching fan who killed the parrot and gerbil, and took my pantyhose.* Tiny, a roadie or a band member remained near her while performing, going to shows, and in the dressing room.

Though Sam and Grant had become distant, at weekly rehearsals, the band wrote, worked on new music, and shared ideas of what to record on a new album since airplay of their 45 rpm single had declined.

Lexa saw Aldar at Teddy's nightclub, and spoke to Tiny in the dressing room. "I need to talk to that guy. I want to pick up any hint if he is who is stalking me…check out how irrational he is."

"I don't think you should do it. He is wacked out crazy," said Tiny.

"If he tries anything you can stop him. I wouldn't consider it if you weren't around me," she said.

At the band's first break, she scanned the club and saw Aldar at the bar. She headed toward him.

"Would you like a drink? I can get you one for free," she said.

"I'm able to afford my own drinks. What do you take me for? Some stupid punk?"

"No, not at all. I'm making an offer."

"An offer using someone else's dime. Girls like you are all the same."

"In your eyes, I guess we are," she said and walked away. *He has the accent I remember. There is no mistaking who he is. His voice is like razors scraping down steel. Milyana, I think I found him. It has taken many years. Now I need to figure out how to get rid of him.*

Aldar left shortly afterwards.

"Tiny, you're right. I'm not going anywhere near him again. Our road crew already pegs him as a lunatic. Does anyone at Dependable Security follow people?"

"I think I know where this is going. It's time consuming and I charge a lot," said Tiny.

"Maybe we can work something out," she said. "I want to know where he lives."

"It can add up to the hundreds," said Tiny.

"I'll pay it," she said. "He is well aware of where I live."

"It's your call," he said. "See you soon."

After the show, the band was invited to a party. "I'm tired of this. It's never fun for me. I can't sing and scream all night, and then spout idle chatter for hours afterwards," she said.

"We're not going to stay long," said Grant.

Lexa walked up the back steps at five am and took the phone off the hook as soon as she walked into the kitchen.

"Stop taking the receiver off," said Sam. "We're going to miss important calls. Don't do it again."

"Then you answer it. It's usually someone spewing obscene words at me when I answer, and I'm sick of it. I thought you weren't going to stay long. The neighbor's dogs are barking and it will be hell to sleep."

Later that day, she called the phone company to have the number changed. Those who had it were sworn to keep it secret. She bought a second phone which she placed on her bedside table.

In the Stone Toad nightclub at the evening's end, Tiny handed a paper note to Lexa, and on it was the address: 1745 W Hopkins St, Milwaukee. He said Aldar Geitlich also spends a lot of time at the Final Rest Funeral home and the Cavalry Club.

"The Cavalry Club, the one Shane Zadrik manages?"

"Yup. That's the one. And Shane owns the club also."

"What do you mean by a lot of time?" she asked.

"Every day."

"And a funeral home? Does he work there?" she asked. "Where is it?"

"He spends at least four hours a day at The Final Rest Funeral home. The Union Cemetery is across the street."

She thanked and paid him, and he left. The road crew packed equipment as Lexa walked down the slick wooden stairwell and opened the club's back exit in the dark alleyway to take in the air of a starlit sky. She zipped up her black leather jacket.

A sculpted, bodybuilding man who stood at 6'4" stood at the door, and his bloodshot eyes stared down at her. His black, wet, dirty mop hair reeked of sweat and Brute cologne, and his navy shirt was half tucked into jeans ripped open down his right leg. "I'm looking for Karl and Grant. Are they still here?"

"Yes they are. Who should I say is asking for them?"

"Tell them it's Nicky." He smelled of alcohol. "You can also tell your damn guitarist he's a jerk and I'm about to squash him like a pea."

"Excuse me?" she said, trying to remain calm while fumbling for the pin. "I'm sure you could." She clutched the pin, ready to use it. He could level her, despite what was shoved into him. She tightened her grip on the door handle and backed into the hallway.

"Your guitar player and my fiancée are going at it."

"He…he's what?" she asked.

"I'm a bouncer at another club down the block, had to break up two fights, then come here to pick her up, and she's drooling over your piece of crap guitarist."

"I'll tell him to get away from her. Who is she talking to?"

"The blonde guy."

"It figures." Lexa shuddered, having almost jabbed a man having a horrid day. "He's not very perceptive."

"She's wearing an engagement ring," he said.

"Sam can't tell the difference, but I'll see what I can do. If I asked you to give him a spanking, can you leave a handprint on him?"

"Don't tempt me."

"I'll have her out here in a minute," she said, and walked into the club to tell Grant and Karl someone named Nicky is looking for them at the back door. She interrupted Sam who soaked in the admiration of a woman whose moves were blatant flirtation. "Your man is waiting for you in the alley. You may want to be extra nice to him tonight."

Heading to the van, Lexa asked, "Did you and the engaged blonde have a nice chat?"

"She's just another fan."

"I came close to letting you get mauled, maybe killed. The fan you were drooling over had a monstrous boyfriend waiting for her."

Sam's chin dissolved, hair melted off his head, his eyes appeared reptilian, and instead of words, he hissed.

I bet you have her number, you snake.

At the beginning of the next show she asked Karl who the body builder was. He smiled and said, "They have an assortment of items."

"They? And what do you mean by items? asked Lexa. "Weed?"

"Nick Nevalla and Shane have good coke too. You should try it."

"Those two work together?" she asked.

"It seems so," said Karl.

"It's not my thing. My brain is already fried by insomnia, and my thirst for alcohol exceeds my worries about how I'm destroying my insides."

"I need to cut back on everything," said Karl. "But first I'm gonna have fun."

That evening Lexa opened another bristly letter. There was no name or return address, and she did not expect a signature on the gruesome verbiage. Most likely it was someone who had reason for anonymity.

Lexa,   *1/20/1976*

I don't love hearing you scream anymore. You think you are too good for me. At your shows, people are always surrounding you.

You're a conceited bitch. I know where you AND Debra live. She needs some of my attention. Her neck needs a good squeeze.

The writing is the same as Aldar's. He flipped a switch since his last letter. He threatened me and now he's involving Debra. We're leaving for an out of state tour, so unless he followed her home, he won't be seeing her at our shows for a few weeks. As soon as I get back, I'm stalking that creep.

She showed the note to Ted, and asked him to warn his wife. Tiny and the road crew had been effective in protecting Lexa and she was grateful for their diligence.

She was relieved to be heading south. A loyal fan base at shows, fan mail pouring in, and stacks of photos being presented, added clubs to Word Locket's out of state schedule in Brownsville, San Antonio, Lubbock and Odessa, Texas.

The trip started after a show at Junnies in Dubuque, Iowa, a night at a motel, and a long excursion southbound, connecting onto interstate 80 to Des Moines, picking up I-35 to Kansas City. In Oklahoma City on I-35 south, Ted got behind the wheel heading to Brownsville, Texas. The weaving of the vehicle at night woke up Grant, who's eyes widened at seeing the van in the oncoming traffic lane.

"Get off the road before you kill us. I can drive."

"I'm fine."

"No you're not. Get off the road. Now."

Ted pulled into a gas station to stretch and ask for directions. Lexa's sleepiness had frozen her curled body to the chair, but in realizing it would be hours before the next stop, she pried herself out of the seat.

"Where are we?" she asked Karl, blinking her eyes and yawning.

"I dunno. The middle of nowhere," he said looking around.

"This is Plano. Are ya'll in a band?" They turned toward an unfamiliar southern drawl.

"No, we're a high wire circus act," said Lexa.

"Yea that's us, the Flying Freaks," said Karl.

"Ya'll want some weed, coke, heroin, speed, bennies, candy dots?" asked the medium built man in skin tight jeans at the pump adjacent to theirs. His black cowboy hat capped slicked back brown hair, and narrow-set brown eyes surveyed his surroundings as he spoke.

"Candy dots?" asked Lexa.

"LSD, sweetie."

"Zip it up, cowboy," she said.

He looked down at his crotch.

"Not your fly, your mouth."

"I'll take some coke and weed," smiled Karl, as Lexa frowned and mouthed 'No', at him.

"Where ya'll headed?"

"Clubs in Brownsville and Odessa," said Karl. In seconds the transaction was complete and he packed his purchase in his suitcase.

"Karl, what are you doing? He's a sleazy dealer who could care less about you. You have no idea what is in that blow. It could be corn starch or ground up aspirin." She buckled her seat belt.

"It's my Texas souvenir. Gonna try some first," said Karl. "He told me to call him Hicks."

"Hicks? Is that his first or last name?" she asked.

"He didn't say," said Karl.

The bleary-eyed band and roadies exited their vehicles at 2:00 am, checked into a motel, and were given their keys. Trailed by Sam and Ebbie, Lexa entered her room, and was greeted by a spiky scorpion crawling toward her. She removed her shoe and smashed it into the carpet, giving two roaches the same fate.

As the weeks crept on, temptations, exhaustion and annoyances over each other's dissimilarities hovered under spotlights and taunted each of them. Grueling nightly performances, nonstop for days in a row, intending to solidify the band's act were followed by parties in a hotel or motel to wind down their energy, and motel guests left by stomping, banging walls and slamming doors in the morning as the band tried to sleep. Shrieking children ran up and down corridors and noisy adults getting revenge after a party they had endured the night before, created sleep deprivation for all, except for Karl.

"I have no problems drifting off and I am not tired," he grinned.

"Wait till you're out of blow and whatever else you bought," said Lexa. She loathed the man who had come to deal, mingle, and count his cash at Boagies night club throughout the week.

Friday, January 30, 1976

A slimy drug trafficker slipped a noose around my bandmate's necks and taken their cash. Not only has he dangled the dopamine drugs before the bunnies, he is intoxicated by the sum he amasses in his bank.

At least I'm not stressed about hostile notes on my mic stand, someone who is addicted to screams, uses rope on victims, and having to pay Tiny.

Our music has drawn out the warped and twisted like carpenter ants who gnaw and destroy the structure that houses them, causing damage to everything in their path, my bandmates included.

CHAPTER 10

TRAVELS AND TIRADES

S he referred to the cowboy in the black hat as Mr. Pee because of
the yellowish tint of his skin, but her bandmates thought the
reference of "P" was for Plano. He approached her as she stood at the
bar on a break, waiting for a vodka gimlet. The bartender handed her
the drink, and she attempted to pay, but the man in the black hat
stepped forward.

"On the house, from Mr. Hicks. Sweetie, the water you're sippin'
on ain't gonna give you a buzz. You're missing out on my sweets. I
got the best stuff. Bennies, speed, uppers, downers, LSD…"

"Downers? Do you have Nembutal?" she interrupted.

"I got the kinda' stuff you can't get at a pharmacy. You want somethin' like coke or heroin?" he asked. Hope you're not sorry."

"My biggest regret is having said the words, 'I do'." She walked away from the bar thinking about Tiny, who kept her posted on anyone who looked like trouble, especially Aldar, whose greasy brown hair and incendiary charcoal eyes fixated on the stage with the kind of intensity that could detonate a bomb.

"So what's your treat from the drug man?" She asked Grant in the dressing room.

"I got two dime bags to kill the pain. I'm not sure why my divorce is affecting me so badly," he said. "I don't like my life at the moment."

"Finality and endings are never easy," she said. "I'm sorry."

The agents who scheduled them at clubs out of state for exposure to new markets made a van, truck, stage, and motel rooms the band's primary residence.

Booked in Fort Lauderdale, the band toured the club circuit doing shows seven nights a week, burdened by fatigue and tension created by noisy motels. As Sam and Lexa looked for a restaurant to have breakfast, a husky, dark-haired man tackled Sam to the ground.

"Stop! What are you doing?" she shrieked.

"Back up, miss. Now." Two undercover police held up badges, frisked Sam and read him his rights. Lexa felt petrified, wondering if someone had set him up for a drug bust. *I wonder if Mr. Hicks was responsible for this,* she thought. "What is going on?" She wallowed in fear of Sam being framed and taken to jail.

"Back away!" The husky man's stubby hand in her face forced her to retreat.

Sam had worn pocketless black slacks, and nothing was on the long-haired freak they roughed up and questioned for an hour. He was given a bland apology and released, but his day was ruined.

Agitated and irritable, he was restless between sets, and in the cramped dressing room, he inched into Ted's face. "Why don't you care about this band? You sound like shit."

"What are you talking about? I care as much as you do."

"You drink too much and play like an old stoner. I can't stand it anymore," said Sam.

"You always criticize me. I'll never be good enough for you, no matter what I do. You get your way all the time. What Sam wants, Sam gets," Ted shouted. Anger filled his bulging neck veins. He gave Sam a forceful shove into a wall.

Grant stepped between Sam and Ted. "What the hell do you think you're doing?"

"This isn't about you," said Ted. His forearm bumped into Grant's chest, igniting him to raise his right fist, but Ted landed a punch between Grant's eyes.

Grant's brick blows matched Ted's heated swings. Lexa's cries to stop were soundless as knuckles smacked into faces, eyes, ears and upper body parts. Grant's bloodied nose dripped onto his white shirt. His left eye disappeared under ballooning, splotchy, strawberry-stained skin. Ted's distorted features, swollen lips, cheeks and a cut on his eyebrow created shock in all, knowing they were late in getting back on stage. They walked to their instruments and stared at the crowd in a stupor, to perform as though a gun was pointed at them, avoiding one another.

At the end of the evening, Grant threw a drum stick at Ted. "That's it. You're done in this band".

"Fine. Finish the tour by yourselves."

Friday, February 6, 1976

Sam apologized to Ted and talked him into staying in the band, but he is as encouraging to Ted as he is to me. The insidious nature of constant criticism is the eventual internalizing of it. Self-berating thoughts plant into one's consciousness, and grow like an invasive weed which strangles out all the good around it. The extra attention given to Sam since childhood, Ted's frequent reminders of being inferior to

*his younger brother's achievements, or the broken relationship
with his first love may have left unhealed scars.*

*I'm relieved to be out of state where my fear of a dangerous
man can ease up, but our best roadies Frank and Thor
announced they are quitting. I can understand how the stress of
the road and our fighting has worn them down, and I'm sad to
see them go.*

Despite words and material gifts given by those professing their
devotion to the band, bonds disintegrated, and the net was fraying.
Since their livelihoods were intertwined, keeping peace required great
restraint and effort. Spot lights, perspiration dripping under hot lights,
crowds screaming, cheering, and tokens of love included letters,
powders, pills, plants, jewelry, books, painted and sketched portraits,
photos, cassette tapes of love songs, and a snake from Kuala Lampur
was offered to Lexa at a party.

"You don't have a problem holding a viper? Aren't you a little
worried about venom? I hope you have the antidote. I prefer common
pets like dogs or cats, or even singing birds."

Friday, February 20, 1976

*I bought a bottle of wine at the club, and drank it sparingly
on our grueling twenty four hour trek home. Today I drove past
Aldar's place, and it's across the street from the Union
Cemetery where my grandmother is laid to rest. It is an ordinary
run down, chipped paint, one story ranch. The front walkway
isn't shoveled, making it dangerous and icy to walk on. I need to
get inside and snoop through his things.*

*My doubts of deviating off the path of the familiar has left me
in a bad marriage and conflicted about leaving the band. Our
meetings are solemn and strictly business.*

"We're getting a new sound engineer," Sam announced to the group on
the way to their show. "His name is Drax, and he can start next week".

"Seriously? Did you get down your knees and beg?" Lexa asked.

"I told him he could live in our upper flat and offered him a great salary," said Sam.

"I can't believe it. It's about time we get someone good," smiled Karl.

"Does everyone understand it means behaving like professional musicians if we don't want him to bail?" said Lexa. "We need to put our animosity aside. We need to compose a song that has airplay written all over it."

Brian Draxton, who preferred being called Drax, had been coaxed from his home in Oshkosh as a result of his technique and expertise of blending sound levels on a mixing board and was fluent in two languages: Party and Audio.

"I see you have full range drivers. Your woofers pack a good clean punch. I like the kick on your subs. I love seeing a signal that's clipped out," he said as he adjusted decibel levels, nodded his head up down and sideways, played air guitar, jumped and danced around. His tousled, short brown hair framed stubbles of hair on his face.

"Grant, I'm gonna notch it up a bit." Drax studied his new console and slid black channels up and downward in grooves to set levels as he pleased. He adjusted the tone of each slam of the bass drum, snare, toms, Hi Hat, crash, ride and splash cymbals. Sound levels on lead and rhythm guitars were fine-tuned in his ears and as the bass guitar was tweaked, he flagged and waved his arms like a director to his orchestra in the midst of the band warming up to AC / DC's 'Back in Black'.

"Ted, turn the mids and treble up on your amp. Karl, bring up the low end. What's your gain set at? Sam, nice three band parametric equalizer," he said as all guitarists concentrated on separate string tuning devices. "Keyboards sound a little hazy," he said twisting more dials, walking wall to wall through the venue to the mixing board, then turned and cranked small knobs as though he was about to launch a rocket ship, stepping around the stage and club until perfection resonated in his ears.

Stage monitors were checked and audio cables, patch cables, mics and stands were tightened, arranged and readied for a show.

"I always say, 'Go outside if you want small talk. Inside this club you party'." Drax's wild brown eyes matched his low, gravelly voice, and at 5'9" he was ready to swing a few punches at anyone who got in his way.

> Wednesday, February 25, 1976
> *This morning on my doorstep, someone left white clothesline rope tied into a noose. I showed it to Sam, and he said he said it was a creep's idea of a joke. I threw it away, but I disagree.*
>
> *Though the slate of antagonism is not wiped clean of what the band has inflicted on each other, the goal of a record contract exceeds our conflicts. We hired a new roadie to replace Thor, who looks as though he can overpower an amateur Sumo wrestler, and we call him Showey. I'm beginning to feel like a rock star for no other reason than to have him as part of our group. Drax, Hound and Showey – I hope they last.*

The new road crew rehearsed set-up and tear down of heavy equipment, dropped dry ice during songs for a fog effect, and kept the lighting synchronized to song tempo changes. Frank's replacement acquired the nickname of Hound, though his dark, curly locks, blue eyes, and handsome face looked nothing like any kind of dog breed.

Hound's job as road and equipment manager made him the puppet master of sorts in making sure the show went on as scheduled per the written contract. If only he could control the behavior of musicians using the same mastery he had of the gear. Until it is thrown in one's direction, there is no predicting what effect fame will have. The enticement for a man to have young women offer themselves is difficult to refuse.

Lexa felt like her insides were twisting as she watched Sam's arms reach around the groupie who hung on him and the outcome was evident. She turned away and walked outside where she sat in the lightless stuffy van. An hour later, the door opened.

"I wondered where you went. I can't get over how you can stand watching Sam and another woman get kinky." Karl held the wheel and started the ignition as Lexa sat in the passenger seat.

"Don't pity me. I don't have another option at the moment, and Sam takes advantage of it. I have to figure out how to navigate this insane life I've chosen. Do married women watch their husbands kiss and hang all over another chick? Tomorrow, do I ask, 'how was your night, honey? Was she good in bed?' He treats me like I'm invisible."

"I hope you don't put yourself down because of him."

"To Sam, new flesh means new excitement," she said.

"He doesn't care who he hurts. He uses people. If you leave us, it would take forever to look for a new singer who would have the same chemistry we have together," said Karl. "I don't think I would like it."

"We have enough talent between the five of us to get a good song on the radio," she said.

Friday, March 27, 1976

I glared at Sam's beady eyes while he charmed some new diva. He hunkered in a darkened corner coveting an adoring nymph like a snake facing its' prey. I regretted attending that party. We are postponing the inevitable, the demise of our life as we knew it.

Sam stands where self-absorption and denial intersect. He has no thoughts about consequence. I need to let go of a man lingering in my memory who once had mad passionate love for only me. I need to sell the silver bracelet he gave to me.

As Confucius said, "Our greatest glory is not in ever falling, but in getting up every time we do." The taste of fame is as delicious as a kiss in passion ending by a hard slap in the face.

Lexa waited until Sam was up and dressed on Monday to confront him. "I once asked you to replace me, but I was referring to the band.

What happened to 'you're the only girl I'll ever want'? If this is how you define marriage, I'm done. I abhor watching you drool all over someone else. I'm filing for divorce."

"Let's have an open marriage...see other people, and reunite when the band ends," he said.

"What a generous offer. Apparently Hindu's can have open marriages. It appears you want a backup, or an excuse if you want a way out, and you don't have a problem if someone else comes along who I like more than you."

"Stop throwing the Hindu thing at me. Lots of people do it and so can we. Marriage is outdated and overrated. Stop being a prude."

"Yes, others can do an open marriage. But I'm not in the 'others' category. I want you to get your things out of here. You can live upstairs. Marriage is for people who at least like one another, and right now, I don't like you." *As much as I want to leave the band, I would flip out to see who replaces me.*

Becoming Drax's roommate, Sam spent the day moving his belongings to the upper flat. She could now take the phone off the hook before she went to sleep, and both bedroom closets would be hers, but she needed to share the refrigerator on the first floor that faced the back entryway at the bottom of the stairwell until he purchased a new one.

Friday, April 9, 1976

I have avoided the news, which makes me unaware of recent murders. Because Tiny is near me during shows, he is most likely perceived as a serious fan, or possibly Aldar is onto him as a bodyguard. I drove past Aldar's house today, but did not see anyone outside. I parked across the street and watched for about 15 minutes, but all was quiet. I need to muster the courage to break in.

A guitarist in another band confided in me that Sam told him he thinks he is a much better guitarist. I guess Ted and I aren't the only victims of Sam's critiques. I wish I had taken the offer of the damn viper snake. 'Officer, I tried talking him out of having a slithering reptile for a pet, but he said it inspired his music.'

"It seems you wanna be skinny because you're in a band, but you're never going to get pregnant if you don't eat more," the white-haired neighbor blurted. Being absorbed in her thoughts, Lexa was startled by the grandmother who surprised her as she walked to the house. "I want to see cute little boys again like Shane Zadrik was."

"I don't want children."

"A beautiful girl like you would have beautiful children, dear."

"Have a nice day," said Lexa, shaking her head, trying to remember if anyone had referred to her as 'dear' or 'beautiful' even once in her life, but could not recall it. *There had to have been one kind word said to me by someone, but I can't remember it. Sam once said I had a pretty face, and now he says I look impish.*

Monday, May 3 1976

There is always a price to pay for being in a relationship, and I wonder what the frail neighbor lady pays. In all the years I've seen her miserable husband, contempt has been on his face. I think she takes a fist, a slap, and caustic words. Maybe it's why she is eager for family visits, perhaps it's the only time he smiles.

I wonder if the Shane Zadrik she speaks of is the same person who sells weed and coke and manages the Cavalry Club; the one who claims he met Jimi Hendrix.

Lexa changed her hair style during breaks and at times wore Sam's blonde wig during shows, which now became hers. She selected what she would wear at the club in Fond du Lac on June 19. The musicians were interviewed by a local music disk jockey, before they packed up guitars and amplifier cords, signed autographs, changed clothes, grabbed bags and headed to the van's reclining seats.

A blue-eyed, curly-haired blonde climbed into the van, onto the bed and she wrapped her arms around her knees. Grant asked why the woozy woman was there.

"She followed you. I thought you invited her," said Lexa.

"Not me. Hey miss, we're tired and need to get home. You need to go," said Grant.

"I'm free!" she shouted, turning the confused faces in the van toward her. Karl, Ted, Grant and Sam asked her to leave almost in unison, and again she screamed she was free. At 2:30 am, the hostility surrounding her heightened, and her screeches continued, as though she knew no other words. Sam shut off the engine.

"Dammit. Get out of our van!" demanded Ted. "We're done entertaining people. We are not your friends."

"What is your name?" asked Grant.

"It's Kalie," she said.

"Kalie, we don't care if you're free. Get the hell out! Now!" Grant hollered.

"No! I'm not leaving! I'm free," she squealed and refused to move.

Band members exited the van to discuss a plan. Ted took her right leg, Grant took her left, Karl took her right arm and Sam took her left, pulling her out of the van's back double doors. She thrashed, gyrated, flailed and howled as though she was possessed by a demonic force wailing and repeating, "I'm free!" Like a scratched record, or a broken doll, her words were an endless yowl.

Plopping her in the alley, Sam, Ted, Grant, Karl, and Lexa ran into the van and locked it up. Sam started the ignition, hammered the gas petal, and tires squealed and veered onto the street.

"I hope she doesn't go for the road crew," said Lexa. "I pity that deprived girl. She is drunk out of her mind and desperate for attention. She has no clue how reckless she is."

"I'm sensing our paths will cross again," said Karl.

"I hope I never see her again," said Grant.

"Why not? She is really pretty," said Lexa.

"If she was so dazzling I couldn't take my eyes off of her, I might be able to tolerate how crazy she is. For a while at least," he said.

Saturday, May 15, 1976
A surprising event occurred this evening. My bandmates turned down easy prey. An attractive blonde offered herself for free as she put it, and no one took her offer. Not even Hindu Sam wanted her. Maybe they feared that once they let her in they would never get her out. Kalie taught me a valuable lesson. Leave if you are not wanted. Never force yourself on anyone. No matter how hard it is, know when to walk away.

Lexa bought a floral arrangement, a man's coat at a thrift store, tucked her hair into a baseball cap, and put large sunglasses on. As she drove to the run down ranch house on Hopkins St., she took deep breaths to calm herself, especially while she rang the doorbell, flowers in hand. She waited a few seconds and rang again, but no one answered. *Maybe he's at the funeral home.*

At the back door, all blinds were down, and she was unable to see inside. She turned the door handle, but the deadbolt lock was secured. She thought about using the vase in her hand to break the window pane, but reconsidered. She took the flowers home and decided a hammer would be more efficient. *I need to wear the blonde wig and a different disguise on my next visit.*

She returned home to pack her suitcase to perform for a Mini-Woodstock party on a forty acre Iowa property. Thirty minutes into their set, gusts of wind shook the stage and mic stands toppled. In a darkened sky, squalls snapped branches off of trees, rattled cymbals and slammed amplifiers together. Rain and torn shrubbery swirled. Everyone grabbed stage gear, guitars and amps, shoved everything into the truck under a deluge, and slipped through mud to the house as lightening arcs crisscrossed the sky during the downpour.

A torrent obscured the road, forcing each musician to spend the night on a chair, sofa or floor, in one room or other. The vote was to return in daylight.

"I feel like crap. I got no sleep. I'm heading home," said Sam in the early morning.

"You can't go anywhere. There is swamp outside." said Grant. "You'll never get out of here through that muck. You'll see."

"I could care less, I'm leaving. Lexa are you coming, or not?" Sam leashed Ebbie, and he and Lexa tossed their bags into the van. He fired the ignition, triggering a slippery, uncontrolled descent down a long muddy hill. A look of eminent death in his eyes, he pumped the brakes, slammed the petal to the floor, steered the wheel toward the incline, then the opposite, but no driving technique existed to stop the sludgy glide downward.

"Jump out!" cried Sam. He pulled Ebbie onto his lap.

Both unfastened their seatbelts, opened doors and as the van slid, prepared to leap out before crashing down the 30 foot drop.

Sam hyperventilated when the van became wedged between two massive trees above the cliff and was at the mercy of the roots supporting them. Fearful of making a move in the creaking vehicle that rocked like a see-saw, Sam opened his door inch by inch, secured Ebbie in his arms, and carried her up the sludge. Lexa remained in the moaning vehicle, peering out of her open door mesmerized by the lustrous foliage and the river streaming over stones. The van creaked. *One wrong step and I'm gone.*

"Do you wanna die?" Sam yelled. "Get out of there!"

Roadies, the land owner, his friends and the rest of the band stood alongside him at the top of the hill. She inched her way out of the van.

"Lexa, look up," Karl said as she trudged to the top of the hill.

"To what? A large bird?"

"It's a red-tailed hawk, and has a wingspan of 43 to 57 inches. They dive at around 120 miles an hour and screech while they hunt for food. It conserves energy by flapping its wings as little as possible."

"It's beautiful," she replied looking upward. *Another day, another brush with death,* Lexa thought as they dialed for assistance of large farm tractors to tow the disabled vehicle to safety. Evening approached when they arrived home.

Sam had gone upstairs. Lexa called out to Ebbie several times, and could not find her. *It's not like her to do this.* She walked outside to see Ebbie absorbed in licking something at the back right corner of the house. "What are you doing?" she asked, bending down to pick up the lid of a jar that appeared to contain raw hamburger and green pellets. "Is this rat poison?"

Their vet's office was closed. Lexa ran to the medicine cabinet, frantic in her search. No syrup of Ipecac. Her shaking hand ransacked the shelf, spilling items into the sink. She poured peroxide and water into a cup, and holding Ebbie in her arms, she opened the dog's mouth and slowly poured the liquid down. She waited another thirty seconds and poured a little more into her mouth until green pellets and red raw meat were vomited onto the floor. Lexa felt herself tremor in fear. *She needs immediate treatment.*

"Sam, I think Ebbie ate some kind of poison," she said, thumbing through the phone book for an emergency veterinarian. "I'm taking her now," she shouted into the house, carrying her fluffy pup to the VW, unaware if Sam had heard her.

Lexa explained what had transpired to a kind and empathetic staff. She was asked if she had brought what the dog had eaten and apologized that she was so panicked, she threw it away.

"We'll give her medicine that will absorb what's in her stomach, meds to help her relax and intravenous fluids. We're not sure if she'll survive the next twenty-four hours," said the vet. "We'll call if she takes a turn for the worse tonight. All we can do is wait."

Saturday, May 29 1976
It is quiet and strange not having Ebbie in the house near me. Nembutal and my bottles of pinot noir and vodka kept me company. Wedging between the wall and bookshelf has become

my safe space. It's where my shoulders and back feel the touch of something, almost like arms around me.

The van nearly falling into the ravine did not frighten me, despite the potential for severe injury or even death. I wonder if I'm becoming numb to the disintegration of my life.

I have lost my grandmother, grandfather, peace of mind, freedom, sleep, my, favorite rock stars, a marriage as I knew it, my relationship with Grant, my family has moved far away, and those who were once friends have become enemies. I can't lose Ebbie. I will feel as though I have nothing.

When the vet called, he said he had good news and bad news.

CHAPTER 11

COLLISION

L exa had percolated her second pot of coffee on Sunday when the vet called and said Ebbie should be fine, but it would take a few days before she would be energetic again. Lexa did see a brown area of grass on the mean neighbor's property line, most likely caused by dog urine, but killing an innocent pet as a solution was extreme. She stopped at a hardware store for a three foot high roll of chicken wire, and sturdy metal posts.

Sunday, May 30, 1976
Ebbie's recovery was a relief, and I took a deep breath after the vet called. Today Sam and I put up a fence to keep her off the evil neighbor's property. Death tapped on my shoulder when we slipped down the sludgy embankment. What are the odds that we would be held back by trees positioned in our path? I was seconds from jumping out. My family has no inkling of the many

close calls I've survived. Each time I faced my demise head on, Sam was involved. Sometimes I wonder if it's a matter of time before my luck runs out.

The band's booking agents set into motion a show at The Palms, a club sponsoring a 'battle of the bands' contest. Crowds would watch ten bands throughout the night and the deal was sweetened by industry reps in attendance, scouting for bands to sign to a recording contract.

"We need to do this show. The club and radio stations will be doing a major promotion. Our name will be repeated on the air and if we win, the prize money is an easy five hundred bucks," said Grant. "Maybe we'll get signed to a record label. Let's write up a set list."

Saturday, June 12, 1976

A small note was taped to my mic stand before our show began which said: 'Lexa. I'm going to kill again and it's all your fault. Debra is still in my sights. She is as easy to track as you are.' I looked around the club, but there were too many people to see if Aldar was there. The club was mobbed. Tiny may want to defer this to law enforcement.

I held up our time slot because I was so rattled, I had forgotten my set list and guitar strap, causing me to run through the club and upstairs to the dressing room.

Lexa scrambled through a thick crowd of dimly lit faces facing the stage and was stopped cold by slamming into a heated body, who wrapped her in an embrace. She felt ill at the thought of holding up the band. "Excuse me, could you I, I..." Her eyes ascended to the sparkling blue eyed gaze upon her and his warm arms folded around her. "Sorry, I have to get back to the stage!" She pushed away, ran up the stairs to the dressing room and back to the stage in enough time to get through the show. The crowd cheered and chanted at the ending of their last song, but no amount of applause could take her mind off of the alluring face that had looked down onto her and sped up her heart rate.

Why am I so unnerved by someone I've never met? She scanned the crowd, her pupils dilated enough to let his body into them, clinging to thoughts of his flickering aquamarine eyes. A smile and a wave of his hand opened a reservoir to wash her into his direction. As he glided toward her through shrieks, music, screams, and applause in the club, she feared the possibility of losing her cool. She wanted to grasp every fact he was willing to divulge from his birth date forward.

"Tarick Tagan. Nice to meet you, can I buy you a drink?" he asked near her ear, where she inhaled his scent through the wall of perspiration surrounding them.

Fresh wood shavings, leather, lime, vanilla, and pine stirred in the magic cauldron. "I'm Lexa. A glass of Cabernet is fine. Put it in a plastic cup to go. Would you like to step outside?"

"Sure," replied Tarick's silky voice. He lead her out of the exit. "I've seen your posters. My band plays at the same clubs yours does."

The music in the building resonated for blocks around the neighborhood. Lexa zipped up her leather jacket. In her eyes, he was model, magazine cover striking, chiseled by Michelangelo's gifted hands. "Let's take a walk to the top of the building across the way. It's quieter and we'll be able to hear ourselves talk," she said.

It was her former apartment, where she remembered her treks up the back metal stairway. They climbed upward in darkness. She gave him a tour of the city, pointing to various landmarks as he inched closer to her. They sat behind the short wall watching traffic and crowds mingling in the front of the club.

"Nice ambience up here, don't you think?" she asked.

"Yes, it is. How did you know steps were back here?" he asked.

"I lived below where we're sitting, long before a nightclub opened across the street. There used to be a grocery store at the corner and the back alley is where I parked my VW. A police car is pulling up." She stared downward. "I wonder if a fight started in the club," said Lexa, leaning on top of the concrete lip of the structure, watching the vehicle park below them at the curb. When the uniformed men stepped outside, she listened to their conversation, wondering why they walked to the alleyway in her direction.

"Someone's always calling from this damn building," said an annoyed male voice.

"The cops are coming up here," she said.

She grabbed Tarick's hand, sprinted across the building, jumped halfway down the iron stairway, raced across a walkway and onto the roof of an adjoining garage. They slouched behind a three foot darkened raised wall as footsteps clanked to the top of the building where she and Tarick had stood moments before.

Lexa turned and peeked over the barrier at three officers using flashlights to scour the roof. "No one's up here. Another false alarm." Echoes of the departing men's complaints faded as footsteps trailed around the building.

Still curled up in her hiding spot, she began laughing. "I'm sorry. That was close."

He said nothing as they sat in the fragrance of each other. She felt drawn to the flickers of light and the glow of this stranger's eyes. He was the best looking man she had ever seen and they were not only alone, she felt the heat of his body beside her. The longing enticed her to within an inch of him when his hand curved around her face. Their mouths joined in a soft caress, not long enough for her. He stared into her eyes and hers were fixed on his. The cool night exposed warm breath as they spoke and Lexa kissed his cheek.

As they arose, the brushing of his hand across her back sent a jolt of static through her and she stared into his eyes, being the first time she could remember feeling electrified from so light a touch.

"Are you hungry? Let's go to a great Chinese restaurant," he said.

"Okay but first let's run back to the rooftop, hop around and scream out to all the people standing in the front of the club to tell them there's a party up here...free beer for everyone." Lexa smiled. "As soon as they cross the street, we'll run and hide here again."

"Yea, sure," he laughed as their footsteps clattered down to his car.

They sat in a candle-lit booth facing one another and she craved the taste of his lips more than the Shrimp Lo Mein on the table.

"What are your plans for this evening?" he asked.

"Anything that includes you tonight," she replied staring up at him.

"I'd like to show you a cool place," he said, opening the car door.

"Will the police be there?"

"Should I ask them to join us?" he asked.

"I dare you to," she said.

"It would be too easy. Thirty miles over the limit, run a few red lights and head westbound on Wells Street," he said.

"True. The police love speeding drivers going the wrong way on a one way street. How much have you had to drink tonight? It sounds like a party in a jail cell. I don't have enough cash to post your bond," she said.

In their banter she learned he was a guitarist in a band named Signal Source and worked at his dad's construction business. She imagined his sculpted body pick up heavy lumber, climb up scaffolding, and carry massive tools.

Their destination was a secluded wooded area. Lexa had paid no attention as to how they arrived, having been so focused on him and his conversation.

"This is a utopia. Where are we?"

"This is my parents' land."

"It's lovely," she said.

He embraced her as they rested their backs on tall damp grasses looking up at the night sky of stars and a full moon, far away from city lights and her wish for another taste of his lips was granted. In that moment, a reckless, insecure, insomniac collided with the composite of Apollo, God of music, holding his golden lyre, and Eros, God of love and passion. Lexa and Tarick exchanged phone numbers as the sun hit the horizon, when he dropped her off at home. She closed her eyes often to envision him as she sat on her bed reliving the evening in detail. She grasped onto her pillow as she wrote.

Saturday, June 12, 1976 continued:

I showed the note on my mic stand to Ted, and I handed my pin to him and insisted he give it to Debra.

A beautiful man and I took in the night on the roof of my former apartment where we escaped the grips of the police. An unlit sparkler, he was a firework brushing against the striking of my match. As he touched his mouth onto mine, a sensation of tingling immersed my body, increasing my heart rate and my breaths deepened as I inhaled his scent and essence. I can't get someone I barely know out of my thoughts. I feel almost the same way I did when Mike and I were kids on the playground, as if the world makes complete sense and I can conquer anything. Too soon for love, this must be the consuming sensation of lust.

He had said his birthday was in early May. She searched through her astrology book and read: A Taurus will not get involved until they have determined whether a person, situation or relationship is of use to them. She felt like this was acceptable, and the party he had invited her to could not arrive soon enough.

While she answered fan mail and placed each letter into a box, she opened a short threatening note on yellow steno paper. She was not able to determine why she had created so much distain in someone who could avoid the band, and there were many other musical acts in the city from which to choose.

June 6, 1976

I hate women, but your screaming amuses me. When I get you alone and I will, you will never see the light again. I will make sure of it.'   A former fan

She called Tiny to discuss Debra's involvement and the new note.

"I was a hired as a security guard. Investigative work costs extra."

"It figures," she said. So no pro bono?"

"Huh?"

"Never mind," she said. "The letter is dated 6/6, and 6 days later, on 6/12, a note was taped to my mic stand. It's a warning."

"Most likely Aldar wrote it," said Tiny.

"I think so too. Is there anything I can do?" she asked.

"Not at this time. Police don't pay attention to that sort of thing."

At noon she called to speak to Debra, and Ted answered the phone. After a long pause, he said, "She doesn't want to talk to you."

"Did you tell her what the note said?"

"I did. She was attacked by a husky man two days ago when she left the grocery store. It was around 8 pm. She fought him off, gave him a hard kick in the balls, and ran like hell. She dropped our groceries and has been freaked out ever since. She won't go anywhere unless I'm along now."

"She needs pepper spray," said Lexa.

"She said she's getting a gun," said Ted.

Tarick and his bandmates lived on a wooded lot. Most of them had girlfriends and were usually elsewhere, but today everyone was at his party, and she knew most of the musicians. She mingled for an hour, and asked Tarick for a tour of his home, but his room is what she was most interested in. Upon entering his bedroom, Lexa wrapped her arms around his shoulders. As she caressed his lips, the iced tea in her hand escaped her thoughts, and frozen chunks of liquid poured down his back. They both gasped and he backed away, startled.

"Oops, sorry," she said.

"Be right back, I'll get a towel."

Damn it. What was I thinking, or not thinking? "Let's hang out in your room for a little while," she said smiling at his return.

"Maybe later," he said smiling.

She wanted him all to herself, and kept him in her sights. The last of the stragglers leaving gave her the opportunity to glue herself to him, and he invited her to watch his band perform on Thursday, June 17. He gave the details close enough to where she could feel his breath on her skin and inhale his musky, masculine pheromones before she left.

On Thursday afternoon, she went through her closet contemplating what to wear to Tarick's show, and entered the club wearing red jeans and a gray tank top. Swarmed by women, a blue-eyed, curly-haired blonde yelled at Lexa. "What are you doing here? I hate you! It's because of you I got thrown out of your van!"

Oh no, it can't be. She's the woman who kicked and screamed like a banshee. Lexa walked in the opposite direction of the female who screeched she was 'free', and headed to the bar to order a drink. *Did she and this band hook up?* Into the fourth song, a group of women instigated by the blonde, started a cat fight and in addition to pulling out hair, pulled on a large cord, unplugging the PA leaving silence in the club. Roadies and the sound engineer hustled to the outlet, jammed the plug back in, and warned the women to stop. In ten minutes, the plug was yanked again, and the fighting continued. Lexa had no tolerance for women who brutalized one another. She informed Tarick the fighting made her edgy, especially the blonde girl, and she had to leave.

"That chick is Kalie Deckler. She dated our bassist. She's a charm, isn't she? We can't get rid of her," he said.

"We had to carry her out of our van," said Lexa. "It wasn't easy."

Thursday, June 17, 1976
I gave Mace to Ted, and asked him to give it to Debra, even if she has a gun. I'll stay close to Tiny, and protect myself. I'm relieved women don't fight to the extreme I saw this evening over my band. It occurred to me for as strong as I feel, I know almost nothing about Tarick Tagan. I wonder if he dated Kalie also.

Tarick called Lexa at 11:00 am, and they laughed about the events of the previous evening.

"Is some kind of combat always going on during your shows?"

"It was the first time Kalie unplugged the PA, not once but twice. I think all bands have crazy fans," he said.

"I agree. People get drunk and do things they regret," she said.

"Would you like to meet and have lunch today?" he asked.

"I have a show tonight, but lunch would be great," she said.

"There's a nice café in Capitol Court. I can meet you there."

She sat on a bench in the hallway of the Capitol Court Shopping Mall staring into the sun-soaked glass doors when Tarick's light blue jeans hugging long sturdy legs stepped in. Striding towards her with a fog of light behind him, he appeared angelic as the sun gleamed into strands on gold flecks of his brown wavy hair. His sea blue eyes smiled into hers and his 6' 2" toned body sat next to her. She craved all of him from the skin on his feet in his slip-on brown shoes, the flesh showing light brown hair on his chest made visible by open buttons on his light weight white shirt, even the light brown hair on his tan arms exposed by rolled up sleeves. Feeling as though she was riding in a hot air balloon, the anticipation of him getting closer to her was excitement in and of itself, and she sat as close to him as the bench would allow. Had he been wearing scented helium, she would have inhaled it and floated upward.

"Let's not have lunch in here," he said. It's too beautiful outside."

They drove into a park off of East Dean Road overlooking Lake Michigan, where he opened his trunk, took his guitar case out, a picnic basket, and he folded a blanket over his arm. They walked to the white sand, and Lexa kicked her shoes off while he smoothed the blanket, strummed his guitar, and belted out 'Heartbreak Hotel' in his best Elvis impersonation. A grin glued itself onto her face. He set his guitar down, poured Pinot Noir into two plastic cups, and handed a napkin and one of two sandwiches to her.

Lexa smacked her lips and broke out in a laugh, "Peanut butter and marshmallow crème. I haven't had one of these in years."

"You like my gourmet sandwich?"

"It's the best lunch I've ever had," she chuckled. "Cheers. To a gorgeous day and beautiful company. I hope we do this again."

They toasted and sipped on plastic cups. Their sandwiches finished, Tarick kissed her slowly, picked up his guitar and sang Joe Cocker's 'Help From my Friends', Elvis's 'Can't Help Falling', and Johnny Cash's 'Ring of Fire'. *I don't want this to end,* she thought, unable to divert her eyes from him. She became buoyant as they sat near waves that hit the shoreline, bubbling outward, swishing, surging and ebbing. The songs of birds jumping through spray added harmonies as though they relished the music as much as she did.

"One of my favorite music festivals is coming up, off of Lake Michigan. I forget what main act we're backing up at Summerfest, but it's always fun," said Lexa. "Those crowds exemplify what it means to party."

"We're playing there on Saturday, June 25th," he said.

"I think I'm free. Maybe we can hang out after your show and watch the other bands, if you'd like."

"Sounds good," he smiled, kissing her at the doorstep, his arms around her waist as their evening together ended.

She chose to wear blue jeans, a gray silky tank top, and long silver earrings to watch Tarick's band perform. During the show, their eyes locked. Sipping on her third glass of wine, she admired how he glowed under stage lights in his black slacks, matching button down shirt opened to his nipple line, peace sign pendant on a silver chain, and black slip-on shoes, her angel of seduction. Eyeing the many women in the crowd who stared at the band including the man of her desires, Lexa attempted to calm herself and popped half a Valium, but instead felt dizzy and euphoric.

When his show was over they met up, and she held onto his arm as they walked around Summerfest enjoying music at all the stages on the grounds. When all of the shows ended, the crowds funneled to the parking lot, forcing them into multitudes headed for the same destination.

"It's going to take us forever to get out of here. Let's go for a walk," urged Lexa who swayed and stumbled, and he agreed. They walked down Chicago Street, turned left onto N. Water St., walked on the bridge over the river onto First Street, and made a right onto Pittsburgh St.

"Let's follow the railroad tracks," she pleaded and they headed south on them.

Though they were near the heart of the city, the deserted area created a sense of wilderness as she staggered over hardwood planks. They held onto each other as they giggled, chatted, and walked for twenty minutes.

"Let's go home. The parking lot is cleared out now," said Tarick.

"Come on, it's only 2:00. The night is young, and daybreak is a few hours away. Sunrise over Lake Michigan is ours to watch for free. No lines or admission fees," she slurred back. Her heart racing in the stillness, she put her arms around him, inhaling his fragrance, his breath and body that swayed around her. The touch of his skin seduced her.

"We're heading back," he said as he led her in the opposite direction, still on the tracks, while behind them a train light glimmered in the mist.

Hearing the drone of a train in the distance, Lexa laughed as she tripped and regained her balance in a drug-alcohol induced oblivion. A long honk wailed. They glanced behind them, and she took off sprinting northbound on the tracks.

"Lexa, get off the tracks!" He yelled, looking mortified.

"It's just a train! I can jump off any time!" She continued to laugh.

"No. Get off now!" His voice quivered.

"There is a sense of lightening on my feet, like a buzzing current is on these rails," she said as she fell again and got back up to run as if she would be able to out run a locomotive charging toward her. "What note is the honk of the train in? I think it's a B flat." Her voice emanated a sound in the same tone as the blaring whistle, but was drowned out by the rail squeal pleading for her to step aside.

Tarick's face became pale as he ran to pull her off the tracks, causing them to fall onto the damp ground inches from the train. Their elbows bracing on the ground, they watched the cars whiz by, noticing his shoe in the center of the track. The cars hummed a chugging melody past them, while they waited to retrieve his shoe.

"I'm looking forward to a comfy bed, and a nice warm body under a blanket. Are we done here?" he said.

Her head on the ground, all was spinning. Salacious giddiness flowed through her. "I need help getting up." She smiled and touched his face and lips, then kissed him. "Have you ever had sex on railroad tracks?"

"No. I think you need some coffee. I doubt if you'll remember any of this tomorrow." He pulled her up, and they quietly walked to their cars. "I'll drive, and we can get your car tomorrow."

"No, it's okay. I can drive. No one's on the road. I'll follow you."

Saturday, June 25, 1976

Sometimes an ordinary day becomes extraordinary because someone exceptional has been a part of it, but I drank too much, have a pounding headache, and will never combine Ludes and alcohol again. I need to be more diligent of where the pills come from. It may have been a combination of narcotics. I was curled up on Tarick's sofa trying to sober up while he slept in his warm bed. He was unaware of what I took, and when my head cleared up at 3 am, I drove home.

Tuesday, June 29, 1976

Tiny called to inform me he intercepted a bomb yesterday evening at Teddy's nightclub on my side of the stage made of steel pipe, dynamite, potassium chlorate, sulfuric acid, and gunpowder. He disposed of all the contents. Aldar was in the club that night, but it was too crowded for him to see anyone set anything near us. He asked if my bandmates had enemies, since we all would have been maimed if it detonated. I can't tell them about this. They are already a bunch of lit fuses, and they don't know I hired a bodyguard. Maybe it's what the letter meant by 'never see the light again'.

Tuesday, July 6, 1976

It's been about two weeks since Tarick called me. Our bands are consumed by our shows. I want to speak to him, but realize I need to let him make the next move. The crowds have been great, people scream and clap between our songs, and we get several encores, but I catch myself looking for his face everywhere and crave seeing him again. I need to use great restraint to keep my hands off of him when he's around me. Has my soul met its counterpoint? Am I treading onto another self-destructive path, or am I lusting to have my fingers on his well-made body? Probably all.

Friday, July 9, 1976

At the Cavalry Club this evening, Shane Zadrik offered me drinks as soon as I arrived at his club. He had champagne chilling for the band and insisted someone take a photo of us. He put his arm around me just as Grant snapped our picture.

I asked Shane why no posters of the band were anywhere, being aware of the promotional package being sent for each booking, which comes out of our pockets. He said our posters are being ripped down as fast as they're put up and to tell your agency to send more if you want them up when you get here.

Aldar was there. He looks at us as though he has lost something, and will find it if he stares long enough. His gaze is hollow as though his eyes were replaced by black glass. He wanders to the bar and to the back of the club, where I track his movements as much as he tracks mine. I suspect he planted the bomb and is disappointed in his failure to maim us. Ted said, 'Debra is fine. Stop asking. She has a gun now.' I wish she would talk to me so I can ask if she got a good look at her attacker.

On Saturday Lexa, obsessing over Tarick, made several attempts to call him, but set the receiver down after the first ring. A few days passed where she stared at the phone, before she felt brave enough to let it ring until it was answered. *I should not be doing this.*

"Hello?"

"Hi, is Tarick available?"

"Just a minute."

His smooth, "Hello" was like a lullaby.

"Hi, it's Lexa. I'm sorry about my bad behavior."

"I thought it was interesting," he said.

"Interesting enough to get together again?"

"Maybe. Are you busy tomorrow?" he asked.

"Tomorrow is fine. We don't have a Sunday concert. I'll try to behave."

They arranged a time and decided to meet where he lived, in the rustic wooded setting of tall trees and high grasses as opposed to hers on a city block several yards from neighboring homes and roadways.

His house in sight, she tried to dampen her anxiousness at the anticipation of seeing him. He met her at the front steps wearing jeans and a loose fitting light blue shirt, unbuttoned enough to reveal his glossy tanned skin, making his clear blue eyes stand out. His hair was slightly lighter than the last time she had seen him, and he offered her a Tab soda over ice. "It's the kind of weather I wish I could hold onto for a long time," he said.

"I agree. My family lives on a waterway in Florida, and this is what it's like almost every day. Is a park around here?" she asked, enchanted by him.

"Yes, about a mile up the road," he replied.

She asked him to take her there.

She ran to the swings, and bet him she could get up higher and faster than he could.

"No way!" He chuckled.

They pumped their legs as high as the swings could take them, and the chains began to buck. Lexa laughed and looked at the sky as she swung.

"It's a rush, doesn't cost anything, and gives my stomach a roller coaster sensation like I get when I dream I'm flying. I've loved swings and monkey bars since I was a kid. In Heidelberg, the TV shows were in German. I understood some of what they said, but the other kids couldn't, so we all hung out at the playground."

She jumped off the swing, noticing the brown wings of a moth fluttering nearby, and held her hand out toward it. The vibrating wings landed on her finger, and she watched it settle on its living perch before traveling upward. "Where do these woods go?" she asked.

"I have never explored this area. Would you like a picnic basket and a red hooded cloak? Watch out for wolves," he said.

"If you have a red hooded cloak, I'll wear it. You can be the hunter who saves me."

"Ha! I don't have an ax or a rifle."

"You do have the nicest lips I have ever tasted, and maybe I can be saved by a kiss," she said smiling, her mouth nearing his. "Tarick, look up. It's a red-tailed hawk. Watch how seldom they flap their wings. They dive for food at around 120 miles an hour and have a nearly 5 ft. wingspan. Hear the screeching? They do that while they hunt."

"How do you know so much about hawks, Miss Riding Hood?"

"One of my bandmates told me."

They spent the afternoon wandering through the park. Drawn to his laughter and banter, she wondered if she may have been overstaying her welcome when they returned to his living room, but he appeared to be enjoying her company.

He walked out to his porch, and offered her a beer as they watched the sunset. A few beers later, they went back to his sofa and picked up their conversation. As the evening passed, Lexa mustered the nerve to slide beside his warm body to place a soft kiss on his mouth, and he lavished a long French kiss in return. He invited her to join him in his bedroom.

She was surprised to see her photo on the mirror of his dresser. It was one of the 4 x 6" itinerary cards they sent out to fans of the upcoming venues. *Did he put it up for my benefit?* "You have our photo…on your dresser? Are you on our mailing list?"

He kissed her lips again, and whispered, "Yes, I am." He pulled his shirt off baring his silky, tanned muscular chest, and kissed her neck down to her clavicle. He slowly unbuttoned her blouse and dropped it to the floor. His hand slid down her chest into her jeans, and he unbuttoned them. Slowly they fell to the ground.

She felt nervous as she anticipated his smooth body on hers. "Let's light candles. I love the ambience they create," she said.

He crawled under the covers as she lit three votive wicks on his dresser which cast an eerie glow in his room. In her black bra and lace panties, she turned toward him. A burning smell caused her to spin around. She had caught her hair on fire and clapped her palms over the burning flames sparking up like a torch on the left side of her head. Bewildered, she hyperventilated, trying to comprehend what had happened. The scent of embers filled the room.

"It doesn't look bad, Lexa. You caught it in time." He sat up in bed and his eyes perused her curves.

"I…I'll be right back." Ash and hair fragments speckled her palms. *What have I done? I've had too much alcohol again,* she thought on her way to the bathroom.

The light over the mirror revealed frizzed hair on her back and shoulders that felt crunchy to the touch. She deliberated how her bandmates and fans would accept the new look, ran the faucet using hand soap to wash her hair to remove the burnt smell, rinsed it as best as she could, and used a towel to blot the water out.

In a few months it will barely be noticeable, she thought upon entering his room. Disappointed at his eyes being closed, she watched his chest rise and fall, his innocence somewhere in a happy place. *He had too much to drink also.* When she blew the candles out, she realized how dizzy she had become. She went to the kitchen for water to dilute the beer she drank.

In a perfect world, I would stay here, but I smell like hand soap and ashes. I ruined my hair, and the room is spinning.

In his bedroom she gathered her clothes, and the temptation of his beauty lured her to stroke his cheek and admire his complexion. The precision by which his skin wove around his firm jawline and perfect symmetry of his face caused her to reconsider awakening him. *Maybe he is as drunk as I am.*

She did not want to diminish herself any more than she already had since she yearned for a memorable night that could begin something real. A relationship with someone who understood what life on the road was like would be invaluable. She placed a soft ambrosial kiss on his lips where she felt his warm breath. She wanted to redeem herself, but perhaps all of her male encounters, especially men she was attracted to would become havoc. What made her feel worse was the inability to change it.

Sunday, July 11, 1976

I did not expect to see my band's photo on the mirror of Tarick's dresser and wondered if it was there for my visit. I get frazzled when I'm around him because his physical beauty rattles my cage.

As if this day wasn't bad enough, I am missing one of my thigh high black boots - my favorite pair.

She contemplated on the times Sam put her down, deceived and disparaged her, and she realized she had become the saboteur. *It appears I'm tightening a choke hold around my own neck.*

She went to visit Nathan, his young sons, and sister-in-law, Polly, who was a hairdresser. She evened out Lexa's locks, in trimming seven inches of Lexa's hair to mid back. Polly asked if Lexa would babysit for an hour while they ran an errand, giving Lexa and her nephews time together. They plopped a book of nursery rhymes into her lap, and the children laughed during Lexa's rendition of the stories.

"...All the kings horses and all the kings men...and women got together and put Humpty back together again. Wasn't that nice of them to fix Humpty? And someday when life hands you challenges and it will, you'll do your best to fix them and make it all better, right?"

"Yes, Auntie Lexa."

A sense of dread overcame her when she opened fan mail. It had stopped being fun after the original dismal letter which was written on 10/3/75. Since then, several letters matched the handwriting, and this was the same.

July 5, 1976
I thought you would be dead. You should be. It will soon change. I'm looking forward to your obituary of what a good little girl you have been. I want to view your face in a casket like I did for all the others.

A sick sensation overcame her in realizing this person had gone to the funerals of the women he killed. His intentions were clear. He would go to great lengths to prove his hatred, his evil heart, his fixation and delusions. She thought about the division of good and bad in the world, of how some will stab another in the back, but have gone out of their way to convince victims of their friendship. And some wear their wickedness like a badge, or an ill-fitting suit under which is heartless and void of humanity.

The band's outdoor the festival show vexed her. It was too late to cancel the show. There was no dressing room and the best place to hide would be in the van. *Aldar wouldn't hunt me down at a fair, would he?*

The road crew hustled to set up equipment, plugging chords into microphones, amplifiers, lights and monitors in the early evening heat, while Sam, Ted, Karl and Lexa stood on stage doing a vocal and instrument sound check. Grant tapped on the bass drum, toms and snare, when thuds and shrieks encircled them.

A cloud of dust surrounded an enormous, bucking, white bull that trampled over equipment, reared and tangled itself in cords, tearing them up. Karl, Sam, and Lexa were on all fours as the bull rammed into the stage, again and again, knocking microphones and amplifiers down. Grant jumped off the back of the stage. The bull became more agitated when cords ensnared its neck and feet. Six wide-eyed workers in jeans and cowboy hats struggled to secure enough ropes around the animal to restrain and pull it away.

Karl, Lexa, Ted, and Sam arose off the stage and Drax ran to the sound board.

"Why, why?" wailed Drax. He knelt on the ground, bent his head downward, placed his hands on the Tangent sound board, which in that moment became a casket where he mourned, grief stricken.

Showey and Hound ran to check the rest of the equipment.

"Damn it! We're screwed!" Grant screamed. We will never agree to do this fair again."

"We can't afford to lose this show, so we have to figure something out. What extra cords do we have?" asked Sam.

What spare equipment is in the truck?" Grant asked Drax, who was in a meltdown and did not hear him. "Drax, get a grip."

Aided by a soldering iron, extra chords and electrical tape, scraps of equipment were pieced together for the show to commence as close as was agreed to in the contract. Due to the circumstance, the band was not held responsible for the delay and performed for 90 minutes.

The roadies and band members got the gear packed back into the truck, and were approached by another road crew.

"You guys think what happened to you was bad? 'Last Measurez' roadie was electrocuted last night in La Crosse."

"Is he dead?" asked Lexa.

"We think so."

"We're only a heartbeat away from the other side of this realm. And I thought our band was having a bad day," she said.

Saturday, July 17, 1976

Our sound board was shredded, power was severed, and most of the equipment was destroyed when a massive bull became entangled in the electrical cords and snake. One minute we were setting up, and the next, our livelihood came crashing down. For the first time, the band will be strapped for cash.

The local music newspaper ran an article of a cow waging war over a snake, the large power cord connecting the sound board to stage gear, but Word Locket's publicity was a minor consolation for the razing of equipment the band needed to secure their living.

"The crew did a great job pulling everything together." Karl said to console Lexa, Ted, and Grant. "But new equipment is expensive."

"This is serious. We've been hit financially by a county fair, and the people involved have ignored all the legal notices our lawyer sent. The insurance policy we had was almost useless. We all have to take a pay cut, or start day jobs again. We don't have enough cash to get new equipment and cover the cost of repairs to our gear and vehicles. We can't cut the roadies pay or they'll quit." *I'll have to cut back on Tiny's services and scrimp on food for a while,* she thought as she closed the band's financial records.

The white-haired, plump neighbor waddled toward Lexa, who lugged her suitcase, and Ebbie trotted close behind. *Not again. Leave me alone, I'm exhausted.*

"Lexa, you look like you got raked over the coals. You need to put more meat on your bones. Are you one of those vegematarians? Do you take drugs? Your hair would look better if you had a short perm like my daughter. You remind me of Julette Zadrik who used to live in your house. I can't believe you're not pregnant. It's because you're in that band, and you want to be skinny like that Twiggy woman." Her mouth flapped like the opening of a pink sock in the wind.

What some lack in knowledge, they replace with opinions, Lexa thought, closing the door behind her. *Even though she means well, I wanted to scream at her to shut up. I bit my tongue so hard, I almost drew blood.*

She sat beside the phone conflicted as to whether she should discontinue Dependable Security. Tiny had discovered and removed a bomb near the stage, provided valuable information, and kept her safe, but she no longer made enough cash to pay for a bodyguard.

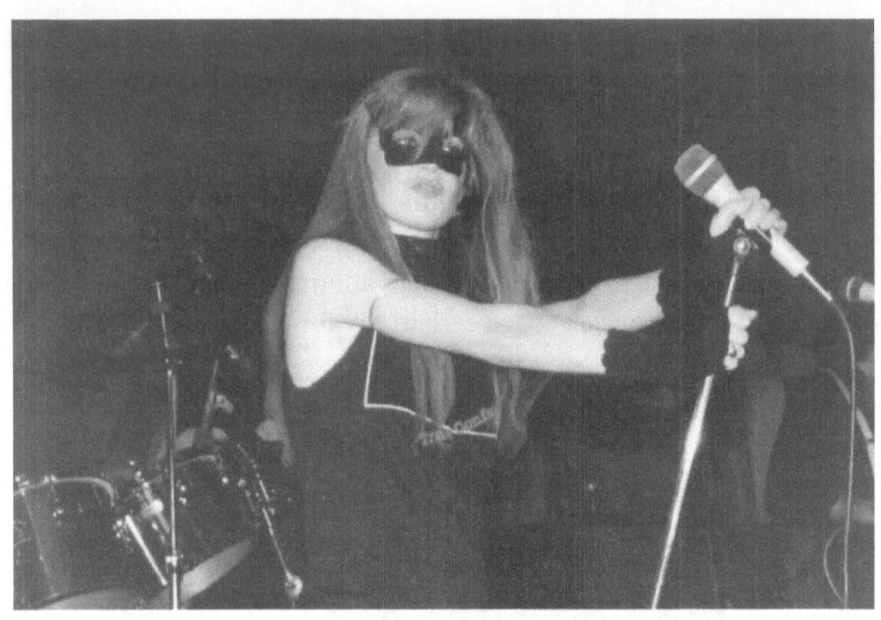

CHAPTER 12

BINDS

Sitting at her bedroom desk on Monday 7/19, Lexa scanned the newspaper for jobs, checked the band's calendar of scheduled performances, and spent her week applying at temporary nursing agencies to work for whomever offered employment.

She rifled through mail and the first envelope she opened was sent by the Milwaukee police department issuing a fine for an unpaid parking ticket, and the fee was now doubled. She had seen no ticket on her VW or she would have paid it. Thinking there had to be some mistake, but the information was correct, she ran through several scenarios as she studied it. Either someone took it off her car, it blew away, or it was deliberately left off of her VW so a subsequent fine would be higher. None of these were acceptable. She took out her checkbook, wrote out a check, stuck it into the enclosed envelope and went outside to the VW. Her screwdriver in hand, she removed the license plates and took a piece of paper to cover up the VIN ID number on the dashboard.

Her smirk became a scowl as she read a perplexing letter signed by: 'devoted fan'. Though it was sent to the P.O. Box, any true fan would not harass her.

7/23/1976

lexa, thiS might be A bit rash For me but Everyone Who has thIs secret Tells me tHat money Makes lifE sweet: NoOn. Jul. tweNty ninth. Lucky $ daY.

cavalry Club. see u 7/29   devoTed fan.

She called Tiny who agreed to meet her near the club on 7/29. She was determined to face the person who wrote the strange message.

Monday, July 26, 1976

I've received another absurd letter on yellow steno paper and the handwriting is different. There is no signature or a phone number, but I have been to the Cavalry Club and know where it is. This person must assume I'll meet out of curiosity. I have to keep Tiny at least until I get through the 29th, especially because Aldar may have had someone write it.

I'm putting the license plates under the front seat of my car. If I get stopped, I will pretend I had no clue they were missing, and to ensure I will get new ones as soon as possible. Always have a plan.

On Thursday morning, Lexa pulled on light blue summer jeans, a snug blue and white tank top, and long silver earrings. She called Tiny to confirm their plans and where to meet near the club.

She left for an electronics store, purchased two walkie-talkies, stashed them, Mace, and a driver's license in her empty tan purse.

It was the first time she had seen Tiny's hair neatly cut and combed. His scraggly beard was shaved and his face appeared thinner. In a black t-shirt and matching vest, he looked as though he had lost about fifty pounds. Two blocks away, Lexa gave Tiny one of the transmitters through her car window.

"If I need you, I'll contact you on this," she said.

"Let's test it first," he said. "Keep it short. Just scream 'This radio isn't playing any music', and I'll be in there in a flash."

"Okay," she said. She drove to the club, parked, and opened the heavy door to Deep Purple's 'Smoke On The Water' blasting while four male patrons at the bar sipped on beers, turned and eyed her up and down as she walked in and looked around.

She signaled to the bartender and said, "I'm supposed to meet someone here…do you know anything about it?" Three of her band's 24 by 36 inch framed posters still hung on the wall behind the bar. She laughed. *It's a great way to keep our pictures from being ripped down.*

"Yea…office…back room," he motioned his head.

She walked through the club, knocked on the door and was summoned to enter. "Hi. I'm Lexa," she said surveying the office, noticing two windows partially hidden by shades drawn halfway down. The latching of the door muted the music. "You wrote me a letter to meet you." *Shane Zadrik, what the hell do you want?*

"Yes, I did. Have a seat." His jet-black, shoulder-length hair was combed into a ponytail at his neck. He stood up and welcomed her in.

"Your Hendrix poster is enviable, she said."

"Would you like a drink?" he asked. An oscillating fan in the corner blew back and forth and onto them.

"No, thank you." As she inspected the room, she was drawn to a framed 4" x 6" photo on his desk, the one that Grant had snapped months before, with Shane's arm around her. A silver skull earring dangled in his right earlobe. A black t-shirt reading 'Live Right Don't Get Left Behind' was filled out by a weightlifting body. Snug blue denim shorts exposed muscular legs and calloused feet shifted under his black slip-on sandals. He smiled, revealing perfect white teeth, and sat down. His dark brown eyes scrutinized her. The light of the sun revealed an attractive, oval-faced man graced by striking olive skin in his early 30's.

She sat in a chair and faced him.

"I invited you here to discuss some business," he said in a mellow voice. "I read about how much damage a bull did to your equipment in the local paper, and when I booked your band at the club for next month's schedule, one of your agents told me how much gear you lost."

"Yes, we lost a lot of equipment. How do you know where I live? How many letters did you write?" she said staring into his eyes, watching for eye spasms.

"I have no idea what you're talking about. I wrote one letter to arrange this meeting, and I mailed it to your P.O. box. Are you sure you don't want a drink?"

"Thanks but no." *I don't like you even though you have a life sized photo of Hendrix and cool guitar strap behind you.* "Your letters are disgusting. Are you admitting you're a pervert?"

"What letters are you talking about? I sent just one letter. This isn't a good way to start doing business together."

She wasn't certain what had possessed him to invite her to his office, but her voice on the radio, TV appearances and the assortment of pictures of her may have been factors. Lexa watched him tap his fingers on the sizable wooden desk he sat behind. *This club isn't as glamorous in daylight,* she thought eyeing dust clumps in corners, spider webs on light fixtures, stains and cigarette burns on the brown floor. "Why didn't you sign your name or leave an address?"

He laughed loudly. "I guess I should have."

"You could have discussed your business proposition during my band's last show here," she said.

"It wasn't pertinent at the time. There was no way we could get one second alone. Is the drummer your boyfriend? No, it's Karl, the bass player, right?"

"I hope it's not why you asked me to meet you."

"I'm curious, but I don't mean to pry. I hope you're interested in what I'm offering." He took a sip from a beer bottle on his desk and rubbed his hand onto the condensation. "We could both make a lot of money. It's…a win-win situation."

"Money always sounds tempting," she said.

"Lots of musicians want their weed fix and I'm sure you know plenty. You sell it and I'd be your contact," he said leaning back. The air around him felt stuffy, and dust particles swirled through sun-siphoned glass, giving him an unexplained gloom.

"I need to think about it. I can't give you an answer now. We're rehearsing to make an album and I travel constantly. What makes you think someone won't turn me in? I don't think so," she said, half ranting.

"I'd like an answer soon. Picture yourself playing in cold, hard cash. Lots of it." He sounded annoyed.

"So…is this a request or a threat?" she asked.

He blurted out a laugh. "Take my number. Call and ask for Shane," he said reaching over the desk to grab a sheet of yellow lined steno paper off of a stack. He wrote down his private number and handed it to her. "I'd like your answer at the latest by next Thursday. It gives you one nice long week, honey."

"Honey? I'm not anyone's honey. If you want me to like you, call me Lexa," she said cringing.

"Okay, I hope we talk soon." As he walked toward her, she looked up at him thinking he was about 6'1". His tanned, toned muscles popped images of Mastiffs and Saint Bernard's into her thoughts. "Have a good day," he said.

"Thanks, you too." She smiled at him, looked at the paper and glanced back at his eyes which pierced through hers. As she walked out into the eighty degree heat, she shook her head, thinking he may be lacking in aptitude.

Back in their cars two blocks away, she retrieved the walkie-talkie and explained to Tiny that she did not need any more help.

"How did it go in there?" he asked. Perspiration dripped off of his face, and sweat stains soaked most of his black t-shirt.

"Shane wants me to sell pot," she said.

"What did you tell him?"

"I said I'll think about it."

"I wouldn't trust these guys," he said. "Not one bit."

"You're giving me an adjuration?" she asked.

"Huh?"

"An appeal to avoid them," she said.

"Oh."

She visited the Union Cemetery and silently sat at her grandmother's grave. *Oma, I keep punishing myself, and I don't know how to stop.*

She drove to the liquor store and bought a liter of vodka. *Maybe selling pot can buy my freedom, a new car, or new equipment. I'll give him an answer today.*

At home an hour later, she dialed the number on the ripped paper, asked for Shane, and was told to hold on. A five minute wait of voices echoing through the receiver transpired before she was told he was unavailable. Lexa asked when the best time to call would be.

"We ain't no babysitters," said a deep voice.

Lexa hung up. *Yea, you don't have a brain, dude. Time to focus on more important matters,* she thought, wondering about Tarick. She wanted to know if he was seeing someone else and decided to pay him a visit as soon as it was dark outside.

She dressed in black, tossed a black knit winter cap on the car seat beside her, drove forty minutes to Oconomowoc, and parked the VW on the side of the road, thirty feet from Tarick's driveway. Walking through thicket, she was able to view lights on throughout the house. Open blinds and sheer white curtains over windows made spying easy. She watched his bandmates in plain sight. Most were sitting in chairs; one was reading the newspaper, and the evening news hummed on TV.

I never keep my shades up after dark, but they have nothing to fear. When I view Tarick, the rose colored glasses I wear cloud my vision. Why did he have my photo on his bedroom mirror? Maybe I come across as needy, but can't seem to mask it. How crazy. Guys are obsessing over me, and I'm obsessing over someone who has me confused and irrational to where I've begun stalking him. She threw the black knit cap onto the passenger seat.

Her house felt like a prison she voluntarily entered. She half-filled a glass of vodka and looked forward to future days of freedom as she took out her notebook and guitar, and sat on her bed against the wall to write songs until 5 am. Sam's feet pounded upward on the outside stairway, and the door slammed. She closed her eyes.

Thursday, July 29, 1976

I dreamt about Julette again. We had a quiet conversation, and all I can remember is her saying, "My son". If only I knew what she wants.

The last letter was written by Shane, not the previous ones. He has no eye disorder. All of the bands tap into his illegal drug activities, and now he wants to bring me into the fold. I could inform the police of his dealings if I wanted to. Perhaps I can accrue enough money to buy things I need, but I trust no one.

Though nursing agencies may have called offering employment while I was gone, I won't be able to fit a new job into my schedule now. I should consider this offer. Since the bull incident, I need the money. I could slip my take into my bandmate's paychecks. They would be none the wiser, and I could continue to employ Tiny.

When you're in a band, people love you for no other reason. It's disconcerting to see my photos in places I've never expected.

Lexa's first thought upon awakening was to dial the number she was given and work out some kind of deal. The phone rang nine times.

"Yea, Cavalry," A male voice asked.

"I'd like to speak to Shane."

"Hey, is this Lexa, the chick who was here yesterday?"

"Yes it is."

"No one has seen him since you were here. We don't know where the hell he is. But you just might. What did he say to you?"

"He did not disclose his whereabouts yesterday," she said.

"You were the last person to see him and several of us can give a good description of you."

"You said you weren't babysitters. Maybe he went to see his mommy." She slammed the phone down, and wondered if they were all drunk at the bar. *If Shane sent letters to anyone else and is mixed up in the drug world, no doubt someone got to him, or he skipped town. It should be easy for anyone to figure out.*

She did not have time to worry about anyone's whereabouts other than her own. Organizing her bag for the show that evening, she checked a full calendar of upcoming performances, and could not rid the image of the man sitting behind the desk who was now missing.

On Monday morning, one of the band's booking agents called. "The police called asking about you. They wouldn't tell me why. Is everything okay? I had to give them your address."

"I think everything…seems to be fine," she said noticing an increase in her heart rate. A short while later her buzzer rang, and two heavyweight uniformed men holding a black day planner stood at her front entryway. Lexa cooperated as politely as possible, and explained she knew Mr. Zadrik because her band was hired by the Cavalry Club, and she had been called…to pick up…a black shirt he thought she had forgotten. Her band performed there. He was fine when she left at around 1:00. No, he did not seem disturbed. No, she was not his friend and only knew him because of her job, nothing more. They held his most recent photo of her standing next to Mr. Zadrik.

"The photo was taken on July 9th. Our band performed at the Cavalry Club that night. One of my bandmates took the photo. I have a witness who can verify my leaving on July 29 and I know him as Tiny. I left the club alone and nothing seemed out of the ordinary. I can provide a phone number where you can contact him."

"Make sure you are available if we have further questions."

She watched the squad car disappear and looked up to the cirrostratus clouds filling the sky. *They think I'm hiding something. What did he write in his day planner? Hmm, more rain on the way.* She pet Ebbie, who spoke to her in human-like sounds. *The police made it clear that I cannot leave town. I hope our agent hasn't told them we are touring out of state tomorrow, and contracts are signed. I'm certain law enforcement is eager to get their hands on Mister Zadrik because he's a big time drug dealer. It is odd he would disappear so soon after our meeting.*

Lexa was sleeping when Sam knocked on her door and asked why she wasn't packed and ready as the plan was to leave at 10 am. Word Locket and the road crew met at the duplex to begin their caravan to Minnesota, where they performed at Boyd's night club in Minneapolis and was introduced to a pro wrestler and his wife. Sam invited him to the stage and let him take over his white Fender Stratocaster to Eric Clapton's, 'Cocaine'.

At the evening's end, the wrestler and his wife gave the band a tour of their gym and the band invited them to party in their hotel room, where he lifted Karl into the air like he was a toy.

August 25, 1976

Conversations in the van focus on equipment, clubs, drugs, highs and all aspects of women. I'm hearing intimate discussions of females as though I'm was one of the guys and read magazines to view things I never knew possible of the human body. Chicks have been inviting band members to spend the night and provide transportation to a party after every show.

a girl a band a diary

The band's next stop was in Atlanta, where the contract required seven days of five sets as compared to the usual three, so the band added extra songs to stretch performing until 3 am. Despite the long night, Karl, Ted, Grant, Sam, and Lexa accepted party invitations and invited members of the crowd to their hotel after every show. By the end of the tour, exhaustion caused the ride home the ride home to be a silent one.

Wednesday, September 1, 1976
We were so tired, no one wanted to drive, so we drew straws. The unlucky straw was drawn by Sam, who took a capsule of speed to stay awake while the rest of us slept. Thank you Mr. Hicks for the one drug that helped us get home.

Our travels are on countless roads in unpredictable elements. I watch our venture through a portal, passing fields of rain droplets in a steady tempo onto wildflowers and fences, open prairies, and rush hour traffic. Trees are showing traces of orange and gold as nights become cooler. My wish is for Tarick to warm me as winter approaches. I'm looking forward to my own bed. Motel rooms and parties have worn us all down.

I think Shane Zadrik skipped town to avoid jail time. Most likely someone ratted him out. I'm glad it went down before I got tangled in his web, but the police have reason to believe I was involved.

CHAPTER 13

RENDEZVOUS

The first thing entering her mind as she woke up and the last thought of each day was of Tarick and the officers, causing her to make every effort to keep uniformed men out of her thoughts. Trying to resist calling the man she craved was futile as she paced, and dialed his phone number. His mellow voice sounded happy when she told him about her travels on the road and the massively built wrestler. She was afraid to ask if he had tried to call while she was away, and made every attempt to sound as excited as possible about the events of the tour. She asked how his band was doing as both bands were rehearsing to release albums.

"The new songs I wrote are going over really well at our gigs. Did you hear about the club owner who mysteriously died?" Tarick asked.

"We've been on the road for three weeks, and I got back yesterday. I've been cleaning, unpacking, and haven't seen local news," she replied. "Which one?"

"The guy who owned the Cavalry Club."

She wondered if she misunderstood as he went on, "His body was in the back of a van, the first week of August. Did you know him?"

"Our band performed at his club. Was it a suicide or was he in the wrong place at the wrong time?"

"Are you sure you didn't know Shane Zadrik very well?" Tarick asked.

"Why do I get the impression you have more to add? What did I miss while I was gone?"

"Word has it you were somehow involved in his death."

Her heart dropped to the ugly design on the old, tan kitchen floor as she asked, "Define 'word'. Did you mean gossip?"

"The musicians I've spoken to said you were the last person to see him alive."

"Gossip spreads quickly, and the juicier it is, the faster it spreads. And it's not the truth. I was out of the state the first week in August. Are you afraid to be around me now?" She laughed, realizing he had witnessed her destructive side but she doubted she would be able to convince him it was coincidental. "I have some open days."

"I'm not afraid of you. I'll have some free time in a few days," he said. "I need to look at my calendar. Does this coming Tuesday work?"

"I'm open that day. See you then." They were to meet at the Chinese restaurant he took her to on the night they met.

She rummaged through mail, spent the next few days cleaning, dusting, doing laundry, grocery shopping and probed her closet to prepare for her date. She emerged wearing snug jeans, black sandals and a multi-colored short-sleeved blouse.

She realized she would have met him anywhere. She parked near the restaurant, and inside she spotted him waiting at a table. Their banter was lighthearted and he laughed during their lunch as he shared stories of his life on the road. One of his fellow musicians was injured and had to skip the last show. What started out as a beer drenching fight between a band member and a roadie, ended when the bass player overlooked a chain stretching across a driveway in the dark and flew down head first, getting knocked out. The homeowner opened the door and screamed at them.

"I'm willing to bet a lot of alcohol was involved," she said.

"Not us sweet, innocent boys."

"Yea, as innocent as Lizzy Borden, I'm sure," she said.

"As innocent as a baby."

"Are you talking about baby musicians who think they're men?"

"Ouch!"

"That little cry is fixable," she laughed. "Put your lips on mine for a while," she said before placing a soft kiss on his lips.

When they stepped outside into the sunlight, Lexa saw a thick, tan piece of paper under the windshield wiper, picked it up, examined it, and laughed to see no license plate or VIN identification of her car on the parking ticket other than the description of a gray Volkswagen Beetle. "Another love letter," she said ripping it up.

Tarick gasped. "You look way too happy for someone who got a ticket. You can go to jail if you don't pay parking fines," he said.

She agreed, not knowing where to start explaining, since he did not notice why most of the ticket was blank. "Down the road is a Dairy Queen. Would you like to join me for an ice cream cone?"

"Lexa, you are by far the most untypical girl I've ever met," he said holding up his carton of leftover food.

"One small cone?"

"Okay. I'll meet you there."

While licking cones they laughed over the ripped ticket she said she would tape back together and send a payment in. She said she would be a good girl and needed someone like him to help her behave. *The ticket will go in the garbage.* "We should go to your place. Licking this cone has put me in the mood for licking skin," she teased, sitting next to him and pretended to lick his cheek.

The back of his 1971 Road Runner remained in her sight and her door opened to the chirping of birds in the wooded field.

"It's so nice out here," Lexa said dreamily, and he agreed.

Their arms around each other, they sat on his sofa and kissed to the sound of the TV on low volume. She wondered if her photo was still on the mirror of his dresser.

"Why did you leave the last time you were here? I woke up disappointed. I thought you weren't interested in me."

"I felt too annoyed for burning my hair. And you were in dreamland." Drawn to his pheromones and flawless skin, she fantasized about her soft flesh pressing into his body. As their lips were about to touch again, Tarick diverted his attention to an anchorman's voice on his television.

"Police are still investigating the death of Shane Zadrik who owned a local music club. Anyone who has information is asked to call the police. They turned their heads to the screen, recognizing the smiling face of Lexa in the photo that Grant had snapped of her and a man she had briefly met.

"Lexa," he said, pulling away from her. "It's you."

Why does some dude's recent picture have to have me in it? And shame on the press for stirring the pot by not cutting my image out, she thought. "I get the impression you think I'm guilty," she said, backing away.

"I'm not sure what to think. You're in a dead guy's photo and I have seen you do too many crazy things."

"I shouldn't be so sensitive, but that stings," she said rising off the couch. "That guy asked for a picture of us when the band was at his club and Grant snapped one. I'm not a murderer." She picked up her black purse and glared at him, her heart grief stricken. Her jacket under her arm, she walked outside to the flickering of twilight on the horizon, fearful of being stopped, having no license plates on her VW.

As soon as she sat down, a dull pain started in her lower chest, but the more she thought about it, the worse her stomach felt while driving home. She parked in the garage, placed her hands over her belly and slumped forward. *My stomach is twisting inside out and I have no idea what to do about it.*

Tuesday, September 7, 1976
When I was a kid running through the woods, I never felt lonely. I always knew someone would be at home. Oma was usually in the kitchen, but in my airless house, I am alone. My stomach ache is so intense I can't sit up straight. I think my constant lack of sleep and anxiety is causing this. I have to gain access to Shane's life and his club. Tarick most likely thinks I'm insane. I caused police to chase us off a roof, had a drunken race on train tracks, poured ice down his back, set my hair on fire, ripped up a parking ticket, and my blurred image is on TV in connection with someone who is dead. He probably thinks I'm as crazy as Kalie who he refers to as a 'charm'.

Tarick's reaction was a call to action and she had no choice but to contact Dependable Security and dig into the whereabouts of Nick and Aldar.

At 9 am she dialed the phone. "Is Tiny available?" She said in an early morning gravelly voice barely holding itself together.

"Who?" A deep voice responded.

"Tiny…he's one of your security guards."

"I'm not sure who you are talking about, ma'am."

She paced back and forth alongside the kitchen cabinets pulling on the phone cord. "He's about 6'5", weighs about 400, has dark blonde hair, usually wears a vest and has worked for Lexa Lynnch, but I also go by the name of Lexa Loxx."

"Do you mean Thurston Tinsky?"

"I call him Tiny, but if he is available, I'd like to speak to him."

"He's out on a job. He might not be back today."

"Please give him a message to call Lexa as soon as he can."

"Will do."

Lexa hung up the phone and ransacked her mind for clarity. *I'll check Mr. Zadrik's address.* She flipped through the phone book. When she scribbled '1745 W. Hopkins Street' on a piece of paper, she realized it was the same address Tiny had given to her for Aldar. She looked for the number of Aldar Geitlich but none was listed.

She checked a map, got dressed, and was in her VW, circling the block to the sound of mowers blowing lawn particles into the late summer air. *The house finally looks occupied. Three cars parked out back. Drapes are drawn and all blinds are down. They prefer the dark? I'll pay them a visit tonight.*

Back in her kitchen, she made lunch of a fried egg covered by a slice of cheese, squeezed ketchup onto two pieces of bread, and while pouring a glass of milk, the phone rang. Grant confirmed their meeting for tomorrow night's show, but she had hoped it would be Tiny. She changed into black jeans and a long sleeve black Henley shirt.

When the sky darkened, she fed Ebbie, let her out, and started the VW engine, the black knit cap and Mace on the seat beside her. She drove around the block a few times, parked on 18th Street, south of Chambers St, tucked her hair under the cap, and walked to the front door facing Hopkins St. She snuck up to the door when loud laughter and a dog's fierce barking caught her off guard. *Either several people live in the house or some dropped by to party.*

Scanning the surrounding area, she noticed neglected yew bushes under the front window. Square patches of dirt and grass wove through the landscape, and a tree stretched its drooping limbs in the back left corner. She walked to the rear of the house, and through the window, she listened in on conversations, and the aggressive barks of a dog scratching on the door caused her to sprint across 18th St to the back of the nearest house just before the back door opened. A deep voice spoke as she peeked out.

"What is it big boy? What?" The dog appeared to be a German Shepherd, and trotted around the ranch-style dwelling several times, relieved himself, and was let back in.

Okay, slight change in plans. She went to the closest grocery store, purchased the cheapest package of chopped meat, returned to her parking spot, ran to where she had previously stood, and dropped pieces of raw meat along the lot line. She raced to the window facing the alley, and spied on laughter, drinking, overbearing voices, footsteps, chairs screaking on the floor, swearing, and a card game going on, but something more peculiar, a voice sounding identical to a dead man named Shane Zadrik.

She crept around the beige house, peeked into the glass pane in the back door, and through a small opening in the bottom of the blinds facing the alley, she spotted a broad shouldered man who had a slight wave to thick, shoulder-length, jet-black hair. At a kitchen table, he sipped on a bottle of beer while talking to three men, all of whom chugged beers and were absorbed in a card game. Conversation focused on the game and whose turn it was to order pizza. One of the men referred to him as Shane, confusing her.

A dog barked, and the bellows around the table increased when a deep voice boomed, "Shut up Boffo! Damn dog wants to go out, come in, go out. Make up your mind!"

The dog sat down facing the men and whined like a child playing the violin for the first time on the same high notes. Smoke filled the room as a joint was passed around. *Nice. Make this easy for me, dopers,* she thought, gluing her ear to the glass.

"I'll see your one G and raise you one G." Cards moved around the table. "I got two rounds left. You did it once. Do it again, baby," as he viewed the contents of his hand.

These guys have a grand to burn?

"I got a straight flush. Time to pay the piper, dudes."

He collected the pile of cash on the table and another man at the table stood up. "Damn. You ripped us off."

"Are calling me a cheat? And you better not be thinking about bailing. The plan goes down no matter what. You got it?" asked the man who looked like Mr. Zadrik.

"It's under control." Another male voice responded in an annoyed tone. "We've heard it enough times."

"Don't go there. Everyone's gotta carry this out like clockwork, every second matters," said the man who was called Shane. "So check your watches." He pushed his cards away and stared at the man across from him. "No last chances to back out. The outcome will be the sweetest revenge."

"No one gets out this late. It's going down. Anyone wanting out now ends up across the street," bellowed a loud, deep voice. A black gun in a leather holster sat under a white t-shirt his over which was a leather vest. All became quiet as ugly glances passed around the table.

I've heard both voices before. They wear guns…in the house? What are they into? She ran to the cars parked outside on 18th St, and wrote the makes and license plate numbers on a piece of paper. A 1975 red, 2 door Plymouth Duster, a 1974 blue, 2 door Dodge Challenger, and a 1975 black, four door Chevy Impala. As she jogged back to the bushes near the window, the back door opened to let the howling dog out. *I've got about one minute to make it to my car before the meat disappears.* She raced, picking up her feet to land onto her toes as quietly as possible to her VW down the block.

In her kitchen at 10:30 pm, Lexa remembered the times she took a glass of wine to the top of a building when she felt stressed. Now the incandescent glare of light bulbs showered her. Outside was a small patch of grass where if a phone rang, all neighbors ran inside, and when drapes were open, she saw what they watched on TV. She dozed on and off until 2:00 am, got up, made a cheese sandwich, brushed her teeth, changed into a cotton t-shirt and shorts, and went back to lie down. *Did the guy who wrote the letter tell his pals where I live? Does he have a twin brother?* She could not calm down. She got back up, reached beside the wall and waterbed for the sword, and pointed it at an imaginary intruder before returning to bed.

Her bedside phone rang at 10:00 am. She turned to clutch it, relieved to hear the thick voice of Tiny as she got up to grab a change of clothes.

"Hello? Did the police call you about me being at the Cavalry Club on that Thursday in July?"

"No. How would they know I was there?"

"They interviewed me. I gave them your name as the witness who saw me leave the club that day. You saw how unhappy I looked when I left that place."

"It doesn't mean you didn't go back inside when I left."

"You think I'm guilty of murder?"

"Lexa, I don't think you'd kill anyone, and I have no idea what information those cops have," he said.

Can you look up the owners of some license plates, and do you remember anything at all on the day we went to the Cavalry Club?"

"Like what?"

"Did you notice anyone outside? Do you remember any cars parked in the lot or the street?"

"Um, I saw lots of different cars. What exactly are you looking for?" he asked.

"Do you remember a blue Dodge Challenger?"

"I'm a little fuzzy right now. I'd have to think about it. You hired me to protect you, not to see what cars were parked on the street."

"You have no idea what it would mean to me to find out who these cars belong to. Here are the makes and plate numbers. Call me as soon as you have something. I have a show later, but you can call me tomorrow. We're at a club in Oshkosh tonight and I have to leave in a bit. So your name is Thurston?"

"Just call me Tiny."

"Your moniker."

"Huh? Harmonica?

"No, your nickname, Tiny. It's your moniker."

"Oh."

Her bandmates pulled their cars into the alley and parked next to the walkway of the garage. She grabbed her suitcase. *I need to devise a way to get my camera into that ranch house before the police pick me up again,* she thought as she buckled her seat belt and closed her eyes in the chair of the van. *No one saw me the rest of the day in July. I have no alibi.* Sam at the wheel, the voices of Grant, Ted, and Karl held separate conversations about women they were dating, songs one wanted to learn, and the sweetest pot one had recently acquired.

Lexa sat up straight and turned to Karl. "Where did you get the sweet pot you mentioned?"

He smiled and said, "The dealers at the Cavalry Club."

"Do you mean Nicky and Shane?" she asked.

"Yes, Nick usually sells it to me," he said.

"Did you know Shane is dead?"

"What?" both Karl and Grant said at the same time.

"It was on the news. He took his last breath in a van. We were at the club in July. When was the last time you spoke to Nick?"

"He was at 'The Stone Toad' two weeks ago, standing at the bar. I got a beer and we started talking. He said he freelanced at Someplace Else as a bouncer. We walked out to his car and I bought some pot. Good stuff," said Karl. "He didn't say anything about Shane. Strange."

"Karl, can you remember what kind of car Nick had?"

"It looked like it was blue, I think. It was dark out."

"Okay, do you remember if it had 2 doors?" Karl laughed again. "I was sitting in the car and that, I can remember. Yes it did."

Grant turned, holding his arm around the passenger seat and said, "I've been buying weed from Nick also. I wonder what happened to Shane."

"Me too. Thanks, guys" she said.

"Do you need some reefer?" Grant and Karl asked in unison.

"No, I'm good." *My spare cash goes to a bodyguard.*

The rest of the conversation was about muscle cars, V-8 engines, thrust and the lurch of 0 to 60 mph in about 7 seconds until the band arrived at the club in Oshkosh. Sound check, changing clothes, free drinks offered by the manager, putting on a show, singing and signing autographs occupied her evening. She ran around the stage, exaggerated gestures during songs and moved in an attempt to tire herself enough to get her body to remember the slumber it once knew, but her mind was lit up like a torch, unable to extinguish itself to sleep.

Lexa pulled her phone off the table next to her waterbed at 10:30 am to grasp the information Tiny gave her, writing the numbers on a notepad. "Thank you. I don't like being a suspect in anyone's death."

"I've been to Shane's club. He and his guys are way bigger and stronger than you are. He owned a lot of other properties in addition to the club. He had lots of cash," said Tiny.

"Why do you think someone would want to frame me for his death? I hardly knew him or anyone in his circle. Some people who may want me to go down would be Sam or his former girlfriend…maybe Grant's former wife, or a crazy person who comes to watch the band. One I can think of is named Kalie Deckler. I'll have to give it some thought."

"I'll check into it," he said. "But it will cost you extra."

"Thanks, and if you want to party this weekend, I can leave your name on the guest list at the Palms, where we're playing tonight or at Teddy's tomorrow. We're at Marty Zivko's club in Hartford next Friday if you're interested."

"I'll think about it."

Lexa now had the names of who the vehicles were registered to: Shane Zadrik, Nick Nevalla and Aldar Geitlich. She rolled over, stared at the ceiling and deliberated whether or not to get up. She pulled the diary out of her suitcase amidst clothes, jewelry, and boots, to catch up on where she had left off.

Friday, September 10, 1976

The men who own those cars have somehow entangled me in a murder. I'm mulling over who my enemies would be. Sam, who graduated with honors from college, is smart enough to burn me, or maybe it's who he's seeing. Is Tarick dating someone who would want me to disappear? The neighbor guy is unhinged, and wants me out of his neighborhood. Debra hates me, but I can't imagine she would take her hatred this far. Grant's ex-wife despises me, and I'm sure she blames me for her marriage ending. Maybe that deranged groupie Kalie Deckler wants me out of the band.

I don't understand why a family member hasn't taken the dead man's car, or put it in the garage. The men hanging out at Mr. Zadrik's place sell drugs to my bandmates and all the bands. Why did he want to incriminate me before he died, and why did that dude in the kitchen who looked so much like him have the same name? The pieces of this puzzle are random, but I had better fit it together soon, or face a rap for something I had no involvement in.

Lexa opened the case of her Leica rangefinder 35 mm film camera and adjusted the light measurement through the lens. The wrong setting would blur all of the photos and render them useless. She remembered the day she opened the camera at her high school graduation party, and thanked her Dad for the gift he had brought back from a stop in Taiwan during his time in Vietnam.

She tidied the house and did laundry. The smell of clean sheets under her, she stared at the white ceiling from the swaying waterbed. The lamp light glowed onto the opened diary on her chest and she imagined what it would be like wearing a prison jumpsuit locked behind steel bars.

In the morning, she prepared her suitcase for what she would wear on stage for the evening at Teddy's Night Club, wrote three copies of the names and plate numbers of the cars parked at Shane's house and hid them in different books of her bookshelf. It would be an hour before the van would be transporting everyone to the show.

She went to the grocery store for three packages of inexpensive beef to keep Boffo occupied, and stashed it in the back of the refrigerator as car engines were turned off and doors slammed. She took her suitcase, headed out the back exit, and locked up.

In the passenger seat, Grant read the classified section of his newspaper as Sam drove. All was silent when one of the papers fell onto the floor. Lexa picked it up to discover the obituary section and read it, being struck by another idea. She would call and ask to search through obituaries of a month ago, and added it to her to-do list for Monday.

Saturday, September 11, 1976

Ted said Debra appreciates the Mace I offered, and has kept close. She has felt scared since her attack and runs everywhere, locks all doors, and looks over her shoulder every few minutes. She has had nightmares, and jabbed Ted in the side. I told him being the object of another's hostility dissolves peace of mind, and to tell her to take a self-defense class, breathe deeply when she's anxious, and don't let perps win. They are never worth it. This event has caused her previous trauma to resurface, but I know her. She will rise above it.

On Sunday, Lexa read the directions on the camera while eating a bowl of cereal, then snapped photos of her alleyway and neighborhood to ensure the focal length was set properly. Her plan was to have the film developed that day and to snoop through Sam's flat for the insurance policy. She sucked in a deep breath to calm her anxiety and walked up the stairs, where she listened to sounds, her ear on the wood. She had to think of something fast to contrive a pleasant conversation as she knocked. Sam opened the door.

"I've been meaning to tell you, if you need to use the washer and dryer in the basement, you can use them any time."

Sam appeared to be stunned. "I'll think about it."

"Give me a little advance notice, so I can make sure my stuff is out."

"My mom likes when I bring my clothes over to her house. She enjoys my visits and we have lunch together to catch up on things while my laundry gets done," he replied.

"Yes, I remember, you're her angel. What has she said about our break up?

"I haven't told her."

"Really? I haven't told my family either. How has Debra been?"

"Not good since her attack, and her dad died last month."

"That is terrible. I'll have to give her a call one of these days, that is, if she'll speak to me again."

"I'm sure she will, and I'm sorry things are so bad between us," he said, catching her off guard. "Sometimes, I think back to how we were before I screwed everything up. It's because of what happened to me when I was a kid. I'm so messed up."

"We all have those kinds of issues. I'll bet a lot of adults had a messed up childhood. Your childhood was much better than mine was. Have you seen my birth certificate or my social security card? It seems a lot of papers are missing."

"I have no idea where your stuff is. I can't keep track of my own things," he said.

"If you run across anything of mine in a box when you are unpacking, you would give it to me, right?"

"Sure."

As she headed down the steps, she looked back at him, and thought he could keep a promise as well as she could lift Tiny, and shuddered at the thought of both. She needed to keep the guilty liar in her sights, and decided to check out if he had an accomplice.

At 9:00, the upstairs outside door slammed and footsteps pounded down the back wooden stairwell, prompting Lexa to grab her small, black, battery powered tape recorder. The van's engine revved and backed up as she ran to the VW to start it up. Keeping her headlamps off, she followed his van down the alleyway, and as his left turn steered him eastbound, she turned her headlights on, tracked his vehicle, and memorized the shape of the rear lights. They wove through the city for about fifteen miles when he turned into the parking lot of an apartment building. She kept her distance, crept in his direction, ducked behind cars, just yards from him as the entrance closed. A buzzer trilled, and a voice let him into the second secured door. She shoved a stick into the opening as it was about to close, while Sam focused on what was up the stairs. Lexa made sure she was hidden, but her trembling knocked her off balance. Keeping her head below the level of the stairwell, she took a quick glance at the direction he headed. After wo quick raps on the door at the end of the hallway to the left, he was welcomed as though he was expected.

If he is planning to frame me, I'm collecting any evidence I can get. She sat on the stair below the upper landing for twenty minutes before rising, walking down the hallway to where Sam had entered, and she cupped her ear on the door.

The music and voices she was able to distinguish sounded like a rerun of Green Acres. She sat on matted brown carpeting and glanced at her watch. It was 10:00 pm when her hand formed around the cold brass knob, and turned it in small increments until the door opened. They forgot to lock it. Good.

From her perspective on all fours on the floor, no one was in the living room lit by the television, but faint voices hummed in the direction opposite the TV, where she saw a bedroom down a short hallway to the right. Her tape recorder in hand, she pressed the record button and crawled toward the room where voices emanated and saw intertwined nude bodies slithering, grunting and moaning. Her heart responded to the sight of her husband's flesh against another female by banging into her chest wall, and she felt faint as she scrambled back to the hallway. She held the banister to steady herself downward. As the cool air slapped her face, she ran to the VW.

Unable to get the imprinted image of her husband straddling a blonde woman out of her mind, sweat soaked her skin as she drove home. She headed to the kitchen faucet, turned the water on, held her face under it, and splashed water onto her neck and upper chest. Her wet hands reached under the cabinet to the left of the sink where she pulled out the bottle of vodka and filled up a glass. She turned on the television in her bedroom, sat on the waterbed, and took big gulps. The humming tape recorder had recorded her silent drive home. She turned it off, removed the tape and threw it so hard, it rattled down the hallway. *He's seeing the woman who he flirted with at the Stone Toad, Nicky's fiancée. I remember her. Yea, sure she's just another fan.*

Sunday, September 12, 1976

Somewhere between the space of calm and chaos lies a catalyst which ignites an event and creates a fallout, the cloud of which can linger for a lifetime.

I can now add covert detective to my resume. Sam's self-absorbed ego obsesses over groupies, not murder. The more attractive he is to other women, the less attractive he is to me. He has lost the ability to distinguish sincerity from vanity, compassion from compulsion, right from wrong. He douses his charm as thick as his cologne, uses women like mannequins he can discard, and is nonchalant about the hearts he breaks.

The weight of judgment is heaviest when it is pressed by one's own conscience. In sharpening my self-perception, I see a woman navigating through strong winds on an icy slope. I have chosen a treacherous road to use as an excuse as to why I cannot attain even the simplest of things like love, acceptance, and truth.

Sam could keep my share of the equipment, the name and reputation of the band, the house, both vehicles, all the furniture, appliances and my guitars. If our bank accounts weren't separate, he would clean that out too. I remember how his face lit up the day we got that check from the insurance company after the fire in the garage. The money was enough for a new roof, new garage doors and a van. Sam has hidden our life insurance policy. It may be at his parent's house.

Though surveillance of my husband was a bad idea, his name has faded off my list of suspects. Unfortunately, I make so many mistakes, a prison cell may end up becoming my next residence.

Krys Graf

The band has become Sam's monster, and has devoured him whole from his soles to his soul. It has pierced his skull, dilated his pupils, and is in full possession of his words and actions.

CHAPTER 14

UNASSAILABLE

On Monday morning, Lexa called the Milwaukee Sentinel and Journal newspapers to make arrangements to read the August obituaries. Old papers were stored on microfiche film and she had to peer through a magnified reader.

"Zadrik, Shane, Born April 4, 1941. Passed to Eternal life on August 4, 1976, age 35 and joined his beloved mother Julette. Survived by many friends. A gathering will be held at The Final Rest Funeral Home on Friday, August 6, from 5 – 7 PM, Memorial Service: 7 PM." *Julette Zadrik. Her name sounds familiar. I have dreams of a lady named Julette.*

Lexa analyzed the developed film and felt like she was ready to photograph what she needed to prove her innocence. As she parked her VW on the back driveway, she looked up and froze upon seeing a squad car in front of her house. Two police officers emerged, saw her sitting in her car and walked toward her at a brisk pace. She was tempted to start the engine and leave, but realizing it would cause more harm, greeted the officers as warmly as she was able, and the icy voices responding to her gave no option other than to accompany them to the seventh district police station on Fond du Lac Avenue for questioning. She deliberated over who had set her up to take the fall for a murder, and held her hands over her intense stomach pain.

The room was an oversized airless closet holding a table and two chairs. Two detectives led her to a chair. One sat down, and the other leaned against the wall when their interrogation began.

"When did you last see Mr. Zadrik?"

"On July 29th. I already told this to officers. Nothing has changed."

"Tell us about that day."

"He invited me to his club because women's items were piling up in a box. He asked if any of it was mine."

The officers looked at each other. "How long were you there?"

"I think it was about an hour."

"Where were you on August 4th?"

Relieved at her airtight alibi, she smiled. "My band and I performed out of state. Hundreds of witnesses can corroborate my presence at those clubs, and our booking agent can confirm it also."

"Your name is mentioned countless times throughout the day planner of Mister Shane Zadrik, including a letter he had written to you, and an entry about him meeting you on July 29. Do you have this letter? You have more answers than you're giving us. A woman's black boot was discovered in the victim's van near his body. It matches the boot on a photo we have of you."

"My band played at his club, and I have no idea how a boot made its way into someone's van, but it isn't mine. A lot of bands perform at his club and I threw his letter out long ago. I don't know why anything of mine would be near him in his van."

"You said he called you to pick up something you had left behind. What was it again?"

"He asked me to see some jewelry he found. Do I need a lawyer?"

"Make sure you do not leave town. If something doesn't check out, we will need you for more questioning."

On the way back, Lexa remembered she had previously told them Shane had called her to pick up a black shirt. The knot in her stomach tightened. She had felt anxious and changed her original story, and was certain the police would be all over it. She felt as as unsettled as the last time she had spent part of a day in a police station, and these officers were as quiet in their squad as the men had been six years ago. She opened the back entrance and Sam was reorganizing the refrigerator.

"I'm trying to put my groceries away and there isn't any room in the fridge because there's so much meat in the back of the shelves. I hate looking at any bloody animal muscle. It makes me sick. You're deliberately trying to annoy me, aren't you?"

"Yea, I want to intrude on your Hindu dharma and keep you from attaining Nirvana. Aren't Hindu's allowed to own a refrigerator?"

"As soon as I have time, I'll get one, " he said.

She closed her bedroom door, checked her camera settings and the band's calendar. She changed clothes and left for the home that belonged to men named Aldar and Shane, wondering how soon she would be confined to a jail cell.

All blinds were down at the dirty tan residence. She slouched in her car and waited, taking glances at the brown trim and matching roof. *Why is the yard in such disarray for guys who should have a decent income as drug dealers, a club owner and who knows what else? Their cars are not pricey. Where are they stashing all that cash?*

She held binoculars over her eyes. The large window to the right of the front door was covered by gold drapes, and blinds over two smaller windows to the left obscured the three windows along 18th St. The rest of the week, including Friday, the 17th when the band was to perform at Marty Zivkos in Hartford, Lexa went to the deserted house once belonging to Mr. Zadrik, only to leave in disappointment at the lack of activity.

At home, she ate, grabbed her suitcase, and sat in the van alongside her bandmates wondering if spying on the house was of any benefit.

She looked upward in a spacious club to the high stage and at the large crowd waiting to be entertained. At the end of the night, a fan reached up as if to shake her hand, and in gaining a full grasp of her, pulled her into the crowd toward him. It surprised her when Showey dropped the cables he was gathering, used his muscular arms to grab her waist and hold onto her. The fan would not let go of her hand, but he relented after Showey threatened him, and he yanked her back onto the stage.

"I saw the absurd look that guy had when he reached up for you," Showey said. "You're a light-weight, and someone's gotta watch out for you. You need to be more careful. Stop trusting people, or you are going to get hurt."

"Thank you," she said. "If I wasn't so tired, I would help you pack up." *I don't trust people, and I don't know why I reached out.*

On Friday night and at the show on Saturday, Lexa's eyes scanned the faces hoping to see Tarick's. She was relieved not to see Aldar as she crawled into bed as the sun was rising.

On Sunday afternoon of the 19th, she wore a cotton black sleeveless top, jeans and black running shoes. She wrapped meat tightly in plastic bags, placed it into an iced cooler, made sure she had enough film, readied her binoculars, leather gloves, checked her camera settings, and drove eastbound. She surveyed the house she was determined to raid. Because of its location across from the Union Cemetery, the words of the dark-haired man, "Anyone wanting out ends up across the street," had new meaning.

In her gray VW, she headed southbound on Hopkins St., east on Chambers Street, and north onto Teutonia. The entrance of the Union Cemetery at 3175 N. Teutonia Ave was flanked by elaborate columns. She turned left into the graveyard and was surrounded by gravestones, some over ten feet tall, and many smaller unobtrusive markers. She parked the VW to walk around, do some surveillance, and use trees as her cover while she snapped photos. Upon seeing a 1974 blue Dodge

Challenger pull up, she knew who the driver was before he got out and walked to the house.

Well, well, Nicky Nevalla, the security guard I almost shoved a hat pin into. What brings you here? she thought, snapping a few pictures of him, his car, and surroundings.

The binoculars magnified shaded windows at the northeast side of the house. She restarted her car, drove southbound on Teutonia, west onto Chambers, parked on 18th St, and snapped a photo of the southwest side. *It's 1:00 pm on a sunny September day. Why are all the window shades down?*

She returned to the cemetery for a few more pictures, parked and walked through headstones, noting many graves dating in the 1800's and early 1900's. A discrepancy caught her attention. *Fresh sod is on this one. What's here is not the same kind of grass as the grave next to it. This headstone is dated 1892. I doubt if a great relative, or a cemetery caretaker would replace grass on an old gravesite.*

Lexa increased her pace through the cemetery to check if other graves were disturbed, and three more 6 feet by 3 feet patches of grass on grave sites appeared to be different. Turning her head sideways, what was most unusual, were graves dating 1887, 1886 and 1873, looking greener than the grasses surrounding it. Heading back to the tree she had stood at, she observed passengers in another vehicle watching the same thing she was.

A spotlight attached near the driver's side mirror, a slow moving, maroon, unmarked police car drove by. The man behind the wheel looked toward Shane's house, and she cringed when his partner looked in her direction. She zoomed her camera lens at the license plates of the vehicle and took a few more photos. She did not want to leave until it was dark, but a premonition of the cruiser turning into the cemetery overwhelmed her. *My VW has no plates, I'd better go.*

She ran to start the VW, and steered through winding pathways toward the exit when she passed the unmarked police car aimed in her direction. She turned her head away, drove past the car, and followed the gravel roadway through snaking paths of the cemetery. The vehicle turned around and began closing in on her. The siren blared, and the light on top strobed. *I'll never outrun a V-8 engine. Stay cool.*

She hyperventilated as she hit the gas heading for an uneven grassy area while pulling the black knit cap onto her head. Her left hand on the wheel, her right hand grabbed the fake moustache attached to the plastic nose and glasses in the glove compartment. *They are not going to get a good look at me.* As she flipped it onto her face knowing she was outnumbered and out-powered, fear climbed into the seat beside hers. The VW swerved and screeched through twisting pavement and onto grass, passing assorted monuments at 30 to 40 mph where sharp turns tilted the VW sideways, whipping along coiling roads. She veered her VW onto manicured grass, alongside a row of carved slabs and back onto the graveled roadway. As a deluge of grit and rocks pinged against the undercarriage, she looped and dodged the heavy, shrieking tank revving behind her that spewed smoke and dust.

She kept the petal steady through turns, and gunned it through straightaway paths, outrunning a light-flashing cherry-topped car at her tail. Through stones of the dead she saw an opening. Inches from concrete and granite tombstones and almost striking one, she grit her teeth. The pursuing car stopped and backed up, its red and blue lights alternating, its siren almost deafening.

"Yea baby!" She peered into the rearview mirror, headed through two trees, down a grassy embankment, over a road curb onto Hopkins St., turned left onto Burleigh and after glancing behind her, she whipped the sweaty disguise off. The gray VW zigzagged through the city until she made it into the garage.

What a waste. None of those shots will do me any good. I have no idea who can help me, and I don't want to drag anyone into this. She tossed the meat back into the refrigerator. *They have no prints, no motive, and no case. When will police tell me they made a mistake? Unless Shane saved the beer bottle he offered when we performed at the club and planted it to incriminate me.* Her pondering turned into a frown when she turned to face the back door whacking against the frame, rattling the house.

"What did you do to the VW, Lexa? It's my car too. Why is grass and dirt all over the tires and back bumper? His words were hurled like a child in a temper tantrum. "You better not ruin that VW."

"I didn't have time to take it to a car wash," she said before shutting the heavy oak door to her bedroom.

"Be ready and packed up for Florida by Tuesday. We're leaving at five am sharp," he said holding his head on the door and his hand on the knob.

She crawled into bed, and awoke from a dream speaking out loud, "I didn't do it, I didn't..." she sat up and finished, "do it," her voice wavered, as she rubbed her eyes.

She devoured an apple and yogurt while packing her bags for the long trip. She took the film to a one hour developing area of the grocery store where she waited and purchased food for the long haul. Studying the photos, nothing appeared out of the ordinary. When the discrepancy struck her, she spoke aloud, "Dirt and sod in their back yard! Dirt and fresh sod! Yes! Is that a sod cutter?" *They are hiding something in the graveyard.*

Shoppers turned to stare at her and she smiled back. *Why am I so happy? I'm a murder suspect...but a free one for now,* she thought running to her car.

Her bandmates arrived and packed up the van. Grant asked if they could stop at a sub shop before they hit the freeway. All agreed and they each got their sandwich. Leaning the seat all the way back, she daydreamed of how she would prove her innocence, as she had nothing useful and no one to trust. She heard her stomach groan and sat up to search for the sub she had placed on the seat between her legs.

"Nobody saw the dog eating my sub? Damn! Ebbie, shame on you. Bad dog!" Ebbie looked happy and wagged her tail. Her noxious gasses filled the van.

"Eww Aww, open the windows will ya?" Karl cried from the back bed, waving his hands over his face.

Lesson learned. Eat my sandwich before Ebbie gets it. I'm starved and it's going to be a long trip. She sat back onto the seat, looked upward and pushed her hands into her belly to stop the aching. "Guys, we need to stop somewhere again. I have to eat."

Sam drove through the humid Florida darkness near the Merritt Island Causeway, tagging thirty feet behind the roadie's equipment-laden truck. The clock on the van showed 4:00 am when he screamed, "Nooo!"

Horrified at the sight, he and Lexa watched the right rear passenger tire roll off and within seconds, the left rear wheel detached from the large white truck, which slammed it to the ground at a speed of 60 miles an hour, bringing an intense display of white sparks in a long, fulminating shriek. The axle split as it crashed onto the road. The back end of the truck scraped the ground, free gliding. Tires rolled alongside the roadway into the ocean water of Florida's coast, and disappeared into the darkness a few miles from their destination. Sleeping passengers jolted upward at Sam's scream, and appeared shocked at the sight of the damaged truck, the doors of which opened to surrender its victims. The pale roadies emerged blinded by the headlights of the van, as though all color had been purged from their faces.

"What the freakin-son-of-a bitch!" screamed Drax who laughed hysterically and hopped around the deserted road. The wind being knocked out of him, Hound quivered, while Showey sulked and shook his head side to side.

The road crew crammed into the van causing the decibel level to go up exponentially as everyone enforced an opinion of what to do next and who was responsible for the lug nuts on the truck's tires. A chorus of loud, ornery voices argued over the best way to handle the disabled truck. They had no choice other than to leave it where it fell and to search for an open gas station and a phone booth.

The band checked in at the Ocean Age Motel in Cocoa Beach as the sun was rising, where Drax said he had enough adrenaline rushing through him to call for a tow.

"Thanks Drax, I can hardly keep my eyes open." said Lexa.

Sam carried Ebbie through the foyer of the hotel past the check-in desk under a blanket like a sleeping toddler.

"I'm fried, and my pillow's lookin' as sweet as a giant marshmallow," said Grant, hauling his suitcase into his motel room being followed by his bandmates.

Wailing seagulls swarmed over the slush of waves onto sand, near the motel. Following a 9 am until 2 pm. rest in her motel room, Lexa called her family to tell them she had arrived, and was picked up by Candy, who beamed about being able to drive, having acquired her temporary license last week. Lexa and her sisters spent the day at the Merritt Square shopping Mall, and went to her parent's house for supper. She helped Candy study anatomy, and aided Abbie in writing a sonnet for English class.

During dinner, Lexa acted as if all couldn't be better in her life, and was happy to converse with her Dad for the first time in many years. When she had called her Mom to inform her of her visit, Lexa was doubtful of her welcome. They discussed her show at the Anchor Club, followed by Brassy's, which impressed her dad, who said Waylon Jennings was recently on the marquee of Brassy's. The icing on the cake was her band's photo in the local paper, and his eldest daughter standing in the center. Near her photo was an advertisement for job openings at Cape Canaveral Hospital.

"If you make it big, will you give up your nursing license?"

"I guess it depends on how big we get."

He smiled and looked as though he had drifted away. "I was glad you became a nurse. I had to visit a few medical facilities and was always impressed by health professionals."

"When did you do that?"

"In Pleiku, Qui Nhon, and An Khe. They were field evacuation hospitals."

She remembered the places he had written of in one of his letters. At that instant it clicked why she never received so much as a memo or note from him again. The sight of blood had always made him weak and queasy, and she knew he would have been puking his guts out at the sight of images he would never be able to erase. His gaunt face and extreme weight loss when he had returned years ago, hung like a veil over his face at the kitchen table.

"Your old clothes are in a box by the bed in the guest room," said her Mom, while they put supper dishes away. "I'm pretty sure they're yours."

Sunlight streamed between slats of the vertical blinds of her parents' empty home when she awoke. Motors of boats vroomed in the waterway, slapping at the water's surface, and the sound of the pool filter whirred. She opened the box, and the sight of her cap-sleeved blue peasant blouse struck a chord of sadness, having remembered the last time she wore it. Moving it aside to rummage through the box, the card given to her by the deep voiced detective in the gray suit jacket fell out of the pocket, and she grabbed it.

"Here's our number. Call right away," he had said. *I found the murderer and now I'm the prime suspect,* she thought.

Outside, she was engulfed by humid warmth and wailing osprey's perched on the tall stakes of the pier. The pool welcomed her to sit at the edge before gliding in. Her head striking the water, she let out a scream that was muffled and disseminated upward in bubbles. She pulled up and gasped for air, pushed herself back into the water, and began swimming. The three laps she swam across the length of the pool exhausted her. She remembered when she could easily glide through ten laps in an Olympic pool when she lived in Fort Monroe, Virginia.

She flung herself out of the water and grabbed the edge of the concrete. Her legs dangled next to the air jets where the Sykes Creek breeze blew water droplets off her arms and hair. The revelation of her father's immersion in mass casualties and disfigured bodies helped her understand why he returned from Vietnam a broken man. The collapse of her marriage, the band's increasing debts, major damage to the equipment truck, and the doom of facing incarceration for murder triggered a second underwater scream. Though she was surrounded by people, loneliness and her inability to connect to anyone other than her family, immobilized her cheek on the concrete. Failing even to spark

Tarick Tagan's friendship and her disappointment in her lack of people skills tapped her last ounce of energy. Having spent so much time alone in her youth, even her best efforts to connect with others was failing. Facing the sanctuary off of Sykes Creek, she watched the seagulls, egrets, and herons float above her.

At 7:30, her bandmates stopped to pick her up for sound check. The van door opened and she sat next to Karl, who was driving.

"What happened to your eyes? They're bloodshot. You been drinking already?"

"No, pool chlorine does that."

"Your family must have been happy to see you," said Karl.

"Yes, they were, but not once did Sam's name come up. They know."

When the first set ended at the Anchor Club, Lexa went to the bar to order a glass of wine and was asked for identification, but all she had as she rifled through her purse was her name on an orange 93 WQFM radio station card. *Damn, that's what I get for a last minute change of my stuff. My ID is in my other purse.*

The bartender laughed, "Get real. What am I supposed to do with this?" he said flipping the card back and forth.

"Grant, here's some cash. Please get a glass of any kind of red wine."

"Sure, I'll see what they've got."

On stage the following evening, Lexa became unglued as she watched two tall police officers walk into the club, speak to the bartender, show him a photo, point in her direction and stare at her. Standing at attention, the bar at their backs, one looked down at the photo he held and up at her. The exit was past the police and the stage being in a corner, she felt her body shake. Her voice oscillated and cracked. She sang horribly and forgot lyrics. Her bandmates looked at one another, shrugged their shoulders, stared at her and wondered if she had snapped. The bulky uniformed men walked toward her when the musicians took a break.

Am I going to jail here in Florida? I didn't do it...

"We're looking for a 16 year old runaway. We need to see some ID."

Had her eyes been able to open any wider, they would have popped out. The band stepped up to her rescue, especially Sam who surprised her. "She's my wife and she's…twenty one, not sixteen."

"Do you have any identification to prove this, miss?"

"No, no, I'm…I don't, but my parents live nearby, and can verify my age and I…I'm married. I'll give you their names and phone number. Call them now if you'd like," said Lexa. She watched one of them place his finger into the dial on the black phone near the bar.

In the dressing room she was greeted by Ebbie, who wagged her tail, licked Lexa's face and hands, and made every effort to speak back to her. Lexa wondered if Ebbie had forgotten how to bark as she pat on her fluffy white puppy's head. She thought about where the real runaway was. "I hope they find that girl," she said.

"I've never seen anyone fall apart like you did when those cops came in," said Karl.

"After how they stared at me? Wouldn't you be a bit edgy?"

"Yea, I would. I guess we all have something to hide. I wouldn't want them rummaging through any of our bags," Karl smiled.

"That was odd. I went from feeling miserable to happy so quickly," she said, resting the back of her head on a chair in the dressing room, taking deep breaths to calm down. "I wonder if it's why a thirteen year old gave me a slobbery kiss. Okay, maybe he was fourteen. He may have thought I was about the same age he was. Karl, here's some cash. Please bring me a glass of whatever kind of red wine they have here."

The van ran out of gas in the parking lot at Brassy's on the last day in Cocoa Beach, delaying their departure, having to hike to a nearby station and return holding a heavy gas can to get enough fuel into the tank to make it to a pump. An argument ensued as to whose fault it was, all the way down Hwy 95 until they exited the van, upon reaching the motel.

By the time they reached Fort Lauderdale, the band and roadies complained about everything. They were sick of restaurant food and grocery store snacks. Sick of motel cockroaches, lizards, and the assortment of insects. They longed for their own beds, and the four walls they called home. They were tired of the nightly gruel in dark, foggy clubs, despite drinks being free for the band.

"Ted, I owe you a whopping smack for what you did to my eye. I plastered make up on my face for two weeks," said Grant recalling the fight in the dressing room on the last tour.

"You owe me a smack? I was so bruised, I could barely lift my guitar for two weeks," retorted Ted as they drove.

Heading west on Interstate 75, the next stop was the Warehouse club in Ft. Meyers for a week of performing, parties, pools, playing and panoramic views of the waterway.

Thrashing alone all night at a motel, unable to delete the image of Sam and a cute brunette he had admired at the show, Lexa rolled out of the furrowed bed, slipped into jeans and a black tank top to meet Karl and Grant for breakfast.

Why, can't I sleep? I hate this crap, damn it. Anger consuming her, she smashed her head into the brick wall near the door of the restaurant and took in deep breaths to calm herself before walking in.

"What happened to you? Grant asked, taking a sip of coffee.

"I'm joining you for breakfast."

"Did you put lipstick on your forehead? 'Cuz if you didn't, what's that red stuff?" Karl looked concerned.

She touched her brow, surprised that her right hand was covered in blood. She had forgotten how vascular the scalp was and how heavily even a minor cut could bleed. The glares of diners holding silverware burned through her during her walk to the bathroom where a mirror showed red streaks dripping into her eyes and down her cheeks, making her laugh. *Was he worth it? Did it fix anything or make you feel better? No.*

Her head throbbed as she ripped a stack of paper towels to wash off the blood. *I'm not going in for stitches,* she thought as she applied pressure to the bleeding. She took the tape off of a bandage to pull the cut together.

Lexa had a few extra glasses of wine backstage to forget about her self-inflicted pain.

After the band's concert, at 3:00 am, Hound's slip into the motel pool, fully clothed in his jacket and shoes caused so much hysteria among the crew, musicians and friends partying, the night manager threatened to call police and kick them out of their rooms, but forgave them after he was offered free admission to all shows at the Warehouse nightclub.

The crew remained the steadfast anchors who could overcome cops interrogating their singer, blistering hot motel rooms and a crash, adding to the truck's bruises, dents and scrapes.

Lexa had no premonitions of the vehicle damage she witnessed at the beginning of the tour. Though there were no physical injuries, all questioned the inevitability of more harm, in weathering the length of time spent on the road as worries of one kind or other tapped a melodic rhythm inside their heads. Lexa's mind hummed details of how she could keep herself out of jail, and after each image of being locked behind bars, she smiled and saw herself enjoying the company of her sisters, walking together on a sunny beach.

"Karl, what day is it?" she asked sitting near him in the van.

"I think it's Tuesday. October 19th."

"Thanks." She began writing.

"When we get back, and if you run into Nicky Nevalla, can you introduce me to him?"

"Sure," he said through closed eyes.

Tuesday, October 19, 1976

I have gained a clearer understanding of Dad, and perhaps he was able to take a deeper look at who I am. We have folded our past onto a sheet of paper, and stuffed it into a book which we cannot remember the name of. Maybe that is how forgiveness works. When the elusive page is found, we each rip it up in our own way, in our own time.

These past 4 ½ weeks of being away have helped me clear my thoughts and devise a plan I can pull off on my own.

Supplies and to do list: 1) One bottle of Scotch, 2) One bottle of Tequila, 3) One bottle of Vodka, 4) One bottle of Whiskey, 5) One bottle of Rum, 6) Three ground up ludes, 7) Three Nembutal capsules, 8) Camera, 9) my brown suitcase and a blanket to cover it up, 10) Practice dissolving the Ludes and Nembutal in a shot glass of the above alcohols.

Photography
by
Marvin Waters

CHAPTER 15

AGENDA

Back in Milwaukee, mail was piled on the kitchen table, where Sam's mother placed a note hoping the band's tour went well. Four and a half weeks' worth of mail sorting, opening and organizing, including a trip to the bank and Post Office to pick up fan mail was not in Lexa's urgent agenda. Her first thought was getting to a liquor store where she put the assortment of booze in a shopping cart. The cashier raised her eyebrows.

"Havin' a paaaty are ya, miss? I need to see your ID."

Lexa whipped out her wallet, and the article about Milyana Milevic fell onto the checkout counter. It was badly disintegrated. She folded it gently and tucked it back into the sleeve. She held out the ID she had forgotten to take to Florida.

"This ain't you. What else you got?"

"Yes it is." Lexa took out every piece of identification in her wallet, including the checkbook in her purse.

"No kiddin', well go on then."

"How much do I owe? Hold on, I need to take a few of these off the bill. What would he most likely drink? Hmm…I think I'll take the whiskey and tequila," said Lexa to the clerk who rolled her eyes.

At her kitchen table, she poured a sample of each beverage into a glass and practiced opening up and dropping the powdery contents of a yellow Nembutal capsule, then experimented as to how fast a Quaalude would dissolve. *The Nembutal dissolves faster,* she thought, taking a sip of the concoction that gave her indigestion, but made her feel loopy and relaxed.

She arranged her camera and the bottles in her suitcase, cramming dish towels between them, and used a blanket to cover the suitcase behind the driver's seat on the floor of the VW. All she had to do was contrive a way to hook up with Mr. Nevalla. As she ran through scenarios of how she would pull it off, she was startled off of her chair by the pounding of a fist on glass, the sound of the lock opening, a foot kicking the door open and feet stomping into the kitchen.

"Lexa! I can't take it anymore. What are these open liquor bottles doing on the back floor of the Volkswagen?" Sam's face was reddened and distorted as he held out the heavy suitcase. "Are you planning to set me up to get arrested? If either of us got pulled over by the police, and they saw this, we would be fined and jailed."

"Get your Hindu dharma together. I'm going to bring that to a party. How about you use the van, and I'll be responsible for the VW. Hand over the suitcase." *Dude, I jumped out of a frying pan and onto burning coals long ago.*

"Okay, but you better not get caught. If you get thrown into jail, don't even think about calling me."

"I never gave it a thought." *Now, stay out of my business.*

The intoxicants behind pots and pans in a kitchen cabinet, she sipped a bit more of what she referred to as a science experiment, and concluded that Boffo was roughly the same weight as she was, so should be able to handle at least a half of a Nembutal capsule. She emptied a red Contact capsule and poured half of the powder of the Nembutal capsule into it, so as to easily differentiate what the dog and Nick would get.

Two of these yellow capsules should give a big guy a nice long nap, she thought before falling off to a solid night's sleep.

She placed her suitcase in the front compartment of her VW instead of the back seat and checked the calendar of club dates that showed Waukesha County Technical College, and Century Hall in Milwaukee. When The Stone Toad nightclub was added to the band's schedule, Lexa relished the thought of being introduced to an unsuspecting accomplice. She rehearsed her spiel and pictured the scenario in her head.

She saw him standing at the bar during their second set at the Stone Toad, and nudged Karl for an introduction.

"Lexa, this is Nicky," smiled Karl looking upward, to a 6'4" solid tank of a man in his early thirties, wearing a gold chain, black leather jacket, and jeans at the bar in the overcrowded, noisy club. His dark brown hair was neatly trimmed to two inches in length and combed back.

"Hi, I remember you. What was it you said to me? 'Tell your damn guitarist he's a jerk.' I agree. He is. How's your fiancée?"

"We're not together anymore."

"That's a bummer. I'm sorry." *But today I'm not.*

As Nicky bent down to hear her speak through the wall of voices surrounding them, she made sure his eyes would catch the glisten of oil she rubbed into her cleavage.

"Wow, nice cannons on your broad shoulders. You must pump iron every day," she said staring into his eyes causing him to blush and smile.

"What are you drinking? Want to do a shot?" she asked.

"Sure."

"We'll have two Red Stag Black Cherry's," she said to the bartender.

"Don't have it."

"Then…Jim Beam, two shots."

"We're out."

"Okay…Jack Daniels?" The bartender plopped two shot glasses on the bar.

"Cheers!" As he bent back to drink his shot, she dumped some on the lower wall of the bar, but made sure he saw her drink her shot when he bent down and looked at her.

"Where will you be later tonight? Maybe we could hang out and keep partying," she smiled. *That was a bit forward.*

"We could do that, Miss Loxx," he said. He waited at the bar like a chained statue. She circled and shook her hips as she glanced toward him while she sang. He kept an open tab at the bar.

She asked Showey to give Nicky a message to meet her at the back door when the show was over. She quickly changed clothes, grabbed her bag, and smiled when she saw him. "Where would you like to go?"

"We could head to my place," said Nicky looking down her snug, black, long-sleeved, low cut shirt, out of which peeked her black lace bra.

"I can't leave my car here, so I'll tag behind you," she said. The scent of Opium perfume wafted around her.

Scene ten, take one, action, cameras rolling, she thought, pulling alongside a road she had visited often as of late. *Stay calm.* "I'll be there in a sec," she said, opening the front compartment of the VW, unzipping the suitcase, stashing the pills into her pocket, kissing the bottle of Jack Daniels. *Remember our rehearsal, now follow the script.* She slammed the front VW compartment shut and caught up to Nicky.

"Uh, sorry about the yard, it's not the best," his deep voice said.

"No problem. You must have a busy schedule like I do," she said as she handed the whiskey bottle to him, and surveyed his kitchen. "I brought some party time."

As he slipped off his leather jacket, Lexa was awed by his defined muscle mass. "Wow, I'm impressed by your workout routine."

"I do a lot of training, and I can bench press 400. No big deal."

A German shepherd sniffed at Lexa's crotch. "Down, Boffo," Nicky said sternly.

"Nice puppy," Lexa pet and stroked the dog's fur. "Can he do any tricks? I taught Ebbie by offering her a treat. She can speak, jump through hooped arms, roll over, and do back flips."

"Naw, he's a guard dog. We taught him to attack and sit."

"Do you have cheese? I'll teach him an easy trick, like roll over. I'll show you."

As Nicky turned toward the refrigerator, she slipped the prepared capsule out of her pocket and walked to the counter where he handed her a piece of cheese. She turned toward the dog and slipped the capsule into it. "I'll give him a simple command, like sit."

"He has a good grasp of the basic tricks." The sleek Shepherd bared its teeth and snapped the chunk of cheddar out of her hand.

"Oh he does," she said as Boffo smacked his lips. *Ouch!* "I get what you mean by attack dog," she said flexing her fingers.

One down, she thought, as she stood in the kitchen looking out at a gold beaded partition between the living and dining room, a chartreuse velour sofa flanked by end tables, a lava lamp on one, a heavy piece of coral on the other, and gold shag carpeting throughout the living room.

A 40" by 36" painting brushed by gold, orange, chartreuse and red strokes hung on the celery colored wall above the sofa. Another similarly painted large picture was on an adjacent wall, two tan chairs faced the sofa, and a rectangular coffee table was centered near the furniture, holding colorful paperweights and two diagrammed books identifying sea shells.

"You have a really nice place. Time for some shots, Nicky. Where are your drinking glasses?"

He opened a cabinet and handed her two glasses. She poured until each was a quarter full of whiskey and said, "Let's chat. Tell me all about yourself." She stared up and down at his mass as he walked to his stereo, pulled a black disk out of its jacket, guided the needle to a Kink's album, and sat across from her in one of the tan chairs.

"I work a couple of jobs and one's a bit different," Nicky's deep voice said.

"Yes, you're a bouncer at a club downtown. What's it called…Someplace Else? I have a crazy job myself and keep even crazier hours," said Lexa. As the 'Kinks' singer wailed out "Lo Lo Lo Lo Lola", her body started to sway in the chair. Intertwining her arms in the air, she began to weave her torso in time to the beat. Nick smiled as her movements became more of a belly dancer.

"A friend of mine and I also work at a funeral home," he said appearing distracted by her gyrating.

"It doesn't sound crazy to me. I've been to plenty of those and the staff was gracious," she said taking a sip of whiskey. "Which one?" She crossed her legs and leaned back.

"It's called The Final Rest."

Lexa choked on her drink, blinked her eyes, uncrossed her legs and leaned forward. *It's where Shane's memorial service was, and where Aldar hangs out.* She regained her composure. "Have you worked there a long time?" she cleared her throat and smiled.

"About three years."

"It must be difficult to be around mourners all day," she said while wondering how she would get the Nembutal powder into his drink. "I'm great at back rubs. Would you like a massage?" she asked.

As Nicky was about to set his drink on the coffee table, Lexa directed him to sit next to her on the chartreuse couch, where he set his glass on the table beside the sofa. She walked behind him where her back pressed against the wall, and began massaging his back and temples, using her fingers to close his eyelids. Her left hand continued the massage, and her right emptied the contents of a Nembutal, only to see the powder sitting on top of the liquid. She panicked, stuck her index finger into the drink, stirred the powder, used the back of her shirt to dry her finger and continued the back and temple rub while talking about calm beach waves, until the contents of the second capsule had dissolved. "Would you like a deeper massage?" she asked.

"You're turning me on, Lexa." He stroked her hand, and tugged her arm towards him.

She sat down, grabbed her drink, held it up and grinned. "Cheers! Bottoms up." She breathed a sigh of relief to watch him gulp his drink down. "If it's turning you on, I'll massage your back a little longer. Then you can show me your bedroom."

"Great." He smiled and laid his head back on the rim of the couch. She massaged his head and back while describing soothing scenes of sunsets and winding brooks through ravines covered in lush leaves until he raised his hand to stroke her arms.

"I can't believe you're here. You're like the breath of air I needed," he said looking up and turning around to face her.

His loneliness made her feel guilty. *What have I gotten myself into?* His arms latched onto hers and he pulled her into his lap. He cupped her face and pulled her lips toward his, closed his eyes and locked his mouth onto hers, pressing his tongue into her mouth. She felt warm and drawn to his vulnerability, his need for affection and his full attention on her.

"I enjoyed watching you move on stage, especially after you invited me to party. Other guys made comments about you, and I hoped it would be me holding you tonight," he said with a dreamy look as her guilt skyrocketed.

His hand at the back of her neck, the other glided under her shirt and rubbed her back, moving toward her breasts. Her mouth watered, and she felt a craving for him. As his kiss became more passionate, she felt the shaft of his penis harden between her legs. He reached down to unzip his leather jeans, and unbutton the fly. *He's hot. Why would his ex-fiancée not want him?*

"Lexa, you're beautiful," he said slipping off her snug black shirt to stare at her skin gleam in the lighting. He pulled off his black shirt to expose his rock solid body.

He moved one hand to her cusp and the other pulled up her bra to fondle her breasts and he closed his eyes. As he stroked her inner thighs, his mouth pressed onto hers. His movements slowed gradually, and inch by inch, his head backed onto the top ledge of the sofa. His body went limp and she felt a twinge of fear, hoping she did not overdose him.

"Nicky?" she whispered, and increased the volume of her voice seeing no reaction. The back of her hand stroked the side of his face and she kissed his cheek, zipped up his leather jeans, buttoned the fly, pulled her shirt back on, replaced the plastic arm on the record player and turned it off.

"Boffo?" The dog snoozed on the orange and yellow patterned kitchen floor. Walls were painted in light lemon and dark beige curtains hung over closed window shades. A clock hanging on the soffit above the sink showed 3:15 am.

She wondered if they had hired a decorator who artfully arranged their trendy furnishings in the living and dining rooms. An extensive record collection sat within a three-tiered console table including all of Hendrix and Joplin's albums. In the corner beside an end table, were separate cone shaped lamps in yellow, orange, red, blue and chartreuse attached to a silver pole. Drapes were a thick gold fabric, ceiling to floor onto a gold shag carpet. At the center of a mahogany dining room table flanked by six chairs, hung a stained glass lamp, and along a wall in the dining room was a bookshelf holding a numerous assortment of books, including chemistry, Advanced Engineering Mathematics, and Thermodynamics. *They're smarter than I thought.*

In the first bedroom, walls were light blue, a royal blue bedspread topped a king-sized brass bed, and a heavy hand-carved dresser sat beside a closet full of designer clothes, leather slacks, jackets and handcrafted alligator boots. *That's where some of Nick's cash goes.*

Across the hallway, she flipped the light switch on and walked into an 11 x 12 ft. room, noting a queen sized bed, brass headboard and a blue rectangular shaped, patterned brown bedspread. Five photos of herself sat on the dresser which were the 4" x 6" schedules sent to fans on the mailing list, and were taken care of by a friend of the band. Upon seeing her photos, she blinked her eyes so many times, she felt like it was she who now had a blepharospasm. The mailing list was so long that even if she had been in charge of it, she may not have made the connection. *Shane saved the itinerary photos of my band. Next mailing, we should only send our show dates.*

Lexa leaned down to take a close look at a framed 5" x 7" tattered black and white shot that had once been folded, of a smiling woman in her twenties with long, dark, wavy hair, wearing a white blouse, slim fitting skirt and high heeled pumps, sitting in a chair, who adored a contented dark-haired child on her lap. The back said:

'Always remember your mother, Julette.'

Another framed photo was an 8" x 10" of a beautiful, young woman with dark, waist-length hair who had similar features to Lexa's, dressed in a colorful flowered form fitting dress, split at the waist, ending near her ankles. Under her tunic, she wore flowing pajama trousers, and her full lips smiled as she lovingly held a dark-haired infant in her arms. *The clothes reminds me of Dad's letters.* Lexa admired the dense foliage of the hilly landscape in the background.

So what makes you tick? Opening drawers, she moved folded t-shirts, socks and underwear aside. More old photos, some black and white, some discolored of the same young woman in the foreground of lush greenery sat among watches, chains, pendants and earrings. At the bottom of the last drawer, were numerous faded and soiled notebooks. She opened what appeared to be a diary and read.

July 5 1972

Decomposing skeletal remains of adults, babies and children who tried to flee the city were strewn along Highway 1 southeast of Quang Tri city, a crucial transportation hub, along the Song Thach Han River of North Vietnam, stretching more than a mile. Paratroopers walking among the remains of the deceased wore gas masks. Deserted trucks, buses, jeeps and bikes were strewn in the dust alongside clothes, toys, M16 and AK47 rifles. B-40 rocket launchers, US jet fighter bombs and B-52's are blasting the area. A North Vietnamese force occupies a heavily fortified bunker line on the southern outskirts of the city. China is moving supplies into North Vietnam through the Ho Chi Minh trail and the Soviets are furnishing among other things, self-guided anti-aircraft missiles.

Lexa looked up. Shane must have witnessed horrid atrocities. The engine of a vehicle at close range caused her to return the book to the drawer and rush to the dining room, but a key unlocking the back entrance to the kitchen forced her to run back to a bedroom that faced the front of the house. She opened the window, climbed onto the ledge to prepare to jump outside and held onto the bottom of the open windowsill while footsteps creaked.

"Lexa?" mumbled Nicky.

"Do I look like Lexa to you? Why are you passed out on the couch? Dude you're dreaming. Get to bed."

"Where's Lexa?"

"What the hell are you talking about? How much booze did you drink tonight?"

She took a deep sigh when doors clicked shut, descended back into the dark room, closed the window and tiptoed into the kitchen where she dried and replaced the glasses at 5:10 am. She took the whiskey, tiptoed outside, tucked the bottle on the floor of her VW, started the engine and put the car in reverse. *That was Shane. If he's alive, what's going on? I'm facing a murder rap for someone who's alive? No way, no damn way.*

She backed the VW down 18th St and into an alley near Chamber's St., giving her a decent view, where she grabbed the blanket and covered herself to wait. Noticing the inside of her windows steaming up, she rolled them down on the driver and passenger side. The adrenaline rush kept her focused.

She refused to redirect her gaze even when the sun peaked in the sky and the car grew hot. She held the camera on the window's edge. A dark-haired male wearing his hair in a ponytail walked outside and slid into a black, four door Chevy Impala at noon.

Thank goodness I didn't have to wait all day. She snapped six photos, started the ignition, headed eastbound on Chambers and continued until she reached the grocery store on Hampton Ave. where she dropped off the film.

The suitcase and blanket back in place, she returned the bottles of her science experiment behind the pans in her kitchen cabinet. While Ebbie was let out and fed, she devoured a bowl of cereal and went to lie on her waterbed.

What do I do when Nicky recalls our evening together? She stared at the ceiling. *I can't afford Tiny,* she worried. Startled by a vivid dream of a gray smoke filled sky, explosions, people screaming and running out of a blackened shell-shocked grocery store cleared of food, she sat up in bed. *Not again.* Her desolation was replaced by birds chirping, and she opened the peach curtains to peer out of the window at a deep blue sky nearing twilight.

Sunday, October 24, 1976
I don't think it's a coincidence that Nicky is a mortician where Shane's memorial service was. My chance to prove my innocence is in the photos I took, but the spit will hit the fan when Shane discovers I've been in his house. Did he fake his death to cash in on an insurance policy, and who is his beneficiary? It can't be easy to fake a death. The police and a coroner had to have gone over him and the van with a fine-toothed comb to check for signs of foul play.

The women on his dresser were once a significant part of his life, and his heart is searching for them in the people he meets.

a girl a band a diary

There is nothing like a good dose of backlash to complicate my insomnia, my dread of being sought after by the law and the Zadrik clan. Nick, Shane, and Aldar know where I live, and with them being on our mailing list, they can find me at the clubs we're playing at. Tiny has been off my radar for over a month. I'm in way over my head and must live elsewhere for a while.

CHAPTER 16

PROGRESS

Lexa picked up the phone to call Debra who had not spoken to her in almost a year and asked if she had forgiven her for her lapse in judgment in telling her secret to Grant. Debra thanked Lexa for warning her about a possible assault, and she was prepared. Lexa told Debra that she needed to get away from Sam and asked if she stay at her place for a few days. Debra politely agreed, both surprising and relieving Lexa, who was anxious to flee. She threw items into her suitcase, and she informed Sam he will need to take care of Ebbie.

The band was to leave for Dubuque Iowa on Friday morning 10/29 giving Lexa ample time to visit Debra.

She lugged her suitcases, food, her guitar, stage gear and clothes, and was waved down by the elderly neighbor. *Go away. I need to get out of here before I'm tailed,* Lexa thought as the plump, white-haired grandmother moved closer to her.

"Lexa, I rarely see you these days. Where are you off to?

"I'm going to visit a friend."

"How nice. You remind me so much of Julette."

"Who?" Lexa gave the elderly matron her undivided attention and dropped her bags.

"The lady I told you about. When Julette lived in your house, her son Shane and my son were friends. He lived there for about 10 years. I watched him grow up."

"I recall you telling me the story a long time ago, but can you tell it again?" asked Lexa.

"He and my son were together all the time, but he moved away after his mother died. He was around 11 years old. I always wondered how he is doing. His dad and my husband didn't get along, so I never knew what became of them."

I knew Juliette's name sounded familiar, Lexa thought, now paying full attention to her neighbor. *All the stories I've listened to, I unfortunately tuned most of it out.*

"What is it about me that reminds you of her?" Lexa asked.

"You're the same height and build…similar pretty face."

"Thank you for sharing this. I have something important to tell you, and I need to tell the neighbors on the other side too. There's been a lot of vandalism in our neighborhood. I thought I should warn you. Here's my phone number. Call me if you notice anything suspicious and I'll do the same for you."

Lexa knocked on doors and informed her neighbors to the south about the nail filled plywood, her twisted windshield wipers, smashed windows of her basement and van, and front porch urn. They said they were already suspicious since the fire. Following the exchange of phone numbers, she packed up the VW and left. *The Julette story and all her gossip over the years. All those names meant nothing to me. I had enough trouble keeping track of who was part of her family. A few more things have fallen into place,* thought Lexa as she drove, now understanding the impact of the photos sitting on a dresser. *I remind him of women who have been significant to him. Is it why he took my nylons and boot? He wanted a souvenir? He offers expensive champagne and displays his collection of my photos. On top of it all, I live in his childhood house. Creepy, but as usual, just my luck,* she thought, recollecting her required college psychology lessons.

Upon her arrival at Debra's flat, Lexa hugged her and told her how much she cherished their friendship. She told Debra to imagine her attacker as a gnat, and Debra has the power to squash him. She said she would try. The description of Debra's assailant matched that of Aldar.

Lexa noticed Debra's late father's Nembutal and Digoxin 0.25 mg bottles on the kitchen counter, and asked if she could have them. One was half filled with capsules and the other was almost full. Lexa said she knew someone who could use that medicine, and since Debra had been planning to throw them away, instead gave them to Lexa.

She thanked Debra for letting her stay at her flat for a while. When Debra informed Lexa she and Ted needed some sleep, Lexa stashed both bottles into her suitcase. She made every effort to get comfortable on a sofa, balled up in a sleeping bag. Unable to relax, she decided to put Debra's gift to good use, and slugged down the contents of half a Nembutal at the kitchen sink. Waiting for the pill to kick in, she picked up an assortment of recent newspapers, scanned over articles and pages when her focus stopped at a name in the Obituary section, kicking up her heart rate. She gasped. *It can't be.*

"Geitlich, Aldar C. Born to Eternal Life on Friday, October 22, 1976, age 29. Preceded in death by his brother Otto and his loving parents, Frieda and Herman Geitlich…Visitation to be held at the Final Rest Funeral Home on Thursday, October 28, from 4:00 PM to 7:00 PM."

She checked a calendar for the date, and made sure she was going to attend this service. She told Ted and Debra she needed to return home to take care of Ebbie.

In her bedroom, she pulled out her new pills and threw herself onto her waterbed. She closed her eyes and drifted off to a daydream where she gulped the contents of both bottles in rapid succession. *These will take me out for good if all goes wrong. I'm not going to jail.*

Startled by banging on her front door, she got up and peeked around the copper curtains and saw two burly well-dressed males on her front porch. Crap! It's those cops again. She ran to the kitchen to the sound of the doorbell, grabbed a bottle of whiskey out of the cabinet, poured a glassful, held the bottle and glass in one hand and opened the door.

"Ms. Lynnch? We need to speak to you."

"Again? I've already spoken to you. Nothing has changed."

"We have a search warrant and additional questions."

Search warrant? Damn it! "So you're gonna barge in here without identification?"

They held up badges and she wondered why she hadn't previously paid more attention to the name of the more rotund, beetle-eyed officer, Harold Humphrey whose mud-colored crew cut was almost hidden under his hat. She guessed his age to be in his mid-thirties.

"Come in officher Humpty. Sat on a wall…had a great fall. Wanna drink?" She took a gulp of whiskey. "You shhhhure? Sho, whatcha need now?"

"Officer Humphrey, Miss. Your statements are not corroborating. We have another photo of the victim, Mr. Shane Zadrik and yourself. The witnesses at the bar have identified you as his girlfriend and his day planner implicates the degree of your involvement with him."

What? I have no idea what the hell is going on. "How'dja like that? I had no idea I was his girlfriend." She took a gulp of whiskey. "I can give you at least ten wishtnesses that I never was hish girlfriend, not ever and maybe you noticed that there happen to be a lot of photosh of me taken with lotsch of peoples. Officher Humpy, I mean Mr. Dumpty, shir. Write down dese namesh." She listed her four bandmates, her security guard: Mr. Tinsky, the names of the booking agents and her sister-in-law Debra Lynnch. "Ashk all of em. They can tell you who is not and never was my boyfriend. Look at my size. Think I can drag around a guy as big as Mr. Zadrik?" She was trembling at the thought of her home being searched even though Sam lived upstairs and the door was locked.

"Do not move from this chair while we search the property."

They started in the kitchen where banging doors, intensified her stomach pain. She held her head in her hands when they opened the refrigerator, walked down basement steps, back up the stairs to ransack the drawers of her desk and both closets of the bedroom. She could hear the medicine cabinet close in the bathroom and felt queasy. Relieved when they approached the living room empty handed, she continued to shake in fear because of their unrelenting focus to gather evidence from the primary suspect of their murder investigation.

"Is your garage door open?"

"I think it is." *What could you all possibly be looking for?*

"Remain seated until we give further instruction."

The officers returned and sat beside her, edging as close as the chairs would allow. "We're going to ask you one last time. What was your relationship with the victim?"

"Our band played at his club, nothing more."

"What were you doing in his club on July 29th?"

"My agent told me Shane had a black shirt and some jewelry he thought might have belonged to me, so I went to see if it was mine."

"Why did you hire a security guard?"

"I need someone to protect me, and lack the strength to defend myself."

The officers glanced at one another, and officer Humphrey gave her his card and asked her to call if she had any information that came to mind. She let the men out, thinking that she did not need to portray herself as a drunken idiot, as it made no difference in their behavior toward her.

That evening, she pulled Sam's old blonde wig onto her head, combed it, dressed in black high-heeled pumps, a slim black calf-length skirt and black blouse, and topped it off with a black and white sweater. She slathered on red lipstick, put on black rimmed safety glasses and used a brown eye pencil to arch her eyebrows and draw a brown mole near her chin. She dug one of her old small black purses off of the top shelf of the closet. Catching a glimpse in the window, she barely recognized herself and was certain no one else would.

The Final Rest Funeral Home, at 1574 W Columbia Street, was across the street from the Union Cemetery and a few blocks away from Shane and Nicky's residence on. Hopkins St.

She scrutinized the people near the guest register and signed in as Jane Dough. While Nicky directed mourners, she held a tissue over her eye glasses, bent her head downward, walked up to the casket and pretended to sniffle. *It's Aldar, the guy who attacked me and Debra. I wonder what they did with his red Plymouth Duster. Was he dead, or did Shane fix his death the way he fixed his own?*

The upper body exposed, the pale face showed no signs of life. His hands folded across his chest, his lower half was enclosed by an elaborate wood casket covered in red roses.

Her head sideways, Lexa studied the remains of a fair-faced, sandy brown-haired man in a gray suit, the depraved man who sent the barbed letters, the one whose voice she remembered from long ago. Taking a quick look at her surroundings, she walked toward a group of women who were huddled in a discussion.

"What a nice young man. He took such good care of his elderly mother until she died. I always envied the wrap around porch on their lovely Cape Cod home. He never married. I can't believe he passed away so young."

"We thought she was healthy, but she died a few months after he moved in. He must have had a broken heart after selling his mother's estate. Heard he got a good sum on it. I wonder who he left all that money to."

Lexa interrupted the chatter to talk about the nice, tall gentleman who has been doing such a wonderful job this evening directing the wake and how she had been to some awful services in the past. "We should thank him for how helpful he's been."

Upon leading the group of women in his direction, she backed away and headed down stairs to a room and peeked in. A faint light showed an assortment of wood and metal caskets and a slightly opened one. Using her tissue, she opened it and saw a supply of rifles and arms that could take out a small army. Some were assault rifles and an M-16 was near the top. Lexa scrambled to the next casket, opened it and three other caskets in the room contained more of the same.

She opened the door to an adjoining room where an L-shaped countertop and sink held an assortment of beakers, flasks, a Bunsen burner, powders, pipettes, and equipment she had never seen. On a long wall behind her, stretching floor to ceiling were cabinets. One displayed rows of different sized plastic containers. She took scrap paper and a pencil out of her purse and wrote. Labels read: "Botulinium toxin- clostridium botulinium, curare- chondrodendron tomentosum, D-Tubocurarine, Tetrodotoxin TTX, Potassium Chlorate, Sulfuric Acid H2SO4, Metal Arsenic, Cacodylic Acid (Agent Blue) Picloram + 2, 4 – D, 2, 4 – D (Agent White) and 2, 4-D + 2, 4, 5-T High Volatile ester (Agent Orange)". *What the hell do they need all these for, especially agent orange, blue, and white? I think those were used in Nam.*

In another immense room were long rows of tall, bushy marijuana plants lit by florescent lights. She was impressed by the massive scale of the operation.

She backed out toward the casket room to leave, but in hearing the door open, she ducked behind the nearest casket, removed her high heels and clutched them.

"I saw you go in here," roared a deep semi-whispered angry sounding Nicky.

The Mace and pin is in my other purse, she thought as she removed the safety glasses, stuck them into the small black purse, pulled on the strings at the top and tied the purse to the belt loop on her skirt to free her hands. Footsteps creaked on floorboards near her while she glanced to her right and left around stacked caskets. Rolling up her skirt to be prepared to run, the screaks continued while she crawled around stacked caskets in the direction of the doorway.

"Show yourself and I won't hurt you," whispered a deep voice to a silent room. "Get out of this room." A latch clicked.

She sat still as she checked for movement around the caskets and turned to sit on the floor. Her watch showed 7:00 pm. She had been at the wake for an hour and wriggled around caskets to get closer to the door. *Are any of those women still here?* She listened for voices and wondered if she would soon be alone in a building housing dead bodies, chemicals, an armory, and a weed growing enterprise. *Getting out while mourners can hear a scream, would be my best option.* She pulled herself upward and looked around.

"Hello? Hello?" *He left.* She crouched behind a crate topped by a casket.

The door reopened, Nicky saw and lunged toward her. He raced around obstacles as she jockeyed in the opposite direction, heels in hand.

"Ma'am, what are you doing in here?"

"I was looking for a cup of coffee and got lost," Lexa replied, raising her voice enough to disguise it while they jumped like a cat and mouse around coffins, moving the opposite direction from him, to counteract his moves. Nick began to move more aggressively until he faced her around a stack of caskets and continued circling her, while she hopped side to side like a scared rabbit about to be pounced on by a lion.

"Lady, I haven't got all day," he said in a tone of outrage.

"So, you'll let me walk out of here quietly?" she asked, disguising her voice.

"Maybe," he said, as they danced around the caskets face to face and she hustled closer to the door.

As she turned to grasp the handle, his bulky arms enveloped her. She picked up her knees, squirmed and pushed herself downward, fell onto the floor, rolled away and scrambled out, leaving him clutching her blonde wig and sweater. She had dropped her shoes in the scuffle and ran out using every last ounce of resolve, around the back of the building snaking through the neighborhood to the VW. She fired up the ignition, pulled the black knit cap on her head as she drove away, and shook so hard she feared she may lose consciousness on her drive.

She jogged up the stairway facing the refrigerator and headed to the cabinets where the liquor bottles were stashed. She reached in, pulled out a bottle of whiskey, and poured a quarter glass full. In her bedroom, she took a Nembutal out of the pill bottle in her suitcase, licked a portion of the powder, and rejoined the capsule.

She sat beside the bookshelf in a dark room. The vent warmed her while she sipped her drink, immobilized by fear. *How am I going to get through our next show? I need to pick up the photos, if no one breaks in and kills me tonight.* She shoved a black plastic flashlight under her bra strap, and balanced it on her left shoulder where she positioned the light to illuminate the pages of her diary.

Thursday, October 28, 1976

The police never found my boot that matches the one near Shane's body because it's packed away in the truck, behind the speaker of my amplifier. I was so annoyed I couldn't find the match, I threw it in there.

Aldar has amassed his mother's estate but lived in a dump. It does not make sense. The fingers of doom snap like the ticking of a clock to remind me that police and the Zadrik tribe wait at each end of my path. What is their plan for so many chemicals?

Curled up in the corner where she had fallen asleep, cradling the flashlight on her lap and the diary on the floor, Lexa awoke to the sound of Sam's voice calling out to her. "Where are you?"

"I'm here," she said crawling out.

"Are you ready to leave for Iowa?" he asked.

"I wonder if they will shoot me while I'm singing on stage," she said looking up to him in a barely audible gravely morning voice.

He furrowed his brow, tilted his head and asked, "Shoot you? What are you talking about?"

"What time is it? When will the guys be here?" she cleared her throat and rushed to wash up and pack a bag.

The after-effects of the powder and whiskey made Lexa doze on and off all the way to Junnies in Dubuque. At the end of the show, Sam, Grant and Ted invited three women who had been in the crowd to the motel to party in one of the rooms. They later left for an open cafe while Lexa and Karl watched TV. She shared the crackers and cheeses that she had packed.

"Did you and Nicky have a good time?" asked Karl.

"He's not my type. We chatted awhile and he nodded off, so I left."

"Was he drunk out of his mind? Why do I think you have more to add to your story?" Karl smiled.

"This might be hard to believe, but the guy could take me out accidentally, by trying to hug me. The night didn't end well. I should write up a will. My share of the house needs to go to my family."

Karl stared at her, raised his eyebrows and said, "Maybe you should hire a bodyguard."

"I already did."

"Maybe you need another one."

"That would be like hiring a babysitter to watch over the babysitter. I need a bodyguard to protect me from myself."

He offered her a white pill. "What's this?" she asked.

"My dad gave me some. It's an Ativan. You're really on edge tonight. I think it'll help you calm down."

"Thanks Karl," she said, recognizing it from when she worked at the hospital. "It's fortunate your Dad is a doctor and can prescribe for you. I am looking forward to some decent sleep." She broke it in half.

They woke up to a phone ringing and Ted's question of where they should have breakfast as well as his reminder of the band's live, on-air interview scheduled at WSUP in Platteville at 5:00 where Lexa, Grant, Karl and the DJ bantered.

"We have Word Locket in our studio today to answer your questions. Caller, you're live on the air."

"Yea, how did your band get started? Did you meet in college?"

"No, we still don't know each other and have to wear name tags, or we would all be called eh, you dere," said Grant.

"Why do you call yourselves Word Locket? Does it have any meaning?"

"Originally, we wanted the name 'Zipper Teeth'. It sounds like this," she said grabbing the zipper of her leather jacket, pulling it up and down rhythmically into the mic. Grant and Karl chimed in, all three zippers at the DJ's microphone.

"Ever consider recording it on your next album? It sounds sexual. Is your real name Lexa Loxx?"

"Enough questions for the day! Thanks, Word Locket! Fans can catch them performing in Dubuque this evening, at Junnies, the largest club in the area."

The band and DJ joked for another 30 minutes before heading back to the club. The crowd noise was almost as loud as the band when the Saturday evening show ended at 2:00 am. Lexa, Karl and Grant went to East Dubuque for more partying, where bars were open. On the way to the hotel, Lexa turned up the radio.

"The defense department is circumventing a presidential ban on nerve gas production by developing new weapons that become lethal when their components are mixed, forming a binary bomb." *Is it what they're working on in the funeral home?* During the drive back she was firm in her thoughts and on Monday evening, dialed Karl's phone number asking if she could bring something to him.

"Karl, remember me telling you I was going to write a will? I wrote something out and had it notarized at my bank today. Keep it sealed in this envelope. My family's information is in here. I think it'll stand up in court if anything happens to me. Can I trust you to keep it safe and get it to my family in case I happen to disappear? Please?"

"I can't say no to you Lexa. Why do you think you will disappear?"

"The wrong crowd and I accidentally crossed paths and I haven't been able to sort out what to do."

"You sound scared. Do you need help?"

"I might. I think about my demise a lot and have nightmares about a major catastrophe, like a war is going on and I'm trapped watching it. It's so vivid."

"Are you going to be okay at the shows we have coming up? The calendar is loaded."

"I intend to be."

Monday, November 1, 1976

Most adhere to the solid world of black and white, or - this is right and that is wrong – end of story. Some navigate well through murky gray rules. My world has innumerable faded color choices, and I jump from cloud to cloud looking for solid ground. I can balance for a little while, but in the end, I fall through and hang onto another wisp of air. What do I have to cling to, really? I'm dangling from a crumbling ledge. We have a constant string of shows and I'll try to hire Tiny again to check if he is willing to hide more than walkie-talkies.

Lexa left a message for Tiny to call her as she paged through the phone book to locate the nearest north side gun shop. He returned her call before she made it outside.

"Hello...thanks for calling back. It sounds crazy, but I have serious concerns about my safety and think someone is going to kill me. Can you recommend a good place to get a gun? I'll make sure your name goes on the band's guest list permanently. I mean all clubs."

He talked her into one of his used Colt Commander 45 caliber handguns, and would meet to make the transaction. Lexa inquired where the closest shooting facility was. She had spent an hour firing her new weapon and laughed out loud. *Am I going to start singing on stage holding a gun? That's not going to go over well with club owners and fans. This is pointless. I'll ask if Tiny will carry heat when he watches me. Either way, I'll learn how to use it and keep it either under a pillow, near my bed or in my suitcase. It has so much kickback; I need to use both hands to get a good shot. I wish he had something smaller.*

At the grocery store, she picked up a few items and the photos, and while admiring her handy work of the six images, was reprimanded by the photo clerk in the white lab jacket. "Ma'am, that's a roll of 24. You developed doubles of 6 photos and it's a waste of film."

What do you care? She smiled at him, turned her head away, and walked to her VW, her innocence in hand. She hid the duplicates in the same books she had placed the license plate numbers in her bookshelf.

She drove to Tiny's office and showed all of the pictures to him.

"That pest is alive," he said. "I wonder what the hell is going on."

"He and his buddies are waging a war. They keep high powered rifles in caskets at the funeral home where Aldar spent his time. He may have faked his death. Can you carry a gun while you watch over me?"

"I will, but I charge more for weaponry. I'll keep the snapshots, but I can't take them to the police yet, and I don't how to help you get out of this at the moment. What do you mean Aldar may be dead?"

"I went to his wake on October 28. He looked lifeless."

A day passed showing no sign of police, Nicky or Shane. She and her bandmates were passengers in Sam's van as he drove them to the show at Windjammers in Sheboygan on, November 3rd.

Upon spotting Tarick in the crowd, she felt nervous and unable to concentrate on song lyrics, being captivated by his broad shoulders, thick, wavy light brown hair, and full lips. When the last note ended, she jumped off the stage and walked in his direction. "So you've come to watch the singing assassin?"

"I was bored. There were hardly any people at our show," he said. "And I wanted to watch the beautiful singer in this band to see if I can get another chance with her." His smile was sweet and shy.

"It's hard to imagine you getting bored," she said, unable to take her gaze off the symmetry of his chiseled face.

"I stopped in when you played at the Toad and I watched a broad shouldered big guy walk you out. Is he your type, Lexa? You looked preoccupied."

"I what? Oh, him," she said wrinkling her nose and frowning. "He's not my type. You were there?"

"Yea, and you left in a hurry."

"Seriously, nothing happened between me and that guy. He and the club owner who died in the van were friends. I wanted to get information. Somehow my boot was near the deceased. I wanted to know if I was framed."

They stared at one another, each waiting for the other to speak first.

"Are you bored enough to give me a ride home to let me show you who my type is? I thought maybe you knew. I've enjoyed our time together more than you can imagine," she said.

"I don't know why I keep coming back to you. Usually when we're together, it goes haywire." he said.

"I hope tonight will be different," she said.

There was a quality about his clear blue eyes, a prism she could fall into and remain for endless hours.

"Let's go," he said. The radio on, the music was soft, and they hummed to the songs. Her attraction to him was intense, and the chemistry of his beauty weakened her resolve. Her skin tingled being near him, as though an electric current surrounded them.

She unlocked the back door, stepped into the hallway, looked into his sensuous face, stood on her tiptoes, touched his mouth and pressed her lips onto his before they walked up the steps. His cold hands on her face slid under her hair and down her back. She melted into his kiss.

She took his hand and led him into her bedroom where he wove his fingers into hers, and stroked her arms. He pulled her shirt up, bared her breasts, and kissed her neck and across her shoulders. Like a magnetic pull, her desire for him had grabbed a hold of her heart. He touched his lips onto hers. She unzipped his jeans, pulled them and his shirt off, her body heating up as she caressed his warm silkiness. They lie in her bed facing each other.

He held her face and his kiss was deep and penetrating. His arms wrapped around her, she savored his velvety skin. She hushed her gasps and released all worldly thoughts. His eyes pierced hers, and sweat pooled between them as she felt him tremble within her. His breath prickled her neck and shoulders.

The heat of his body around her made her feel safe. He stroked her hair, her chest, pelvis, and legs. He caressed her again and again.

With her head nestled in the cradle of his arm, she felt tranquil when he fell asleep. She watched his chest rise and fall. *He's fortunate to sleep in such peace.*

His beauty was straddled in youth, all of it perfect, exotic and all that was fleeting. It was a moment she wished she could enclose in glass and revisit when her darkness became too unbearable, to be immersed again in the purest form of pleasure where time slowed to a near standstill. She curled up beside him.

She awoke to the sounds of birds chirping, surprised she had slept through most of the night. When she opened her eyes, she felt the warmth of his aquamarine eyes focused on her.

"Good morning," she said through sun-illuminated walls, unsure of what to say. "Are you hungry?"

"A little," he smiled. His arms embraced her while she stroked his chest. They took their time getting up.

"I'll make breakfast for us." She made coffee and cracked three eggs into a pan.

He took a sip of coffee, and standing behind her, wrapped his arms around her waist while she made eggs, buttered toast and orange juice.

"I have a show at Carroll College in Waukesha at 4:00, which gives us time to hang out."

They sat at the table enjoying breakfast when a scratching sound at the back door, then glass shattering onto the landing, jolted her out of her seat to the hallway.

Nicky Nevalla reached through the broken glass and unlocked the door. She ran for her suitcase, grabbed the gun and pointed it at him as he walked up the back steps. Tarick sat at the kitchen table in horror watching her clasp a gun and scream, "Stop!"

"What do you want?" she asked.

"Lexa," Nicky said in a deep sing-song tone of voice. "Someone wants to talk to you and I suggest you cooperate. You owe me."

"I owe you what?"

"After my evening with you, I couldn't get out of bed the next day."

Tarick looked as though he was about to cry.

"I'm sorry I drugged you. I'm not going to jail for something I didn't do. My band will be here in a little while. You owe me a new window. Ever hear of knocking...or using a doorbell?"

"Like you would've let me in. I'll have you back in an hour."

"Where do I need to go for an hour?" she asked, pointing a black gun at the brick house of a man.

He looked at Tarick and back at Lexa. "Someone I'm close to is in trouble and needs your help. This person knows you're a nurse and is willing to pay you."

"I'm not sure what I can do," she said lowering her gun. "Is the person ill?"

"The man is in terrible pain because of an infection, and is in grave need of medical assistance. I can't leave here without you."

"Stop, pleading," she sighed. I'll have to meet you there. Am I going to your house?"

"Yes you are," said Nicky.

"I'm sorry Tarick, things aren't going the way I wish they would," she said as she turned towards him.

"Lexa, what are you messed up in?" he asked.

"It's a complicated story. I hope I'm able to tell you about it sometime soon, if I get out of this alive. I'd better go," she said staring into his sad face. "I am sorry things get messed up every time we're together. I don't know what more I can say." She opened her purse, stashed the gun into it and walked out to start up her VW.

She stared at the back of the house surrounded by whirling orange leaves, before she was let in on her first knock, where Nicky welcomed and led her into a bedroom she had seen before.

In a messy bed was a slender, short-haired blonde man wearing rounded eyeglasses, a white t-shirt and pajama slacks, who grimaced in pain. He turned to her and spoke in almost a whisper.

"I need your help."

Though his appearance had changed and his voice sounded weak and distraught, she knew it was Shane. "What kind of help do you need and why are you involving me?"

"You've been through my house and funeral home. I need medical attention and have no one else to turn to." He lifted the right leg of his pajama slacks above his knee to reveal a deep red lump and reddened streaks traveling toward his hip. There was no mistaking an infection in the early stages of septic poisoning.

"You need a doctor and antibiotics."

"It's not an option for me," he said in a sigh.

"That's not my problem," said Lexa. Shane and Nick closed their eyes.

"Can you suggest someone else?" Shane turned toward Nick.

"Okay, I'm here already. Nick where's the nearest pharmacy? Can you get me to one?" she said, noticing her photos were no longer on his dresser.

He opened the door of his blue Dodge Challenger and she took a seat. "There is one about a mile away," he said.

Inspecting the shelves at the drug store, she picked up an eight ounce bottle of povidone-iodine, several boxes of gauze, three rolls of medical tape, a 500 cc bottle of sterile irrigating saline and faced Nick.

"Can you take me to my house?"

She jumped down the basement steps and rifled through the supplies she had saved during her days at the clinic. Despite being old, the items would be sufficient. She took a sterile scalpel #11 blade and 4 x 4 gauze pads, Kerlix gauze, grabbed a box of sterile gloves, ran back up the steps and took Sam's Penicillin pills which had outdated, but in having been forgotten at the back of a fridge, would still be of benefit to someone who had no other choice.

Her arms full of supplies, she climbed into Nick's car. "I'll do my best, but I can't guarantee anything. It's none of my business, but do you embalm the bodies too? In the hospital, it was tough tending to the dead. The worst part was consoling the family."

"Yea, I embalm bodies, apply a preservative, load on cake makeup and sometimes I have to reconstruct the face."

"Al almost looked like he was still alive," she said.

"What did you put in my whiskey?" he asked. "I couldn't think straight the next day."

"Nothing I wouldn't take myself. It was Nembutal and I'm sorry. I was distraught. I thought you were trying to set me up for a murder rap. I'm the primary suspect because of Shane's day planner, the photo of him and me which seems to look like we're a happy couple, and my boot at the crime scene. Cops and I aren't the best of friends these days."

"Your boot?"

"Didn't you know it was beside him in the van where he was discovered by the police?" she asked.

"What the hell? I didn't touch anything of yours."

"Someone did. If it wasn't you, how did it get there?"

"I have no idea," he said.

In Shane's room, she pulled her hair into a ponytail, organized items on the bed and bedside table, opened up the gauze, the scalpel, sterile water and iodine. A thermometer showed a fever of 104.2 degrees. She scrubbed her hands, pulled on sterile gloves, poured the brown iodine onto gauze and wiped the reddened area above his right knee in a circular motion, repeating this process several times, the singular sound being the mechanics of a clock in the room. She palpated the lump to check for any weakened area of infection at the surface of the skin, took the scalpel, looked at Shane and said, "Grit your teeth."

Thick white fluid seeped onto the dressings around the wound, and she pressed on the outer edges of the inflammation in a circular motion as the remaining fluid oozed out. She poured the sterile saline over the area.

"I wasn't sure if you would help me. You're the only medical person who knows I'm alive," he said weakly.

"Your disguise makes you unrecognizable. You could go to an Emergency Room."

"No, I can't take that risk."

"Your fever has to come down, and your body needs to fight this infection. I'm going to wrap sterile, warm moist compresses on this to help the abscess drain out. If you have a heating pad, make sure it stays on the lowest notch, keep a moist towel under it and do not let it dry out. A few of these antibiotics were taken, but you should have enough. I also recommend a daily vitamin. You don't look like you're eating too well. You've lost a lot of weight."

"Tell Nick what I need. He'll take care of it."

"You're the jack of all trades," she said to Nick. She wrote out a list of instructions for them to follow, and said she would return tomorrow. As she turned to walk out of the room, she was met by a face she recognized.

"How's he doing?" said a familiar voice.

Lexa gasped at seeing a brown eyed man with shoulder-length black hair named Al Geitlich enter the room. *I liked him better when he was in the coffin, preferably dead.* His voice made her want to grab his neck and choke him. *Are they all going to fake their deaths? I'm certain they used one of the chemicals in their lab.*

Boffo's barking could be heard in the room she had not searched.

Back at the house when her bandmates arrived, she met them near the garage so they would not see the missing window.

Thursday, November 4, 1976

I held onto Tarick as though my life depended on it and maybe it did for the moment I shared so deep a connection to another human. I'll be amazed if he has the courage to call me again. I think what he saw today has driven him away forever. The flicker of a chance for us to become a part of each other's lives has been stomped out. My life is too crazy for any man in this world to consider being a part of it. His eyes spoke of his own loneliness and loss before I left. Love appears as elusive as a recording contract. It seems after having spent so much time alone, being detached is becoming my comfort zone.

I called Tiny to send a bill for what I owe, and to inform him I won't need any more assistance.

On Friday 11/5, she inspected Shane's leg wound, and the red streaks had faded. She changed the dressing and smoothed down fresh tape. "It looks better, but finish every last antibiotic, take your vitamins, drink lots of fluids and keep the compresses on. So, you're a blonde now?"

"Yea, scissors, hair color, glasses and I'm free to walk around again."

"Did Nick tell you he broke my back window? At least it's not freezing outside yet. Or I should say…the window of your childhood residence."

"Childhood residence? What are you talking about?"

"Your former neighbor lady, and now mine likes to talk…a lot."

"I remember her. She was always nice to me and my mom. Nick and I made sure your window will be repaired today. Sorry to drag you into this," he said sitting up in bed, propped up on three pillows, his voice sounding stronger.

"Maybe you can give me some suggestions of how to get off the radar of the police," she said. "I've met almost the entire second shift in my district, and now I'm getting far too acquainted with the day shift. I am not happy about facing incarceration," she said eyeing the life-sized poster of Hendrix, now on a wall in his bedroom.

"Are you going to sell me out?" he asked.

"The info I have about you won't be told to law enforcement, if it's what you're asking. I'm guilty of illegal things also. So, I need to ask…why do you want to kill me?" She wished she had given Karl a copy of her most recent photos and the men's license plate numbers with her will.

"You've been here. I'm not your enemy. I hoped to help you take in some cash because of how much equipment your band lost. We had a hunch the FBI was onto us, but didn't know how close they were until one of my men spotted a federal agent in the parking lot the day you stopped in, and I had to disappear fast. I wouldn't be surprised if they're keeping an eye on you."

"You think the FBI is watching me?"

He laughed. "I wouldn't doubt it. I have your address. We get your band's itineraries, so it's impossible for you to hide. You have no idea how easy you are to track."

"Is this some kind of truce?"

"I don't think we need a truce. Nick told me why you were in here, and we haven't been hostile to one another."

"I think your mother's spirit is still in the house I live in," she said. "I know she died when you were young and I wonder if she's searching for you. Would you consider coming over to talk to her? She's been waiting for you for a long time."

He turned away. "Why do you think it's my mom?"

"You can thank my neighbor, and I have had many dreams about your beautiful mother. I never understood what she is trying to tell me. I have to get going. My band is meeting soon and they already think I'm wacky. By the way, do you have my new phone number so you don't have to break another window?"

"No, but it would be nice if you gave it to me. Do you want your wig, shoes and sweater back?" he smiled.

"Yea, I'll take them and your phone number. Too bad the police won't return my boot. Someone stole it and it's evidence now. They think I was involved in your death. I'll see you tomorrow to check on your leg at around one thirty." They exchanged numbers.

She returned home to shower, pack and await her bandmates, her mind full of questions as to whether she was now an accomplice to criminal activity by exercising her nursing skills.

Driving to Shane's house on Saturday, Lexa thought about the words by Abraham Lincoln, 'I destroy my enemies when I make them my friends.' She was led to Nick and Shane for a reason. 'The plan goes down no matter what,' weapon filled coffins, chemical lined cabinets, and altered grave sites concerned her. *Were the trucks in the parking lot of his funeral home also part of this plan?* She was let in after her second double knock.

"You look much better today," she said.

"I think you cured me," he said welcoming her in, wearing navy pajama slacks and a blue t-shirt. They walked to his bedroom where gauze, tape, sterile saline and antiseptic sat on his bedside table.

An examination of his leg showed healthy pink skin as she changed the bandage and reapplied fresh antiseptic.

She touched his forehead. "No fever." The thermometer showed his temperature was at 98.6 degrees. "Are you going to tell me how you knew I was a nurse?"

"I make it my business to be informed a lot of things," he said.

"Oh, that clears it up for me," she smiled. "Well, I think you can get your discharge papers sir. I'll write up a summary for you, what to watch for, wound care and dietary instructions. Make sure you finish all of the antibiotics. Do you understand?" she said, as he walked her into his celery colored living room where she was greeted by Boffo's sniffing of her lower body. "You smell Ebbie, don't you?" She smiled and stroked the Shepherd behind his ears as luminous brown pools of coal stared up at her.

"Thanks for your help. I was a bit anxious and made a guess you might help me. Nick didn't think you would come anywhere near here even if a gun was pointed at you."

"It sounds like you and Nick go way back," she said.

"He's been my best friend since high school. We joined the army together and managed to make it out of Nam in one piece," he replied.

She sat on a chartreuse sofa listening to Pink Floyd's 'Dark side of the Moon' while Shane sat across from her on a tan chair. He offered cashews from a gold patterned glass bowl.

"So you discovered I had lived in your house long ago. I was driving past it one day, and saw you wearing a nurse uniform, gathering the pink roses my mother planted, and almost hit the car in front of me. So you met my former neighbors," he said.

"She probably looks nothing like she did when you knew her, but once she starts talking, I have to interrupt her to stop."

"Her kids were her life, so now that they've moved out, she must need some distraction. That husband of hers was an asshole. But so was my Dad. Her son and I used to make up stories to antagonize them, but the fight we planned never happened. Each story became more agitating, and we wished they would both go down, and hard. Dad was more interested in his new flame and moving to his house in Shorewood overlooking Lake Michigan after Mom passed. She looked like she was asleep, but wouldn't wake up no matter what I said or did. Dad never showed any emotion about her death."

"I'm sorry," Lexa replied, remembering the evening Oma had fallen into an unshakable coma. "How did you like living in the mansion?"

"My stepmother was a bimbo. I couldn't stand her, so Dad shipped me off to my mom's mother who was kind and caring. She insisted I go to college and made sure I studied. She bribed me by making sure we always had warm chocolate chip cookies," he said smiling as though a cookie was in his mouth.

"What was your major?"

"I went to UW Madison where I majored in chemical engineering and worked alongside Dr. Ira Baldwin, the professor of bacteriology and scientific director of the labs where chemical defoliants were made, but after getting arrested for dealing weed in '61, it was over. Long story short, I shipped out to Fort Campbell Kentucky, trained with the 101st Airborne Division and who do suppose I met? James Marshall Hendrix. Jimi. It's why I like your band so much. I haven't seen anyone who can rip through Hendrix licks like Sam can. If I close my eyes, I can't tell the difference. When he played the Star Spangled Banner at your show, I thought I was going to lose it," he said leaning his head back looking up to the ceiling.

"A lot of people became guitarists because of Jimi," she said.

"Jimi was in his element on a guitar. He rigged the strings and finger picked it upside down, so I couldn't ever use his. He wasn't a gun man. All of us thought we could get shipped out at any minute. I knew he not up to the task of killing anyone. The army was going let him go, and when they did, I felt like I lost one of my best friends."

"You met one of my idols. Hendrix is a musician I would have loved to have seen live in concert, and you became a friend of his. I felt his loss the on day he died."

"So did I," he said.

"You live in an area that serves you well, like the graves across the street. It must be convenient for you to hide dead bodies there."

He threw his head back. "Yea, there's dead bodies, but I didn't put them there. My biggest worry was if the house got raided, I'd land in prison. If drugs and paraphernalia were out of sight, they would have nothing on me."

"This place is the perfect hideout. How did you fake your death?"

"An exact combination of chemicals and Aldar's help, if you want to wake up again, which gave me a death certificate, thanks to the coroner and police. I made it look like a suicide. The club had loads of empty booze bottles, and I scattered them and a pill bottle around me."

"Did the chemicals involve D-Tubocurarine and Tetrodotoxin?" She said reaching for the cashews.

His face took on a serious look. "It's not a pleasant experience."

"Do you know why someone would frame me? The police are pointing fingers at me."

"If I knew, I would tell you and I don't know anything about your boots. I don't understand why they suspect you."

"They were carrying your day planner. And the picture of us together."

"Hmmm," he mumbled and said nothing.

"How did you avoid having an autopsy done?"

"Because of the funeral home, Nick and Aldar have connections at the morgue. They switched the tags, and carried me out. A car salesman who's hub was in Plano, Texas and I had a lucrative business together, but once they took Mr. Hicks down, we were all going down. He grossed half a billion running the largest drug smuggling operation in Texas, selling cocaine, heroin, and weed, but didn't keep a low profile and he went down hard. The feds took down his entire empire. On the day you stopped by, a DEA agent was snooping around, so I had to disappear fast."

If you had Aldar's help, it explains why something of mine was near you. That creep rummaged through our dressing room, she thought. "I met Mr. Hicks. My band took a pit stop in Plano. He zeroed in on us when we stepped out of our van, and nosed around the clubs where we played. He made lots of transactions all night long. It was as though everyone knew him," she said.

"He was a good salesman. Cars, drugs, whatever he got his hands on. We were both wanted by the FBI and the DEA. I would have never seen the light of day if they got a hold of me, but soon I won't have to worry about it anymore."

Lexa leaned toward him to pick up a cashew. "What do you mean?"

"You better go. I'll give you some cash for your help."

"No, it's okay, I hope there's another way you can pay me back."

Sorrow fell into his dark brown eyes as he watched Lexa walk out to her VW. He appeared more fragile than the first time she had seen him, having lost 30 pounds. Blonde hair, hollowed cheeks and weight loss had made him almost unrecognizable. Bluish-purple circles started under his eyes and crawled up to his brows. She pulled her jacket collar over her neck, braced against the wind as swirling snow camouflaged the remaining patches of withered grass. Turning the windshield wipers on, she pulled on her gloves, drove southbound on Hopkins St., made a left onto Teutonia St. and turned onto Columbia St. to pass the Final Rest Funeral Home.

So the Texas tentacles of Mr. Hicks have reached throughout the U.S. He provided the drugs Shane and Nick were selling. I need to keep an eye on the storage facility where Shane keeps weapons and chemicals. A plan that goes down no matter what. He has seven white large cargo box trucks parked in his lot. They're like the one the band has, she thought as she swerved to avoid the curb. She slowed down to take a better look. Each white truck had bold black digits on the door of the cab: C7T. The D.O.T. number.

The note Shane wrote to me had those digits. Maybe I don't have to worry about getting killed yet, she contemplated, looking across the street to the Union Cemetery.

NIGHTBEATS

CHAPTER 17

NUMBERS

She ran down the basement steps, and ransacked a few boxes. Shane had given a plaque to her a year ago. She examined it in a new way, twisting and turning it under a magnifying glass. *As if I would find anything on this piece of wood,* she thought, when a small date in the lower right hand corner of the protective sheen stood out: 1/1/77. She raced up the steps, took her diary, and almost ripped out pages until she zeroed in on the entry of the date this gift was presented to her: 10/3/1975. *He gave the plaque a future date. He has been planning something for over a year, maybe more, and I'm not sure if this clue is intentional or not.*

She checked her watch and realized the library would close in 15 minutes, sped into a parking spot and checked out a book on Numerology.

In the same aisle, she picked up another book and read: "In Tarot, the meaning of the eight of swords is that of a woman who is blindfolded and trapped by the swords of her own prison. By releasing the blindfold and bindings, she can weigh her options, make a choice to free herself from her own trappings and reclaim her inner power." She checked her book out as they were locking up for the night.

At her kitchen table she scribbled and added up the numbers on the plaque. 1/1/1977: $1 + 1 + 1 + 9 +7 + 7 = 26$; $2 + 6 = 8$. Then the first letter: 10/3/1975: $1+ 0 + 3 + 1 + 9+ 7 + 5 = 26$; $2 + 6 = 8$.

Rifling through the box of fan mail, she read the dates on the other letters:

9/22/1975: $9 + 2+ 2 + 1 + 9 + 7 + 5 = 35$; $3 + 5 = 8$.

1/2/1976: $1 + 2+ 1 +9 + 7 + 6= 26$; $2 + 6= 8$. The letters written 1/20/1976, 6/6/1976, and 7/5/1976 all added up to 8. The numbers on Shane's cryptic letter: 7/23/1976 added up to eight, prompting her to look up the numeric meaning in the book.

Did I receive a message, or is it incidental? The numerology book says that 8 refers to Power, Control, Sacrifice and Strength, so it could be a cipher. I wonder how much thought they put into my discovering a connection. I don't like this game. Power over what? It's close to eight weeks away. I think the will I gave to Karl for safekeeping is useless if I don't have a solid plan by then, she thought, as she fell backwards onto her waterbed. She closed her eyes.

Sweat beads covered her when she awoke, having relived another dream of darkened skies and obliterated scenery. She worried this realistic dream may become a reality as she packed clothes for Sunday night, where the band performed at Apollo's Lyre in Kewaskum, and Drax went into a tirade.

"This is my last night in this band. I can't stand it anymore!" He screamed at everyone in the dressing room at the top of his lungs. "I'm quitting and no one can stop me. Sam thinks he's so perfect announcing into the mic that the PA sounds terrible. He can run the sound for all I care," yelled Drax.

"Sam is in another one of his crappy moods. He probably didn't get laid last night. None of us want you to quit. You're the best there is," said Lexa. "He treats me like I don't matter all the time. We've all gotten a taste of how he is."

"Some folks love football, some live for baseball or basketball, but for me it's all about the sound. I breathe it in, breathe it out, hear it like no one else does, and it's my life. No one puts down my sound. No one. Especially having to use that piece of garbage sound board."

"Drax, I'm sorry about Sam's meltdown on stage. We all need to talk to him. His bad behavior is annoying to all of us," she said.

Sam apologized, and Lexa bought Drax a beer, which quieted him down.

Monday, November 8, 1976

We had a good crowd tonight. Terror stopped gnawing at me long enough to hear the wind and moon harmonize a tune resonating against shutters, gutters, vinyl siding, and shingles - the binaural beats maybe in the key of G. Sam's ugly words into his mic about the PA set Drax off. I wonder if he puts his groupies down when he has had enough of them.

On Saturday 11/13, Lexa entered The Palms and walked up the stairs to the dressing room, lit by one light bulb hanging over a table. Facing the doorway of the dressing room, the brown sofa was dimmed by twilight sifting through the windows behind it. She looked outside at her former apartment, and to the left of it on State St. was Ricky's strip club. Sound check was uneventful, and the band waited to take the stage at the opposite end of the entryway of the large rock club.

Wrinkled newspapers sat in a magazine rack near the sofa. While Creedence Clearwater Revival's "Who'll Stop The Rain" reverberated from loudspeakers of the PA, Lexa picked a paper and read the Milwaukee Journal of 10/29/1976 to pass the time. Headlines read: "President Ford Bids Nations to Halt Sales of any Plutonium Making Plants", banning commercial atomic fuel recycling...Fords order was...to determine ways of guaranteeing that terrorists cannot turn spent reactor fuel into plutonium...for nuclear weapons. She stashed the article in her suitcase and turned to Karl, who sat next to her on the sofa to ask what time it was.

"I have no idea. I'm not wearing my watch."

"Then what's ticking? Do you hear that?"

Both pulled off sofa cushions and looked around. The ticking got louder. Lexa stepped to the left side of the old couch and a 12 inch pipe stood upright attached by several wires to a detonator and small clock, near a plastic container wreaking of gasoline.

"Here's the ticking," she said holding it up to Karl. "Do you have nail clippers?" She snipped the wires and pulled it off the pipe. "The alarm is set for 7:00, and the dressing room explosion would have demolished us. The front doors would be blocked, and club would be incinerating. The road crew could have gotten out of the back doors. Someone keeps track of what time we do our sound check. The doors are never locked when there is live music. Anyone could have walked up here."

"Why does someone want to kill us?" asked Karl.

"Deranged people walk among us." She walked the pipe outside and dropped it a dumpster. She asked the road crew if they had a use for a red five gallon gas container. *Damn it. He thinks I know too much.*

The following day she called the number Shane gave her. Nick picked up on the second ring. "Hello?"

"So you planned to pay me back by mutilating me and my band?"

"Wait a minute. I have no idea what the hell you're talking about," said Nick's deep voice.

"I need to talk to Shane."

"Keep it down. That is not possible."

"Tell him we neutralized the bomb he set. You failed. And it was possible for him to speak to me when he needed my help. Ask him why he wants to return the favor by terminating me," she said before slamming the receiver.

Her mind was tired, heavy, and anxious in planning her next move. The calendar showed no out of state shows. *Tomorrow I'm buying more ammo for the 45. If I have to take out the entire group or hack up their truck tires, I plan to. How many low lives work for him?*

She took the newspaper article out of her suitcase and reread it, wondering if a story she had read the previous year about nuclear fuel being shipped to three Wisconsin Atomic Power Plants at Point Beach 1 and 2 and Kewaunee were related to Zadrik and those who worked for him. The outside of his residence did not reflect that which was therein; the mind of a brilliant man who was a victim of innumerable injustices. She deliberated whether she should do a more intensive search through his house, but knew another visit could be her demise. The ringing telephone startled her.

"You wanted to talk?" asked Shane.

"What happened to letting me live in peace? Did we discuss a truce?"

"I believe it was your words."

"You failed to kill me. I dismantled the bomb."

"I have no idea what you're talking about. You must have made some kind of crazy enemy, and it is not me."

"I need to talk to you in person."

"No. I would rather you didn't."

"If I come over will you let me in?" Five seconds of silence passed. "It was sickening to almost be killed by a bomb in our dressing room, and I can't shake the gloom surrounding me. Please let me stop by." A heavy sigh blew into the mouthpiece.

"Fine, but don't stay long and make sure no one is on your tail. Watch out," he said.

She checked the safety lock, placed the loaded Colt Commander into her large black purse, opened the zipper halfway for easy access, pulled the shoulder strap over her head, and stepped out into the 20 degree night. Wrapping her knit scarf around the shoulders of her tan coat, she watched the steam of her breath fade into darkness. She started up the VW and studied car lights behind her. While checking her rear view and side mirrors, she drove around the block three times.

Shane answered the door and invited her in. They sat in his living room in silence for a minute. He did not wear glasses, made little eye contact, and did not smile. "I can't let you come here anymore. It's too dangerous for both of us."

"If you aren't trying to kill me and I can't think of anyone other than Sam who might want me dead, can you help me figure out who wants to eradicate my band?"

"Sam?" He looked up through the black and blonde uncombed hair over his eyes. "Why would he want you dead?"

"He wasn't anywhere near the dressing room when Karl and I discovered the bomb. Maybe he thinks he'll get everything if I'm out of his way because of an insurance policy we signed years ago. I have no idea where it is so I can't cancel it. The publicity of my death would increase the band's following. He made sure everyone else was on the stage by the back doors, except for the bassist."

"Lexa, I already told you my thoughts aren't about killing you."

"My dad wrote letters to me from 'Nam, but they stopped after six months. He was a changed man when he returned. I feel some guilt now for the way I left home," she said.

"I remember my first day in the field. A Huey helicopter was shot down about a hundred yards away in a rice paddy. I resigned myself the minute I saw the crash that I'd never make it out of there. We dragged so many dead soldiers out of the fields. I couldn't allow myself to get attached to anyone."

"It sounds horrific."

"You could see tracer rounds shooting into the jungle and fire flares of howitzers shooting all night long. I broke the squelch on the radio every ten to fifteen minutes so they knew I was still alive in the blackness. I thought I saw imaginary things and kept getting told to shut up, but we were all on those bennies, I mean Benzedrine, to keep awake for thirty hours and it starts to mess up your brain. I was not a fan of the government and how those in power use people, even before I ever landed over there. My grandmother knew if I didn't control my anger it would destroy me."

"And has it destroyed you?"

"Maybe. About thirty clicks from Saigon, I fought for my life to protect the corporate interest in the Michelin rubber plantations which stretched for several miles. The betrayal I felt was consuming."

"The men who supported the war, Lyndon Johnson died in '73. The Gulf of Tonkin incident which started the war was in '64. Richard Nixon who was almost impeached, resigned in 74. I have no sympathy for either of them," she said.

"What the men in power did was cause the Viet Cong to form alliances with not only Russia who supplied missile crews and weapons, but China who supplied weapons and helped set up the Ho Chi Minh trail, the elaborate underground tunnels. We were nothing more than living targets."

"There are no words to make you feel at peace about what happened," she said. "Who is the beautiful woman in the flowing clothing? She was holding a baby. The photo…on your dresser."

"One was of me and my mother. The other was my wife, Kim–Ly and my son. We met during my R and R, rest and recoup," he said.

"Wars chew people up, and they are never the same again".

"It's easy for men in fancy offices to lay down rules for people who must obey them, while they have little remorse for the devastation they've caused," he said.

"I think I've taken up enough of your time," she said. "Thank you for seeing me."

"It's okay. I can't believe I vented so much to you. I've never talked about it before," he said.

Lexa held onto his forearm as she stared at him. "Now I have some idea as to why my Dad came back so messed up. What torments you is worse than what I'm going through. If you ever want to talk again, you have my number, and you get schedules of where my band plays. I will leave your name on the guest list, and my invitation for you to make peace with your mom still stands." She stepped outside, shivered in her coat and turned around to face him. "I'm serious about visiting your Mom. Her energy is in those rooms, and she's waiting for you." When he closed the door, she measured the glass of the window on it.

In returning her books to the library, Lexa referenced where the headquarters of Michelin was. *I think I may have figured out where three or maybe four of his trucks are headed, she thought. If he's not trying to kill me, who is? Aldar? The wacko groupie Kalie Deckler? Sam? His ex-girlfriend, Janie?*

Back in her house, she opened the box of fan mail and studied the letters written on yellow steno paper. The letter Shane insisted he wrote had capitalized letters within words, which she previously thought didn't signify anything. She took out a pencil and counted out every eight letters which were in caps. The message read: SAFE WITH ME ONLY. Then, C7T. She remembered the Department of Transportation numbers on the trucks.

Socrates words, "The only good is knowledge and the only evil is ignorance," shifted her thoughts in determining how she could stop the doomsday dreams that stole what little sleep she could attain.

Monday, November 15, 1976
On June 10, 1963, John Kennedy had given a speech, ending it with, "The United States as the world knows it will never start a war. We do not want a war, we do not expect a war. This generation of Americans has already had enough - more than enough - of war and hate and oppression." Five months later he

was assassinated, and within nine months of his death, president Lyndon Johnson lit the torch on the Vietnam war.

Shane is agonized by the inhumanities of Vietnam, and is plotting more carnage.

I believe he plans to send explosive trucks to the corporate offices of Michelin in Greenville, South Carolina, as well as the place of the constitution and headquarters of the FBI: Washington DC. The other cities would be a guess, maybe New York, Dallas and Los Angeles, and I cannot let him in on what I know if I wish to be around much longer. I picked up five more magazine clips for the 45 and will have a gift ready for him if he decides to "visit his Mom". Little time is left before he deploys and carries out his itinerary. Despite insomnia and stomach pain, I must have a plan ready before 1/1/77. I will need gunpowder, potassium chlorate, dynamite, sulfuric acid, and seven steel pipes. Tiny can easily get this for me.

CHAPTER 18

GIFTS

She walked through aisles at the Harry Schwartz bookstore, browsed through fiction and non-fiction, opened several books including 'Handbook to Higher Consciousness' by Ken Keys, Jr., fifth edition and 'Johnathan Living Seagull', by Richard Bach.

It is not enough, Lexa thought, opening a cookbook and writing out a recipe for chocolate chip cookies. She paid for her purchases and left. *I need to convince him his plan will do more harm than good. Innocent deaths only accomplish more heartbreak.*

The drive to the Milwaukee Public library was under thick gray snow clouds. Fascinated by the ornate architecture, she opened the doors, approached the reference desk, and asked where the work of

Leo Tolstoy was. She was directed to 'Classics of Non-Violence no. 3, translation by L Perno, published by Peace Pledge Union, London 1943. Inside, a letter written by Leo Tolstoy titled, "A Letter to a Hindu", comprised insights of the Hindu Kural, one of which was: "The Punishment of evil doers consists in making them feel ashamed of themselves by doing them a great kindness." *Beautiful words, but beyond difficult to accomplish.*

She discovered words of courage documented on parchment by Martin Luther King: "Hatred paralyzes life, love releases it. Hatred confuses life, love harmonizes it. Hatred darkens life, love illuminates it. In the end we will remember not the words of our enemies, but the silence of our friends."

Words of Mahatma Gandhi became visible in her notebook: "An eye for an eye makes the whole world blind...all through history the way of truth and love has always won. There have been tyrants and murderers, and for a time they seem invincible, but in the end they always fall--think of it always."

"I need to be prepared if Shane shows up," she said closing her notebook. "He's enmeshed in his personal war."

Gift wrapping the books and a notebook comprising words of peace, she baked chocolate chip cookies, allowed them to cool before freezing them, and studied quotes, remembering the old adage, 'The pen is mightier than the sword'.

En route to Gateway Technical College in Kenosha, she wrote these words in a notebook. She memorized the quotes while she changed her clothes in the Chemistry room the students had offered as her dressing room, and during breaks of Word Locket's show.

Monday, November 22, 1976

I'm not sure if Shane and his entourage will buy into Doctor King's words, though profound as they are; "Only light can banish darkness; only love can banish hate." Does anything exist to erase one's obsession with revenge? It appears he may have already buried himself across the street, where tombstones and the dead hover in his thoughts. Of my own strategies to work through, one will bring peace and the other will leave lifelong torment. Both are the flip of a coin.

On Thursday, 11/25, Sam invited Lexa to have Thanksgiving dinner at his parents' home. After dinner, Debra and Lexa helped put dishes away while Sam and Ted had video game competitions. Sam's dad wanted to join and he asked Lexa to be his partner. They played against Sam and Ted and lost both times. Leaving at 11:30, Lexa thanked everyone for the lovely evening, including Sam during their drive in the VW.

"When your parents discover the truth about us, they will blame me because you're their angel. I had a good time tonight. By the way, I read about Hindu's. They can get a shot if it's medically necessary like anyone else. I don't think that excuse will work for you next time."

"Yea, but the doctor and nurse won't have a clue," he laughed.

"It's a good thing they gave you those antibiotics."

"Where are those, anyway?"

"I...needed them," said Lexa.

On Friday, 11/26, Lexa woke up in a panic. Five weeks remained to convince a deranged genius to stop a plan of annihilation. She ate an egg and toast, brushed her teeth and packed for the show.

What is it that always calms me? What got me through those thunderstorms and loneliness as a kid? Lexa drove to an art supply store where she purchased a 24" by 36" canvas, numerous colors of acrylic paints and brushed on the primer, to allow it to dry while she would be romping on a stage in a club, where the owner had to handle irate police regarding noise complaints. As she sang, smiled, moved, laughed and danced, none of the 450 fans could tell how dizzy, nauseous and exhausted she felt. She ran off the stage to hide a nose bleed after their final encore.

At Saturday's show, she ran off the stage during the last set. Her bloody nose took a while to stop. Target practice was added to her list of tasks for Sunday, 11/28, but she felt so wilted, it took extra exertion to get to a shooting facility where she improved her skills on the heavy weapon. Back in her room, she began painting on the canvas.

"Lexa, where were you? I was thinking you could do some vocal tracks in the studio today," said Sam, who knocked on her entryway.

"Sure." She secured her painting supplies and sang for an hour until her throat felt dry.

"I'm getting some water," she said. "Be back in a few." At the kitchen sink, she looked over her right shoulder as she took a sip of water, and sitting near the outside doorway was a hardware store bag containing the same steel pipe attached to the bomb near the sofa at the Palms night club. *How convenient. He sells my songs and music after I'm gone.* Under the sink, she dredged through detergents, dish cloths, towels, garbage and engine oil. *Where would he hide an insurance policy?* "How much longer did you want to record today?" she said loudly.

"At least another thirty minutes," he said.

"No problem. Be right there."

On Wednesday, Lexa ran up the steps as soon as Sam left the house, dug through all of his drawers, closets and cabinets, but there was nothing of value to her. She returned to her bedroom, admired the painting she planned to give to Shane, rehearsed original material during sound checks, hustled through gigs, and wondered if the cold weather brought on a virus.

Queasy and tired when she awoke on Saturday December 4, she opened the Yellow Pages to look up the glass repair shop that had fixed her basement window and was told they would be able to fix a 17" by 18" pane, provided it was at the time of their business hours: 8:00 am to 4:30 pm. She jotted down the phone number, placed it into her purse, and knew her schedule would give no opportunity to sneak through Zadrik's belongings until Monday, 12/6.

At noon, she parked her Volkswagen on a gravel road in the cemetery and as she was about to cross the street, a five second vision of a fiery blaze engulfing Shane's house disappeared in a blink. *If I warn him, he'll never understand,* she thought clutching the black purse at her side held by a shoulder strap. She rang the back buzzer, and knocked repeatedly. If anyone answered, she planned on giving them the note she had written to Shane.

"Lucky break. Thank you," she said looking upward.

She pulled leather gloves on, took the hammer out of her black purse, backed away while holding it over her face to protect her head and smashed the window of the back door, creating an array of chimes in different tones raining down along the step. She used the hammer to smooth out sharp edges, reached in to unlock the entryway, took the phone off the kitchen wall and dialed the number to Same Day Glass Service to send someone out as soon as possible to 1745 W. Hopkins St.

She opened the container of cooked meat, dumped the pieces into Boffo's bowl while stroking his fur, telling him what a good dog he was and swept every last shred of glass into the doubled paper bags she brought. To make a quick getaway, she placed the bag outside the front door, making sure to leave it slightly open.

Lexa headed to the bookshelf, opened random books and picked up one that explained how nuclear fusion creates less radioactive material than fission. It detailed how fission increases the number of unstable atoms, releases more energy and starts a chain reaction. She ransacked through most of the books and carefully replaced them.

The inspection of Nick's room was uneventful. She felt sadness when she picked up a diamond ring sitting in a small black velvet box at the bottom of his sock drawer. *I wish you love and happiness.*

In her search of the medicine cabinet of the bathroom facing the kitchen, she saw toiletries, toothbrushes, razors and boxes of several different hair dye colors, including one called golden blonde. The bathroom across the hall from Nick's room had more of the same.

Across from Shane's room, next to Nicky's, which she guessed was Al's room, Lexa rummaged through his closet, bedding, and in the bottom drawer of his dresser, she uncovered pantyhose, 5/8" white utility nylon rope, duct tape, and ten faded newspaper articles about strangled women, including the one she had read in December of 1973 in the college cafeteria. Three photos were of women on their backs, their eyes and mouths half open lying near gravestones. *He took pictures. Why would this sleazy man have these? Souvenirs? He has a preoccupation with death in all forms. He took my nylons and socks. He's disgusting.* She spotted ten itineraries of her band with the photo on one side and schedule of the month's performances on the other, and could not believe what she held as she returned the items under t-shirts and underwear. It was the yellow steno notepad.

He wrote the other letters. He is alive, and reporting a dead man to the police will not go over well. I have your damn address, you sadist, and it's my turn to leave a letter. She arose and answered the doorbell to the man from the Glass Service who began measuring the window. While she waited for the installation, she ripped a page out of a notepad.

Hi Al,

Thanks for all your nice notes. How good of you to inform me of your whereabouts. I told all of my friends, my bandmates and Debra. We don't care about a lowlife like you any more than you care about us. Maybe we will pay you a visit late at night while you are sleeping. I know you would like to meet the women you tried to murder, but failed -wouldn't you?   *LXa*

She left the drawers open and the letter on his dresser. *His anger will notch up his eye spasms.*

The new window is too clean, Lexa thought as she counted cash in the young man's hand before he left, then removed the manufacturer's sticker and alongside the ground, cupped a handful of dirt to blot onto the window. She rubbed it off to appear as close to its previous condition as she was able.

The locksmith she had called, arrived at the time agreed upon, ten minutes after the window was repaired and she played the role of a ditzy housewife, as the nice man in the van, advertised by keys painted on its side, stepped in while she stroked Boffo's fur. Six pennies remained in her wallet after paying him. She returned to her snooping.

In Shane's room, she opened drawers, saw the Hendrix guitar strap and her photos in a shoebox and in opening the bottom drawer, she removed old, discolored notebooks, scanned through his diaries and read.

"While stationed in Saigon, we were informed of the US sanctioning a single-party election and in the months that followed, we were fighting for our lives."

She skimmed through countless words, some disappearing under smudges.

"Americans were stirred into the quagmire of Vietnam's cauldron of complexities and ended up at the bottom of the heap in the hell of a holocaust that devastated its own country. Bodies were bulldozed into mass graves. Their wounded and starving people proved that no one won. Generations there will suffocate from chemical warfare and an entire generation of Americans will contend with the aftermath."

Four more dates were boldly written.

11/02/63: Leader of South Vietnam: Diem is killed.
11/22/63: Leader of the US: John F. Kennedy is killed.
4/4/68: Martin Luther King is killed.
6/6/68: Robert F. Kennedy is killed. No Coincidence.

She wondered if this was related to his fixation of numbers and what kind of guilt hung over him for being a factor in the spreading of chemicals that destroyed food, decimated foliage on leaves so planes could visualize the ground, and would sicken or kill not only the enemy, but fellow soldiers who had been exposed. She replaced his notebook.

Back in Al's room, she grabbed five pairs of underwear and three pairs of socks, and threw them up into the tree. Suitcase in hand, she double checked the lock, and taped a note to the window.

Hi Shane, don't forget that someone is waiting for you at your former house. I've decided how you can repay me. Please call. X.

Her breath searing through the graveyard and a heavy purse banging into her side, she ran holding a flashlight in one hand and in the other, a paper bag clinking glass shards. The horizon closed in on the sun, fighting to shed its last flickers of light between the headstones. Spirits of the deceased sat up to smile and some floated around her grinning and pointing the way, not to her car, but to sites where fresh sod lay. She turned around to track their wispy auras that faded into the diminishing twilight. Her flashlight shone on a gravesite where she scraped the snow off of fresh sod and pulled it up to expose a twelve inch diameter gray rock emitting heat.

It looks like a ring of Uranium I saw in one of Shane's books, she thought, using her boots to stomp the sod back. She had read how Plutonium is made by bombarding Uranium with neutrons to make nuclear weapons. Her steps crunched into icy terrain as she walked to the Volkswagen, aided by the light of the full moon.

Monday, December 6, 1976

Three weeks and six days until a deadly radioactive fallout. I'll have to work around all the upcoming shows and ask Karl to help me let the air out of the truck tires, or blow up the rigs. I've become weak and tired all the time because of insomnia. It is as though I am walking under water and have no stamina or balance.

a girl a band a diary

Going to police will cause more problems. My story of Shane, whose death certificate is on file, as well as Al's, will not be believed. Lacking tangible proof, I'm still a primary suspect.

In picking up the phone ringing at 12:30 on Thursday, Lexa's drowsiness cleared enough to comprehend that it was Shane's voice, and she sat she straight up hoping the right words would come to her to extend an invitation for him to visit. He agreed to meet her that evening. *He read the note I left.* She pulled out her recipe and baked several batches of chocolate chip cookies.

Julette where are you? She dressed and ate a sandwich, ran to the elderly neighbor woman's house to acquire details about Julette, as to how her hair was combed, what her scent had been like, what words she often said and was given a few ideas.

"Thanks for your help. I baked some cookies for you and your husband."

The woman looked surprised in accepting the gift and thanked Lexa who then drove to the grocery store, and at home vacuumed and dusted, made baked potatoes, a salad of mixed greens, and sautéed a steak, and carrots. While food waited in a warm oven, she pinned her hair into a French twist, wore her black knee-length pencil skirt, chose a plain tan sweater and fastened a strand of pearls around her neck.

She wrapped the cookies into a gift box, and sat it alongside the books, the notebook she had written in, and a 24 by 36 inch canvas of a painting done in acrylic, of a beach sunrise was wrapped in brown paper packaging.

She lit incense and three thick white candles on her dining room table, and guided the needle onto the grooves of the Aretha Franklin in Paris album.

The doorbell rang, she opened the door, and felt sadness.

Shane's once well-fitting black leather jacket hung on him, unkempt black and blonde hair was pushed behind his ears, and deep, dark circles rose above his cheeks. He shivered in baggy dark blue jeans and black snakeskin boots.

It was her father walking in the door five years ago, into a kitchen where her family ate dinner together, the room where they celebrated birthdays and Candy and Abbie giggled until Dad being tormented by the choke hold of his past, silenced any hint of laughter.

"Hi. I'm glad you could make it. Come in," she said smelling the food wafting around them and her scent of baby powder. "How is your leg?"

"Doing well, thanks. It's almost healed," he said removing his jacket and handing it to her, exposing an ill-fitting blue thermal shirt. She led him into the living room where he surveyed her large bookshelf, fireplace, paintings and plants. "It's strange standing in my childhood home. It didn't used to be a duplex. My parents slept downstairs, and my bedroom was upstairs," he said. "It looks nice. I like the artwork."

"Thank you. Painting is therapeutic for me. It's nice to see you again. I hope you're hungry. My schedule is busy, and I haven't made a decent meal in ages. I also have a few gifts for you," she said.

"Why did you do that? I can't accept them," he said turning away.

"I thought you'd like some home-made chocolate chip cookies. You looked so happy when you talked about your grandmother making them for you."

"My grandmother passed away while I was in Nam. I never made it to her funeral and never said goodbye," he said in a tone of bitterness.

Lexa glanced at the corner next to the bookshelf where she had sat the day she was told of her grandfather's death, remembering her sadness in never having the courage to say what she wished. "I've often had a suffocating sensation in the back room. Sometimes I think I'm feeling what your mom may have when she passed on. Did anyone tell you why she died so young?"

"I always knew it was my Dad. Always. I hated him."

"After I moved into this house, I felt a sense of darkness and gloom. In one of the closets, the socket made light bulbs fizzle like sparklers. I thought it was an electrical problem, but when the neighbor told me about the death in the bedroom, it made me wonder if there could be a connection. Especially because I've had many dreams about Julette. If her spirit is still lingering, she may have unfinished business and maybe I was meant to bring you here if nothing else, to let her know you're okay and she can move on."

"I... I can't tell her I'm okay. I think she'd know it's a lie."

"I'm sorry. Let's eat before the oven dries out our dinner." Lexa accompanied him into the kitchen where she had preset the table, and arranged the spread of food.

"I reread the letters my Dad sent from Nam. I barely recognized him when he got back," she said as they ate.

"This is really good, thank you," he said. "I haven't had a decent meal in a while. As much as I don't want to think about that hellhole, it stays with me 24/7. So many things trigger memories of it. Even you," he said staring through her.

"Memories of Nam or of someone you knew?"

"Of Kim-Ly and my son. They're buried over there."

"I'm sorry. I doubt my gifts will ease your pain, but please take them anyway." she said dropping her eyes downward.

"In my heart I was an American doing my job even though it was the farthest thing from my mind to be thrown into a war. When fellow soldiers lost their lives around me, I would think, 'he died for this place'? Every day there were casualties and snipers. The Viet Cong were quick, hardcore, ruthless and prepared to die. They had no problem killing soldiers, civilians, peasants, merchants or anyone who got in their way." He pushed his fork around the plate.

"I can't imagine how horrid it must have been."

"My hands were dripping with so much sweat, I worried I might drop my machine gun weighed down by 100 rounds of ammo. When our squads got thirsty, we dipped our containers into rice paddies and puddles, knowing chemicals were sprayed by our own men. The stench gagged us even though we plugged our noses and tossed in a couple of Halizone tablets. The smell became putrid in the heat where bodies deteriorated. The constant air strikes stirred up the bloody muck."

"When I'd get home after my hospital shift and had nights of caring for those who battled an illness, or lose their life, I was rattled and couldn't sleep. I repeated to myself over and over, that I signed on for it, but it didn't make it any easier. Their gray faces never left me. I can't imagine how you must have been affected." she said. "In the end, it's up to you if you let bad memories destroy you. I guess if you're ever ready, you'll be able to let go and move on."

"My grandmother used to say something like that," he said.

"For me, I've thought of evil on this planet like certain kinds of cancers. You can't chop off one part when aberrant cells are roaming through the rest of the body and expect healing. I saw my share of death in the hospital, both young and old. I had to somehow cope, keep my head up, and get through each day."

"What did you do?" he asked.

"We're not designed to last forever. Some never make it out of the womb and some live more than 100 years, but ultimately, the body will face its day of reckoning. My job became the helper of preserving dignity, of making peace with the inevitable. I did my best to bring on a smile or a laugh. When someone walked out of the unit healed, they never knew how happy I felt for them. When the band dates escalated, I had to switch to a clinic."

He stared at the gold band on the ring finger of his left hand, using his thumb to spin it around. "I don't know how you talked me into coming here. I'll never be able to get near the back room. My dad knew about the ingestion of chemicals long before I did."

"Is it possible we were meant to connect and speak to one another? Because of you, I ended up on a path I would never have begun."

"I don't know." Shane's head dropped downward and he rubbed his temples. "Thank you for this delicious meal. I've been eating a lot of junk and snacks."

"You're welcome. What did your parents' bedroom look like? The walls were white when I moved in," said Lexa as she stood up and set dishes in the sink.

"It was ordinary. A bed, dresser, nightstand. Dad gave it all away when we left. It meant nothing to him, and might be what got me through Nam…being forced to let go of people and things."

"Learning to let go…sounds like my life. Then, oddly one day you see me picking roses outside and now here you are, looking at old familiar rooms and talking to me. Let's visit your former neighbors," she said, grabbing his hand, leading him out of the kitchen. "She wondered what happened to you and I know her husband would love to see you."

"No way." He pulled his hand away, and let out a small chuckle.

"Just kidding, but it's nice to see you laugh. And you can pay me back for helping you heal, with a little D-Tubocurarine Tetrodotoxin."

"What are you talking about? I don't give that stuff away. It's too hard to come by and it's perilous," he said as Lexa pulled him toward the bedroom until he was close enough to look inside. She grabbed her presents off of her desk and placed them into his hands.

"These are for you. Take them."

"Thank you," he said.

"You have more than enough powder. You can spare a little bit."

"I don't think so," he said. "Why do you want it?"

"For the same reason you did. I need to be prepared for any unusual circumstance," she said. "I lit some candles on my dining room table in the hopes you may want to speak to your mom."

"What are you talking about?" he asked.

"Let's try a séance. Do you think Julette will respond?"

"I'm not interested. At least not today. I really agonized about even coming over here," he said. "Before I forget, Aldar went into a rage when he saw your note on his dresser. I don't know how, but he will retaliate. And I won't be able to stop him."

"I wrote it because he stalked me, harassed me, and wrote the same kind of letters."

"I don't put it past him," said Shane.

"I'm glad you visited, really, even if you aren't able to make peace with your mom." She accompanied him down the steps, turned on the porch light and both saw broken cookies strewn across the ground.

"Wait. I'll get a broom," she said. She swept up a path for him.

"Did you share these with your nasty neighbor?" he asked.

"I pity the wife who puts up with him," said Lexa.

Thursday, December 9, 1976

Sometimes no act of kindness exists to make another like you. There is nothing I can say or do to give the evil neighbor any concern for me.

No one is immune from emotional or physical pain. It tends to remain in our memories. I may be nailed to a see-saw of up and down days, but Shane's detached wings lie crumpled on a war zone, entrenched in his pain fields of mud, blood, shrapnel and mortars. Though I have my days of guilt, he is engulfed in it; powerless to stop his father from killing his mother and powerless to stop the death of his wife and son. His friend Hendrix went on to share his music with the world and died physically. Shane died emotionally and still walks on a battlefield.

a girl a band a diary

CHAPTER 19

FADING

Lexa leapt into her desk diary and submerged herself in the numbers, dates and club bookings on the calendar. The band resonated their music to fans who acted as though they had been best friends for years. The musicians were let in on personal secrets, infidelities and divorces almost as though they were confessionals for strangers, ears which listened to grievances and having no one to tell, made the secrets safe.

On the calendar, the saying for the week was: "Praise: something a person tells you about yourself that you suspected all along."

"Not a bad idea, praise someone whose self-esteem is at rock bottom," she pondered while tapping her fingernails on the pages, sitting at her kitchen table. Photo sessions, rehearsals in the studio, dates at Bunky's, Shuffle In and Headliners in Madison, Jackson Pavillion in Iowa, and Crazes in Chicago were lined up. She jotted down ideas of what gifts she might give to her family. She packed her suitcase, and drove to the shopping mall until she had to leave for the show. At home, she made it to the bathroom in time to vomit and took a cool washcloth to swab the sweat off her skin. Snacking on a few dry crackers, she pulled herself together and left.

Her bandmates got situated in the van for the long drive. She settled on the bed in the back, where she slept until they arrived. The dressing room at the show revealed how pale she had become.

"Man, I need to pull myself together, or no one's going to go out of their way to watch me sing anymore," she said to Karl while applying extra make up to her face.

She felt dizzy on stage, but a surge of fear stabbed her when she saw Al Geitlich bathed in red stage lights staring at her through of the crowd of faces. He unbuttoned his shirt and pulled it out of his jeans, pushed his hand between his legs, exaggerated a stroking movement with his right arm, and blew a kiss to her. Though her stomach tightened as he traced her every move on stage, she pretended to be unaffected, and kept close to roadies and band members. She hid on the back bed in the van at the end of the night.

Sunday, December 12, 1976
Karl thought I was joking when I asked him to help me let the air out of truck tires. When I explained I was serious, and it was related to the bomb in our dressing room, he said he would help me, but he will have to explain his whereabouts to his new girlfriend who recently moved into his apartment. I asked if her name was Kalie. He laughed and said 'No'.

Al's frozen stare fixates on me as though his thoughts are elsewhere. His dilated pupils are like radar guns. He has no moral compass, no empathy, and I am onto him. My note most likely gave him a tantrum.

Sam walked down the steps to get the food he stored in the refrigerator and Ebbie cried to be let out.

"Lexa, where are you?"

"In the bedroom." She kept her eyes closed and hovered under blankets.

"You don't look so good," he said, keeping his distance from her.

"I have a virus I can't shake," she said.

"Do you want me to take you to a doctor?"

"I have no health insurance and I hate doctors. I'm sure I'll be better in a few days. I need longer stretches of sleep. Would you throw a piece of bread to me?"

"Uh...sure."

Dragging herself out of bed took added effort, but she managed to down an egg, toast and orange juice, and added vitamins and green vegetables to her shopping list. At home she unloaded groceries and made a meal, convincing herself she would have more energy soon.

She practiced her guitar and scribbled out numerous ideas of how to stop a group of renegades, but her brain felt muddled. She fell asleep on her waterbed, holding the guitar and notebook on top of her.

On Tuesday, she finished her Christmas shopping and purchased a gift for Shane, a brown thermal long-sleeved shirt.

On the afternoon of Thursday 12/16, Lexa selected clothes and reorganized her suitcase to prepare for a show that evening, when she was interrupted by Tiny's voice on the phone.

"You sittin' down?" he asked.

"No, why? I've been meaning to call you," she said. "Where can I get gunpowder, potassium chlorate, dynamite, sulfuric acid, and seven steel pipes?"

"Lexa, stay away from those Zadrik people. If you blow up their trucks, it will destroy the entire city like an atomic bomb. They're messed up in some heavy stuff. They're dangerous. All of them."

"I saw a lot of explosives at their funeral home. They are unhinged," she said.

"I saw them loading stuff into trucks at the Final Rest on Columbia St. wearing haz mat suits," he said.

"Haz mat?"

"Hazardous material suits. Serious body protecting gear. I think you should pretend they no longer exist to you."

"I appreciate your taking the time to check it out, but I don't understand why," she said.

"I don't trust them, and when I get a bad sense I scope things out," he said. "And what you said about them rattled me."

"Are you going to help me stop them?" she asked.

"No, I called to warn you to stay as far away as you can."

"What do you think they're going to do with what's in the trucks?"

"Are you serious? They will flatten a city or two," he said.

"Exactly. Probably several cities. Think about it. It could be someone near and dear to you who becomes a victim. Ask yourself if you want your conscience weighed down by guilt."

"There are a gang of heavyweight men involved," he replied. "I prefer to stay in one piece. We'll be dead if we interfere."

"We'll be dead if we don't. How many trucks did you see?"

"Seven," he said.

"Do you know when they'll nuke these cities?" she asked

"I have no idea."

"Inscrutable," she said.

"Huh?"

"Unexplainable…baffling," she said.

"Oh…listen, I'm taking time out of my day to tell you to stay away from those guys. I don't want to become an unidentified body shoved into a morgue."

"If they obliterate your home town you won't have a choice." she replied, and hung up.

Tiny was proficient at his job and despite his mass, he knew how to disappear in a crowd. He had clientele who paid him more than she could, and it was not the first nor would it be the last time she and an associate had different views. She returned to her pen and notebook.

Thursday, December 16, 1976

Shane has to be calling the shots, Nick is his strong man and the rest are in it for the paycheck. Nick is most likely the beneficiary of Zadrik's life insurance policy and they have no money worries. They have an armory of weapons and explosives. Aldar, who changes his hair color to fit his moods is most likely a psychopath and has no problem ending lives including his mother's to collect on her insurance and the sale of her estate. They are carrying out a vengeful plot of destruction and I haven't figured out how to put a crimp in it yet.

The sight of Tarick as he had strummed his guitar on stage during his shows wearing a black shirt and peace sign choker made her smile for a moment and she imagined herself giving him a sweet kiss.

She checked her watch and had one hour to find a peace sign pendant and chain before sound check started. She threw her suitcase into the front compartment of the VW.

She bought a red and white Santa Claus cap and sleigh bells attached to a band of red ribbon, a three foot pine tree, a string of white lights and two boxes of multi-colored ornaments. *It's worth a try. Hopefully it will trigger memories of their past.*

She made it home in time to climb into the yellow van, where her bandmates argued about how to change the set lists, whose turn it was to pump gas, and what they were going to do about the broken channel on the sound board.

Friday, December 17, 1976

I have felt too fatigued to acquire supplies to make bombs. I managed to hide my stomach pain at the show tonight. I'll be treading on thin ice, but have nothing to lose by showing up on Hopkins St. bearing gifts. Karl has my will in the event it doesn't go well.

a girl a band a diary

Used in nuclear bombs and reactors, toxic, radioactive plutonium can boil water from the energy it releases in alpha decay. Once in the bloodstream, it remains in the body, bones and internal organs forever.

The successive days involved traveling, including Edgewater in Twin Lakes. At Elmo's Ballroom in Platteville, the band became rock stars having a fabulous time on a stage to dancers and partiers.

On Sunday afternoon when Sam made his daily trip to the refrigerator, he looked to his right, to see Lexa's head nestled on the kitchen table. "Are you sure you don't want me to take you a doctor?"

"I don't like doctors," she said straightening up and turning her pallid features to him.

"You look awful, but it's up to you. Did you want to go to my mom and dad's party this Saturday on Christmas Day?

"Why…will your parents think something is wrong with our perfect relationship? Sure. I wrapped a few things for everyone. I bought Ted some new guitar strings and a strap, since his is frayed and for Debra, I bought silver filigree earrings with a matching necklace."

"You didn't have to do that," he said.

"I got them a while ago and was going to give them to you anyway. *I must look really bad for you to pity me.* "Why aren't you taking your new girlfriend to your parent's house?"

"My Mom would freak out. Are you going to be okay tonight?"

"I'll be fine." She brushed the sweat off of her forehead.

To get to Headliners in Madison, they left at 3:00 pm, stopped at Taco Johns, where Lexa took over driving so Sam could eat, then stopped to pick up Ted, Grant and Karl, who were waiting at Karl's flat. Karl had a sore throat and had lost his voice, so the set lists had to be rewritten to cut his songs out of the show. *I hope he doesn't think he got sick because of me.*

"You're a trouper, Karl," said Lexa after the show. "It isn't easy."

"You should talk," he said. "You aren't well either, but we managed to get through the night."

The roads were icy and the van slipped and slid all the way back to Milwaukee. Relieved after returning Ted, Grant and Karl to their residences and parking the van in the garage, Lexa made a decision to rehearse her role as Mrs. Santa.

When she awoke, she baked a batch of chocolate chip cookies and wrapped them in three separate containers. Annoyed that her jeans felt so snug considering how little she had eaten over the past week, she ate a small bowl of cereal that seemed more difficult than usual to swallow. She applied extra makeup to cover her pale cheekbones and buttoned up her tan suede coat.

Her items stuffed into large shopping bags, she arrived at her destination, pulled the plush red cap trimmed by white fur onto her head and rang the front buzzer.

"Ho, ho, ho, Merry Christmas," she said shaking the sleigh bells stitched onto the red velvet ribbon as a chill rocked through her. "Mrs. Santa has some presents," she smiled as the door opened.

Shane stared at Lexa in disbelief. His body was hunched forward and his arms were wrapped around himself shivering as he looked at her through matted blonde hair with black roots. His opened mouth, said nothing, and his gaunt appearance alarmed her.

"You okay?" she asked, receiving no answer from him.

"Who is it?" said Nick's deep voice.

"Hi Nick, it's Lexa. I won't stay long. I wanted to drop off a few things." She began to tremble.

"What the hell is going on?" bellowed Al Geitlich who now had auburn chin-length hair combed behind his ears. It was hard to miss the spasm-like blinks of his left eye. "Well looky who's here. Miss Santy Claus." He stood beside her, wrapped his arm around her neck, and breathed into the side of her head. "Ain't she cute, fellas?"

"Merry Christmas," she said, raising her fragile courage like a white flag. "I brought something for all of you," she said unbuttoning her coat, pulling away from Aldar.

Except for Boffo's sniffing, all was silent as she opened the first bag, took out the narrow cut pine encircled by lights secured to a small tree stand, and the scent of evergreen filled the room.

"Where can I place this?" she asked surveying the living room.

"Put it in my room. I'll show you what to do with it," screeched Al.

"Al, stop," said Shane. "Put it by the window. You can plug the lights into the wall outlet.

"Thanks," she said, trying to remain calm. "Would anyone like to hang ornaments?"

More quizzical looks were exchanged between the men. She pulled out the wrapped gifts. "This one's for you," she said to Shane. "The nice plaque you gave me is on my hallway wall," she lied. "This is for you, Nick and this is for you, Al," she said shuddering. They appeared stunned as they held onto boxes void of a clue as to how to interpret the unexpected visit.

"I need to get going," she said as she left the sleigh bells and remainder of the ornaments on a chair to soundlessness.

She let herself out, taking one last glance at the dumbfounded men who looked as though they had witnessed an apparition from the graveyard across the street. "Merry Christmas," she said as she waved at them and scrambled to the VW to start up the engine. White lights on a green tree twinkled through the window.

That went well, she thought, or maybe not. She began laughing. I am still alive. She tossed the red and white cap on the seat next to her, and wondered if the trucks were still parked at the funeral home. In driving past it, three black digits on the door of the cabs stood out. All were marked C7T, the Department of Transportation numbers.

Wednesday, December 22, 1976

I'm not sure what Shane means by 'safe with me'. He hasn't asked me to join him on his venture. I wonder how he intends to keep me safe. My unwelcomed visit has irritated Al, but Shane and Nick didn't seem to mind. Al may plan more retaliation after what I did to his things. I've put a few more pieces into place, but I still have a long way to go. Will Shane wear the peace sign necklace and read the letter I tucked into the shirt?

She wondered if the effort she had put into writing the letter and wrapping cookies into colorful paper would be worth her while and she reminded herself if they didn't eat them, Boffo would devour them and leave another present for them to think about.

Dear Shane,   *December 22, 1976*

On the day you were born and a beautiful, dark-haired new mother held you in her arms, I have complete faith it was one of the happiest days of her life. She thought about all that she needed to share with you to guide you to a happy and successful future. Though your lives did not go as she wished, and if time could be turned back for you to relive the happy memories, she would know you have become a great and thoughtful man who has an amazing future unfolding before you. Although perhaps it may not seem like it to you, she and your grandmother did their best to show you that you were loved and an important part of their family. They would be proud of your brilliance and how you are able to achieve whatever it is that you dream of. I hope you never underestimate the abilities you possess. My wish for you is to live your life to its fullest in great health and happiness. May you continue to grow into a better man each day with the conviction to reach your dreams, and may the door of opportunity always be open to bring you the best this life has to offer.

Sincerely, Lexa

She wound small, colorful lights around the branches of a pine tree in her living room and hung ornaments, and then wrapped presents for Nathan and his family as well as Sam's family. She arranged them under the tree.

It was time to reattach the license plates to her VW, having avoided being pulled over and ticketed.

Lexa asked Sam if he would join her at Nathan and Polly's on the 24th where an assortment of appetizers, desserts, cookies, and a generous meal was served to the music of Christmas carols. While gifts were exchanged, Lexa sat next to Nathan.

"Did you know that Dad toured field evacuation hospitals?" she asked.

"Yes...I did. He was in body bags registration. Made sure the belongings and all the body parts they could find were sent back with a letter of condolence. Whether it was from mortar fire or a heroin overdose," said Nathan.

"Most likely I never heard about it because I left home so long ago," she said.

"I thought Dad told you."

"He and I never spoke much," she said.

"Nam sucked the life out of him," said Nathan.

"Yes it did," said Lexa. "Wars are the deadly aspect of humanity."

Her young nephews opened gifts, and happily played together. New toys surrounded them. Nathan and Polly had made an elaborate dinner, and invited everyone to eat. Lexa and Nathan discussed their family dynamic for most of the evening.

The drive homeward was quiet, and she and Sam went their separate ways after letting Ebbie play in the snow. She wondered where Tarick was and assumed he had family gatherings also.

At Sam's home the following day, Debra, Lexa, Ted and Sam sang Christmas carols while he worked his fingers on the keys of the baby grand piano. His mother soon accompanied him. They exchanged gifts as though no one had a worry in the world, as though time had wound backwards to happier days. Then all sat down to a generous meal. Lexa and Debra helped clean up while the guys adjourned to play video games and in a short time all teamed up to compete. Lexa took a few photos.

"You're so lucky to be with my son. I remember when I was young and so much in love," Sam's mother said dreamily. Lexa glanced at Sam, Debra raised her eyebrows and Ted burst out laughing. Sam looked mortified.

"He's like drinking a glass of sparkling, silver mercury." *Pretty on the outside, toxic on the inside.*

"I'm glad you appreciate him. He deserves someone who does."

She thanked Sam's family for the invitation before their journey home in a light snowfall.

Worried that her illness was not improving, she thought about getting a new doctor if she wasn't better in the next few days. She appeared so worn out on stage on Sunday the 26th, that in the dressing room during their first break, Karl and Grant insisted that they would take her to a doctor whether she liked it or not.

"Okay, guys take it easy. I'm fine. Let it go. Fans cough and sneeze on us all the time. I'd be okay if I could get a little sleep."

"Here. Take some of my Ativan," said Karl. "I'll give you seven tablets. My dad can get more for me."

"Thanks, Karl." *I need to conserve my pills.*

"Let me know if you need more," he said.

Tuesday, December 28, 1976

After our show ended at the Stone Toad, I went to look for Sam who had driven us to the club. Roadies were packing equipment, and no one had seen him. Grant and Ted had left. Karl and his girlfriend were getting ready to head out. I thought Sam may have been in the club somewhere, since I couldn't imagine him leaving without saying something to one of us, especially me who had depended on him for a ride. When I ran toward the back steps to the door to see if he was in the alley, the heel of my boot slipped on the slick wooden stairwell, and I fell down the stairs, slamming my body onto the landing. I banged my legs up, skinned my knees, scraped my hands and had to pull splinters out of my palms. I asked Drax to take me home after the equipment was packed up. The back steps were a brutal hammered assault. There isn't a spot on my body that doesn't hurt. If I saw Sam burning in hell, I would offer more gasoline.

Thursday, December 30, 1976
Stabbing pains started yesterday and became more intense with cramping as though my insides were working their way out. I writhed into the late night soaked in sweat. The contractions ended to reveal a tiny, lifeless stillborn.

Friday, December 31, 1976
I wrapped the remains in a towel, took a shovel and drove to the Union Cemetery to dig a shallow grave. As I struck the frozen ground, a glowing figure who looked like a young Oma arose toward me. I asked her to watch over the departed, but it was clear by her gestures, that what I placed on the ground was a traveler who had not yet taken a breath in this world.

I mounded snow over the towel as both will disintegrate by the elements of passing days. I curled up onto the hardened earth, where frost seeped into me. If it wasn't for the familiar woman veiled by light who swirled around me, motioning for me to arise, I would have allowed the icy sting carry me to the spirits below.

I remembered Nathan and how we played football together as kids, and holding Candy and Abbie's teeny hands to walk them to the swings, taking them trick-or-treating, and getting them dressed in the morning when they were so small.

As I lie on the ground, my eyes were drawn to the billions of stars above me, the galaxies, the nebulas. Those who have perished are immortalized here by stones bearing their names, and dates of each birth and demise. I gave much thought of how I wish to be remembered. I needed to rise off of the ground and do good things, to be remembered fondly. Never did I hear any of my patients who were facing death in their final moments say they wished they had harmed another person.

CHAPTER 20

FUMES

Undecipherable vocal sounds echoed off of concrete gravestones into the cold, crisp air. Lexa pushed her hair out of her face and raised her body onto her knees. Grabbing onto a grave to pull herself upward, She thought she was delusional, being unable to comprehend so much as a word of what was said, but soon realized she understood it all. That's German.

"Wir machen eine Menge Gelt wenn wir das Plutonium verkaufen."

"Sie werden nie uber dieses wissen," said a voice that sounded like Al, who bellowed a roar. *They will never know about this. They will never know about what?* She thought.

"Mach Schnell. Wir werden es in diesem Eisenbahn abschleissen."
They'll lock what in the truck? Plutonium? Uranium?

"Wir brauchen Sie nicht. Unsere Leistung schmeckt ganz toll," brought on more laughter, and muted voices became distant.

She peeked around headstones in the darkness, left the shovel on the ground, and snuck in the direction of the Final Rest. *Who don't they need? Why don't they speak English?*

Lexa was unable to tell whether she had seen three or four men, and continued in the direction of the voices toward Teutonia St. using gravestones for cover. As she neared the trucks parked in the lot, she saw flashlights moving. Vehicles started up. *They're getting ready. I have no gun and no Mace,* she thought as she crawled closer.

"Teilen wir alles zwischen uns vier.

They're going to split everything between the four of them. He has his own agenda.

"Pass auf! Haben Sie jemand gesehen?"

Damn, I think they saw me. She ran to Shane and Nick's house, took the key given to her by the locksmith, and unlocked the back door. Within minutes, the men stormed inside. Al and his loud chortling army cracked and scraped up walls, clearing the contents out of his room. Looting, ransacking, laughing, German conversation of them selling Plutonium to Russians, and how much cash they stood to make, echoed into her cubicle where she remained motionless.

The closet door opened, and light filtered under the sheet where she was balled up in, and within a five minute span, perspiration covered her body. She closed her eyes and took slow deep breaths. When the back door slammed, she waited another few minutes before wiggling out of her tiny hiding space. Spider webs and dust clumps remained in Al's empty room.

They're going to destroy a lot of lives, she thought, rifling through a kitchen drawer where she took a piece of paper, and wrote:

12/31/76: Al is double crossing you. I know for a fact, watch out, X. She tucked the note under Shane's pillow, retrieved her shovel, and returned home at 11:30 pm. She opened her travel bag and picked up her diary.

Friday, December 31, 1976 continued:

The faces on a ten foot statue of an angelic woman and child facing a man appeared to breathe in the darkness. I watched my breath rise into the air and become the vapor that separates the living from the dead. It was the life force I felt as each cold breath entered and warm breath left my body. Keep breathing, Oma said, You must keep breathing. She blew a kiss to me and vanished. Then I heard a voice say, "You found him," but it may have been the cold wind flowing around me, or perhaps I heard Milyana.

As she returned her journal, Debra's small plastic bottles peered out of the pocket of her suitcase. She opened and stared at the contents of each. She took out a Nembutal, opened the capsule and stuck her tongue onto the powdery contents. The bitter taste numbed her mouth. *I don't need Shane's chemicals.* She stared at the handful of pills for a few minutes and returned them to the cloth compartment, rested her back onto her bed, and closed her eyes.

The phone ringing at 8:00 am startled her, as did the rapid fire voice of her neighbor living to the south who rattled to Lexa that it looked like someone was breaking into her van.

"Thank you for calling." The bruises and scrapes on her legs, torso, and arms slowed her movements in rolling to the edge of her bed and pushing herself upward. She headed for the window to see the back of a man who appeared to have a kitchen knife in his hand.

Butter knife versus a sword, she thought, reaching alongside the waterbed. She headed to the hallway to slip into plastic snow boots and outside to the man who was crouched down with his butt facing her. Lexa swung the blade flat side toward him like a baseball bat connecting a home run into his backside. His scream shrilled into her ears. She backed away from him.

Glaring at her was the mean neighbor who had been traumatizing her for years. He shot up, stared at her, and flashed the deep grooves in his face caused by years of anger.

"What are you doing? she asked.

"I've had enough of this spaceship and I'm getting rid of it," he said pointing the knife outward to Lexa's chest. "The government planted you here to infuriate me. Admit it."

"Excuse me? Is butter on your knife?" She noticed a long scratch down the side of the van. *The guys are going to be furious.*

"I've known you were aliens all along. I hear your strange sounds at all odd hours of the day and night."

"Our guitars? You put the board filled with nails behind my car, didn't you? You tried to kill my dog!" she screamed.

"Doors slamming. Engines revving. 3 am, 4 am, whenever. No normal person does that. Your weird screeching noises could only be made by aliens. Go back to wherever it is you came from!"

Lexa ran to his house, rang the buzzer, and watched the delusional man's evil look close behind, the knife in his hand aimed at her. His wife answered the door.

"Ma'am, do you think you can calm your husband down? I think he needs help," said Lexa to the elderly woman, while hyperventilating and hopping up and down to stay warm, still clutching the sword. *She must have some idea that he isn't coherent today.*

A look of fear overcame the weary lady at the door. "I need to call my family," she said and turned to pick up her phone. Lexa ran to the front of her home, reentered the side entrance, locked herself in, and through the windows, saw the man walk around her house, looking for her. *After all this time, I finally understand. I hate to do this, but I have to call for help,* Lexa thought, feeling her hatred toward him melt into pity as she dialed the police and explained the scenario. Sirens surrounded the street in ten minutes.

She pulled a loaf of bread out the refrigerator and grabbed a jar of peanut butter from the cupboard. Opening up the silverware drawer, she examined a black handle with the name Rapala imprinted into it, that she had purchased years before. She was resolute in what she intended to do today. Between bites, she thought of its many uses and checked the gun in her purse.

She washed her face, brushed her teeth, and combed her long snarled hair. The green and blue spots and scrapes on her legs were dark and tender. She pulled up thick tights and jeans, and a long-sleeved pink top over her bruised ribs. She layered on several more sweaters, loosely wrapped her scarf, pulled on black boots and her shoulder strap purse over her head.

Outside, the standoff between police and the man who had long hated her was blaring to where the neighbors stood in the cold to gawk, and his family's vehicles began pulling up like a parade. I don't envy them today, she thought, turning the key in the VW ignition.

She drove past the funeral home. The trucks in the lot were parked in different places than when she had last seen them. Beside the curb, she turned the engine off, scanned the houses lined up along the street, the shoveled walkways, and traffic splashing sooty snow onto edges of the roadways. Lexa knocked on Shane's back door, noticing the trampled, icy, uneven paths.

Al stepped down and grabbed Lexa around her throat, squeezing until her face reddened. His mouth open, he grit his teeth as he pulled her into the kitchen. "I've been wanting my hands around your neck for a long time. All of your kind deserve death," he said as she lost her balance, unable to breathe, blood pulsating hard in the arteries of her neck. "I liked hearing you scream, but you couldn't mind your own business."

She dragged the blade of the Rapala over his right wrist. He squealed, his eyes widened, and he pulled his bloody arm back. She picked up the right heel of her boot and stabbed it into the flesh of his left foot, stepped back and slammed the pointed leather toe into his crotch. As he bent forward, she grabbed the pin and jammed it into his left upper arm, and pulled it out. "Feel the love, sleazebag."

"You bitch!" he screamed into the numbing air.

Lexa turned to run to her car clutching the knife. Hunched forward, he regained his composure, and opened his jacket. "I assembled the firebombs to waste you at the shows. Take your last breath baby," he said, squeezing the trigger, ricocheting a gunshot off the sidewalk.

She ran, missed the bullet, and hid at back of the house. Al's blood oozed into the snow, but he clutched his black 45 caliber Glock while his left hand supported his right arm. He followed her.

She turned hard to her right, lunged forward onto the ground and another gunshot popped into the air as she pumped herself back up to run southbound through the snow. Al's breath flared in the cold and his uneven footsteps limped behind her.

She hid alongside the house, and as he rounded the corner, she flooded Mace into his eyes. His twisted face spewed vile profanities as he scooped handfuls of ice and rubbed it over his eyelids. His body was hunched forward and blood poured from his right wrist, saturating his clothes as he rubbed snow into his burning face.

Lexa ran into Shane's house, locked the door, and ran into each room calling his name. Boffo led her into Al's empty bedroom. On the floor, blood trickled through Shane's matted black and blonde hair. Boffo whined and licked his cheek.

"Shane wake up! Get up," she said, pulling his torso upward. "Come on, get up." As she pulled on his dazed body, his eyes opened, having little awareness of his surroundings. His head nodded downward. "Shane, where's Nick? Shane!" She shouted.

"Fu...nrl" he said weakly and blacked out.

She placed a pillow under his head, and glass crinkled down the doorway from the window. She jumped up to run out of the front door to the funeral home, holding onto her purse which slapped onto her hip. She tore across the road through traffic and honking horns, past cemetery stones, headed to the funeral home, threw the door open, and screamed out Nick's name at the top of her lungs. "Shane needs help." She bent forward to catch her breath. "Al tried to kill me. Shane's in a pool of blood on Al's bedroom floor."

Nick nodded at her, walked into the coffin room, searched for his weapon of choice as a woman would scan over a box of jewelry, grabbed an M-16 assault rifle out of a casket, and barged outside through the frosted gray cold. Storming past icy markers of the dead, he marched across the cemetery, and caught sight of flickering yellow and orange streaks rising on the front window drapes. Now charging at full speed, he was hit by a stream of smoke billowing toward him, the gun planted in his arms, pointing outward. Lexa struggled to catch up and stood inside the inferno within seconds. Nick dragged Shane to an outside exterior wall grasping his shirt, refusing to drop the rifle in his right hand. She ran for the kitchen sink, turned the faucet on full force and sprayed the kitchen walls, floor and ceiling, then aimed at the dining room. Outside, Boffo whined and hovered over Shane.

"Lexa, give it up. You're never going to save this place," Nick said. "Keep an eye on Shane. Boffo, come," he commanded, reaching to stroke the shepherd. "I have to terminate Al."

Nick ran across the street, Boffo glued to his side. Shane's head bobbed downward, blood crawled along his hairline over his nose, and dripped off his chin onto a brown thermal long-sleeved shirt. Lexa bolted into Shane's room to grab his notebooks and shoebox, soaked down dish towels and covered their faces. She took the painting of the beach sunrise, sat his things outside on the snow and used his bedspread to cover him. Kneeling at his side, she wiped the blood off of his face and he began to regain consciousness. He sniffed, sat up in a trance, and turned his head toward the smoldering fumes.

"Lexa? Where am I? What did you do?" he said, pulling himself up onto all fours, his skin deep pink being saturated by the heat. In an adrenaline rush, he ran into the incinerating house.

"No!" she yelled, and in seconds he emerged, pointing a black pistol at her face.

"What have you done to my house? If this is your way of stopping me, you will not succeed," he screamed as the burning structure forced them away.

"We need to call the fire department," she said. They were jolted by an explosion coming from the direction of the Funeral Home, distracting him long enough for her to grab her Colt Commander and aim it at his face. "You aren't serious, are you? I wasn't here when you got smacked on your head. Think about it. You think I'm responsible for this?"

"I can't remember," he said, leveling his gun barrel at her.

"We're both going down if Al is around here."

"He might be a loose cannon, but he supported our mission and said you were throwing a wrench into our plans."

"I don't recall a discussion about your plans. Didn't you get the note I left about Al double crossing you?"

"Stop it! My head's messed up. I can't think straight, damn it."

"We have guided missiles, but misguided men. Darkness can only be banished by light, and hatred can only be banished by love," she said lowering her black handgun. It's Martin Luther King's words. The world's a mess, but making the innocents suffer solves nothing. Everyone loses. Call off your attack on humanity."

"I have no idea what you're talking about."

"You may not have let me in on your agenda, but it didn't take much for me to put together that you're in another war zone."

"I'm not calling anything off. We surrendered when we left Nam. I'm not doing it again. They played a game with our lives and now I'll show them a game they'll never forget," he shouted, pointing his gun at Lexa's chest.

"They? Who is 'they'?"

"Our government, tire manufacturers, the good ole boys whose hands are soaked with the blood of good people who were their pawns."

"Who is it that you can't forgive? Them…or yourself when you had to kill in the name of your country? Men who create power determine whether they use it wisely or if power uses them," she rambled, remembering part of John F. Kennedy's quote. "If you keep doing the same thing, thinking the same thoughts, how can you expect a different outcome? You have no problem destroying innocent lives? Future leaders will be smart enough to learn from the mistake of 'Nam. Wars are over."

"My blood has become burning liquid searing through every cell of my body. I have more anger and hatred consuming me than anyone you'll meet in your lifetime. I've made peace with revenge and my ending."

"Then what? You'll be happy? The world will be a better place? You'll think of yourself as a great man?"

"You think I give a damn about what anyone thinks of me?"

"Since no words exist to end your torment, take me out. I want your eyes to watch the life sucked out of me. Then I won't need your damn powder." She opened her right hand to let the Colt 45 slip into the snow, held her hands upward and took a step toward Shane.

"I swear I'll do it."

"Get it over with." A gunshot rang in her ears. "It didn't hurt as much as I thought it would," she said, closing her eyes. Hearing a second gun blast at close range, she opened her eyes and looked downward at her body. "How odd, no pain or blood. I think I'm still alive," she said," patting her chest, arms and legs. "Where did you learn to shoot?"

"Like I could kill you," he said shaking his head.

She moved toward him and touched his arms. "Shane, the fortunate know how to live. I'm trying to figure it out myself. You're brilliant enough to have an extraordinary life. I grabbed as many of your things as I could. Nick has Boffo," she said, picking up her gun and Shane's things under falling cinders.

"I guess I needed to let go of my things eventually." He watched the blazing heat dissolve his home.

Lexa knelt on the ground. "I don't feel so good."

"What's going on?" Shane said as he grabbed her.

"I fell down a wooden stairway, and everything hurts like hell. I need to sit down," she said placing her head between her knees at the curb.

Shane opened his red Duster, helped her into the passenger seat and started the engine. She saw the silver peace sign pendant she had gifted to him dangling on the chain as he adjusted the rearview mirror.

"You okay?" he asked.

"I'll be fine. So, am I safe now? Safe with me only C7T?"

He smiled. "You figured out the message and the digits on the trucks. Sometimes the best laid plans fail. Nothing happened like it was supposed to. Nothing. I have to find Nick. Thanks for the necklace."

"You're welcome. I hope you wear it someday. Don't be so hard on yourself. Wait…take your things," she said.

Shane grabbed his belongings, put them in the back seat, drove eastbound on Chambers, north onto Teutonia St. and onto Concordia, where they watched the funeral home spew flames. Two of the seven trucks were missing.

"I saw your note, so Nick and some of my guys packed everything into one truck and only Nick has the key. I told him to get it out of here while I kept Al busy and now that I think about it, he probably would have killed me if you hadn't left a message and unexpectedly dropped by. All the trucks look identical, so only Nick and I knew which one was loaded."

"I think Al and his crew have acquired Plutonium. Did you know he murdered several women? But I'm not sure how many."

"I did not know. What makes you think that?"

"Not only did he admit it in the letters he wrote to me, but he had rope, nylons, and newspaper articles which reported the names of who he killed in his dresser. I'm not sure how far he will make it. I carved up his wrist. I think he'll need medical attention. How did you guys hook up?"

"We met at the bar. He was a regular, and knew a lot about explosives, firearms and numerology. It didn't take long for us to combine forces. When you talked about evil being infused among people, I thought about the futility of demolishing particular places."

"Al sent the other letters I had originally thought you did, about women screaming and using rope on them," she said. "It was on the same paper you used. I'm sorry I called you a pervert".

"I had no idea he wrote to you. He'd do anything for money and we were both into numbers. Eight was our code. We planned a chain reaction of eight detonations across the country from New York to LA as spectacular as Hiroshima," he said.

"Eight places? You had seven trucks."

"I'm ashamed to say it, but when Al saw your itinerary listing Crazes in Chicago, he discovered out how easy it was to break into your truck, so he insisted that we use yours. Replace the equipment and your roadies would have been driving through Chicago at 4:00, but it's when I knew things had gone too far and I wanted out. If Al decides to take someone down, he could care less about anyone else."

"You were going to kill our road crew? Drax, Showey and Hound are good men."

"They were supposed to help our venture, but I couldn't do it."

"It's hard to believe," she said shaking her head. "My band and I would have been in Chicago not far behind the truck. Now I understand all the vivid dreams of charred landscape. I was there. So that's why Al and his pals joined forces. He made a guess you might bail. Where's Nick going to dump a load of radioactive explosives?"

"He's got the chemicals too. We're going to meet up. We'll dump them in some deserted place," said Shane, driving in the direction of Lexa's VW.

"I'm glad you asked for my help, and I got to know the real person you are. Will you be able to give your life a second chance?"

"I don't know. You have no idea what I've been through. My world is black. It seems like nothing is worth doing or seeing anymore."

"Those who chase the light eventually find it. Countless places on this earth are worth seeing."

"Name one," he said, as they neared her vehicle.

Lexa closed her eyes and reminisced, "After you get to Denver, head to Colorado Springs, then to Pueblo. Continue west on Hwy 50 to

San Isabel National Forest. Drive to a small white sign posted on the right of a dirt road that says: Old Monarch Pass. Take it 2 - 4 miles to the top of the pass and keep going. About eight miles from the top on the left, there may be a white piece of cloth as a marker. I'm not sure if it's still there. On the next small dirt road, drive about 100 feet, and turn left," she said, remembering her camp site in the pristine beauty of the mountains.

He asked her to write it down, opened the glove compartment and handed her a piece of paper.

"I had gone to the mountain top in summer. You may not be able to get there now. This time of year, a warm beach would be where I'd be heading to. If you read a sign that says, "Dangerous Undertow", take it seriously. Learn how to navigate the waves if you see it.

"Thanks for your concern for me. I looked at your painting of the waves, of how they move and catch the light when I woke up each morning and realized I couldn't remember the last time I saw a sunrise, heard waves slap on a shore, or had my feet in the sand. Nick told me my hatred was fading, that it was good to see the old Shane he once knew, and maybe we could move on. You'll be hard to forget, Lexa."

"The same goes for you. What was written as the cause of your demise on your death certificate?"

"It said heart failure, but the autopsy was done on the cadaver they mistakenly thought was me. Nick was listed as kin and got the result."

"I have to know what was in your day planner. Why were police so insistent that I was your girlfriend and their primary suspect?"

"I…had a crush on you. Your name was everywhere. While I talked to agents on the phone to schedule bands, I scribbled hearts and flowers around your name, never giving a second thought that cops would ever have it. I'm sorry." He said.

"The police don't have anything on me at all. They were trying to intimidate me into giving them information about you. I told them nothing useful. So…did your guys point out the large federal agent before you ran?"

"Yea. When my guys saw that big blonde gorilla from the DEA hanging around outside of my bar the day you came, I had to make a break for it," he said. "He wore a black t-shirt and a vest to disguise what he was. Mean looking schmuck. They saw him using a walkie-talkie."

"Big blonde gorilla? *Tiny?* I hope you'll stay in touch, and let me know how you are occasionally." she smiled.

"Yea, it's shorter than we think it is. I'm going give more thought to the choices I make," he said.

"I wish there was a device which could tell us the outcome of every decision," she said.

"There are so many variables to any choice," he said. "Like how we perceive of something, our attitude, our outlook."

"Now look who is being the philosopher, Mr. Black."

He laughed, I guess my world isn't as dark as I thought it was.

The reddened skies, created by the fire from both structures, wove a haze of pink and indigo into the air as stars dotted the sky. Shane's house on Hopkins Street raged in smoke. The Final Rest Funeral Home was being cremated as it crackled and sizzled in long radiant flames. Shane and Lexa stared at one another as she opened the door and stepped outside. His eyes remained fixed on her as he hit the gas petal on the black Chevy and revved the engine as sirens shrieked.

"I hope to hear your voice again," she said.

"I hope so too," he replied and leaned forward to reach into his back pocket. "Take it. I won't need it anymore. Be careful how you plan to use it," he said, handing her a two inch by four inch sealed brown envelope. "You saved my life in so many ways. It's the least I can do. Just take it."

She examined the letters TTX written in ink on one side, stared at the worn, bruised face in the red Duster and said, "Hang on to your keys. You'll know what I mean when you get to the mountain top." She kissed his cheek. "Don't get distracted by how surreal the summit is. I hope you can move on."

"I'm gonna give it my best shot," he said.

"It's a process and is easier said than done."

Shane gave her a nod and the red Duster's engine roared, tires squealed, and smoke billowed behind his vehicle. She headed the Volkswagen northbound onto Teutonia St. as flashing strobes closed in on the neighborhood. Sirens wailed, firefighters shouted commands, hoses were attached to hydrants, and water streamed at swirling, hissing, golden spirals.

Once home, she bolted the door shut, stepped onto the landing and in her bedroom, removed her gloves, purse and sweaters, lowered her injured body to the waterbed, but was unable to relax. Aldar was now missing. Feeling exhausted, her eyelids felt heavy. She took her Colt Commander out of her purse. *I shouldn't have come back here.*

She deliberated for a few moments, went to the hallway closet, pulled blankets out, and threw them into her bedroom. She picked up Ebbie, carried her up the inside stairwell to Sam's flat, closed the door and locked it. She grabbed sofa pillows and tucked them end to end under the blankets of her waterbed. Tossing her shoes out of her bedroom closet, she smoothed her sleeping bag and comforter on the ground, threw in two pillows and the blankets. She placed the gun under her pillow and drifted to a light sleep.

Awakened by glass smashing on her back door, she slid her fingers into place on her gun, while footsteps screaked in the hallway, living room and into her bedroom. Three gunshots blasted at close range, a half a minute of silence, and the floor creaking nearby caused her to point the gun outward toward the closet door.

Footsteps pounded to the refrigerator where items were thrown around and ransacked. Clunking down the hallway was followed by slamming of the back door. In the dimness she turned on her flashlight, saw three holes leaking water through the blankets, and crept out of the closet. *He thinks he killed me. In the dark, it looks like blood seeping into the peach comforter. I better siphon and drain the water before it floods the room.*

The last of the water was drained outside when she shut her bedroom window, wound up the garden hose, and replaced it in the basement. Back in her closet, she fell asleep on the floor clinging to her pistol, but was awakened by a cold house. Shivering even though blankets were wrapped around her, she called Same Day Glass Service, and a van arrived within the hour.

"Thank you for coming so soon. Here's a tip. Have a Happy New Year."

She turned up the heat, filled Ebbie's food and water bowls, walked up the stairs, found her sitting by the door, and they ran down the steps and outside for a few minutes before Ebbie ate.

Lexa sat next to the bookshelf with blankets covering her where she dozed off, and snuggled Ebbie who plopped at her side. The house was warm when she awoke and went to the fridge to see what food was left.

She cracked two eggs into a frying pan. With her breakfast plate on a book, she opened her diary to write. Sam knocked on her door and walked into the living room as she sat in her familiar cubicle.

"I have been to the best parties ever. The food was excellent. All the great local musicians were out and about, even our bandmates. Ruby Starr asked where you were. You missed all the fun. Why are you always sitting in this corner? You're so predictable. It looks like your bedroom's a mess. It's one of the reasons why things could never work out between us."

She smiled. "Yea, one of the countless reasons. So you're saying I'm a boring slob?"

"Be ready by six for tonight's show." He turned around and walked up the steps to his flat.

"Happy New Year to you too," she muttered under her breath. *I need a few glasses of wine to celebrate the new year.*

Saturday, January 1, 1977
I realize I don't have to destroy my enemies, though the temptation is intense. Instead, I will let the path of self-destruction implode on those who have chosen to take that road. I will stand aside as karmic energy rains into those who give

their worst to others. Do I think I lacked fortitude in not killing Aldar when I had the chance?

Courage will find you at unexpected moments. It taps on your shoulder and jumpstarts your conscience to stand its ground and right a wrong in this world.

It means embracing love even in what feels like the absence of it, and happiness doesn't mean a life of perfection, though it helps. It means having the free will to say just for this moment I will be happy. Just for this hour I will be happy. I will be grateful for small things I take for granted. One thing became two and soon the list was longer than I expected.

At Crazes nightclub, the carefree faces this evening and those enjoying life on the dance floor filled me with a sense of belonging - to them and to the stage. As I helped pack up gear, soon everyone joined in, and the roadies were able to leave earlier than usual.

Julette visited me in a vivid dream. She said, "You found my beautiful son." Thank you. She said she can move on now, but I asked her to stay until I sell the house, and she agreed.

Sunday, January 2, 1977

Long rays of sun stream through gray skies and stretch out to fields of snow covered fields. Blessed Trinity Parish's church bells ring beyond the three miles to the Union Cemetery. The melody of the chimes echo a symbolic peace. I'm relieved a war was aborted, and will be thankful for each tranquil day. Shane and Nick have an uphill battle ahead as they try to redefine themselves while repairing shattered spirits and forgiving not only those who betrayed them, but forgiving themselves for what they did in the name of their country. It was they who decided it was time to change, and only they can determine what was holding them back from attaining piece of mind. Like my dad, they were traumatized by war and will never be the same again. Any step toward healing the wounded, the fallen, the broken and the lost is a step forward, in being able to lose everything, grasp onto the impermanence of this world and find hope in each breath that renews and restores. I will always wonder if Shane had self-inflicted his leg infection. Was it a painful ruse to determine if I had told the police about his and Nick's drug dealing? He could have died.

People rarely change unless they are thrown down the rabbit hole, and in my case I managed to crawl out of it a few times.

My own New Year's resolutions include forgiving myself for all my failings, and learning to forgive others. It is always my wish for the New Year to be a better one than the last.

Monday, January 3, 1977
This morning I drove to the Union Cemetery to place flowers on Oma's grave. As I walked, I glanced at names and discovered a small plaque which made me feel as though I was meant to see the name Milyana Milevic, dates of birth and death: 11/1/1952 - 11/3/1970. I knelt on the ground and placed a rose. "I found him sweet girl, but it will not bring you or any of the others back. I hope there is splendor in your heavenly realm." I knelt on the ground remembering her beauty under the streetlamp, of how she should be dancing in the wind, running through the sand, picking colorful flowers, and laughing. Though I said farewell, she will not be forgotten. I also placed a rose on the nearby grave of Julette Zadrik.

Shane called to tell me that I'll never have to worry about Aldar again. Somehow I already knew, after picturing it all these years, and I wished him and Nick well on their travels. They were headed to warmer skies and Florida beaches. I reminded him to watch for signs that said 'Dangerous Undertow', and I told him my story. I apologized for not rescuing his Hendrix poster, but he assured me he knew where to get another.

I did not tell Shane that the massive man he thought was a DEA federal agent in his parking lot when I had met him last July, was my bodyguard Thurston Tinsky. With his two-way radio at his mouth, Tiny unknowingly set off a chain reaction in the chemistry lab of experiments gone awry. Tiny, the gargantuan domino changed the world for a moment, toppling a set of events and altering the outcome.

I called my parents' house to check on everyone, and Dad answered the phone. I decided that today would be a good time to tell him I was sorry for the way I left. I think he waited all these years for something as simple as an apology. We had the nicest talk I can remember for the first time in my life, and we even had a few laughs. I asked him to say 'Hi' to Mom and my sisters. A sense of calm overcame me after reconciling with Dad, and I feel like we are going to be okay. If he has not beaten the memories which agonize him, he has pushed them aside for now.

I made Oma's recipe for beef Rouladen, mashed potatoes and a salad, and brought it to the neighbor. She said she's been lonely since her husband was taken to the Mental Health hospital. She asked if I would join her for dinner. When she sells her house and gets packed up, she'll move in with her daughter.

I was stunned to hear Tarick Tagan's voice at the other end of the phone to wish me a Happy New Year, and ask how I was doing. He said he couldn't stop thinking about me after he saw a red-tailed hawk that made him think of our rooftop run when his heart raced faster than his legs could. I told him I was fantastic, and all couldn't be better. We talked about our upcoming shows, some we looked forward to and some we dreaded. Dare I dream there is the faintest possibility that we may have a future? I'm not ready to start tearing my walls down for anyone yet, but will give it some thought...maybe. When I saw the world as ugly, it was. When I see the world is beautiful, it mysteriously changed.

ABOUT THE AUTHOR

When I traveled the country in a rock band, events became so surreal, I began diaries to document the events. Had my short sentences about what had transpired not been written down, I may have forgotten much of it. I discovered the legal documents of the incident where the white bull destroyed our equipment at a State Fair.

When the truck tires rolled off of our equipment truck in the dead of night near our destination in Florida, I remember thinking, 'this cannot be happening'. It seemed like the never ending series of unusual events, letters, fan mail, gifts, and drug offerings were part of the job.

JD Hicks was a car salesman and drug dealer from Plano Texas, who was convicted of numerous drug charges, and spent the last days of his life in a Federal prison. We did not meet him, as his time was before the band toured through Plano, Texas.

Many of the clubs in this book are no longer in existence. The Palms, Century Hall, and Someplace Else have all burned down.

Someone who read this said to me, "like that could ever happen," and I assured her it did. There is sometimes a fine line between fact and fiction. Did an impaired, cute blonde climb into our van, refuse to get out and have to be physically removed? Unfortunately yes.

Version two is the result of fixing grammar errors. Revisiting one's darker times is never easy.

Rock on, Krys